the
daughter

DATE DUE

ALSO BY LUCY DAWSON

LUCY DAWSON
the
daughter

bookouture

Published by Bookouture in 2018
An imprint of StoryFire Ltd.
Carmelite House
50 Victoria Embankment
London EC4Y 0DZ

www.bookouture.com

ISBN: 978-1-78681-330-5
eBook ISBN: 978-1-78681-329-9

This book is a work of fiction. Names, characters, businesses,
organizations, places and events other than those clearly in the
public domain, are either the product of the author's imagination
or are used fictitiously. Any resemblance to actual persons, living or
dead, events or locales is entirely coincidental.

For James, with love

PROLOGUE

I stop running. Everyone is shouting and my ears don't like it. I want to go home. Mummy would say, 'You poor bunny', and make me a bed on the sofa. My body feels all hurty and hot.

'Mrs Fey?' I go and find her. 'Can I take my jumper off, please?'

She does her nice smile and bends down. 'It's too cold out here, sweetheart. You should really have your coat on.'

'I feel hot.'

'That's because you've already been doing so much rushing around! It's not long until the end of playtime; why don't you come and sit down for a minute?' She reaches out and puts her hand on my head. 'You do feel warm, actually. Do you?—'

But then she stops because someone calls her. Emily from the other class is crying next to the climbing frame, and she's got sick all on her dress and on the floor.

'Oh dear!' Mrs Fey stands up again. 'Just a minute, Beth, I'll be right back.'

It's gone on Emily's shoes too. Everyone is looking, and the boys start shouting 'Urgh! That's really smelly!', holding their noses, and falling over. Mrs Mottram gets cross and tells them not to be silly. We watch Mrs Fey and Mrs Mottram move the climbing frame away from the sick, and Cara whispers: 'I'm going to hang upside down', which we are *not* allowed to do.

Cara climbs up really fast, then sits on the *top bar,* swings backwards and TAKES HER HANDS OFF so she's hanging upside down, but Mrs Fey doesn't say anything because Emily is still crying. Cara's hair is all over her face and her dress has gone up. I can see her tights and a bit of her tummy where her vest isn't. She looks funny and I laugh.

'You do it!' she says.

I really want to, and I don't even feel hot any more now I'm not running.

I start to climb up. The bars are colder even than when I go to the shop with Mummy and she gets the frozen peas to put in the trolley but lets me hold them first.

It's wobbly and slippy at the top when I sit next to Cara and I have to hold on hard. She thinks it's funny to try and tickle me, which I do NOT like, and I ask her to stop it, but she doesn't. I try to wriggle along the bar on my bottom, away from her, but she chases me. I take my hand off to stop her because she's going to tickle me again – her hand is out – but then the sky goes the wrong way and the surprise makes me scream.

Mummy.

PART 1

CHAPTER ONE

22nd November 1999

I didn't see the woman approaching our car. Nirvana had just started playing on the radio; the DJ crashing the vocal with the helpful observation that he couldn't believe half a decade had passed since we'd lost the great Kurt Cobain to suicide. I reached over immediately – Beth was only five – and turned it off, bracing myself for the inevitable 'What's suicide?', but actually all she said was: 'Can I undo my seatbelt, Mummy?'

'Yup. I'll come and get you, hang on.' I grabbed the book bag and drink bottle from the passenger seat, got out and walked round to the pavement. Opening her door, I put a hand out to steady her as she wobbled precariously on the edge in readiness to jump down. 'Careful, sweetheart.' I tucked the bottle in my coat pocket and the bag under one arm. 'Let's just zip you up first, OK? It's freezing. Where are your gloves?'

She squinted up at me worriedly, the sharp sunshine shining right in her eyes. 'I think I left them in my tray at school.'

'Oh Beth!' I scolded gently, letting go of her now-fastened coat. 'We talked about this! Always keep them in your pockets so you've got them when you need them. Will you please make sure you put them on at playtime?'

'Yes, Mummy.' She nodded obediently.

'At least you've got your hat.' I grinned at her to lighten the tone. 'Come on. Let's go. We don't want to be late. I'd better hold onto that paw to keep you warm, I think.'

I offered her my hand but she slipped past me, a little puff of breath visibly clouding as her feet landed squarely on the floor – her head only millimetres from the car door.

'Beth!' I exclaimed again before I could stop myself and, ignoring me, she snatched the bag that I was now holding out, ducked past and ran onto the enclosed grass of the square on the other side of the pavement, where she started to twirl, freely. I slammed the door shut, just as the female voice said: 'Excuse me?'

I turned round with a ready apology, thinking I must be blocking the narrow pavement for someone trying to get by, but in fact the unfamiliar woman was on the road behind our car, astride an old-fashioned pushbike, complete with wicker basket. One lace-up clad foot was down on the road for balance as she panted slightly, having just stopped pedalling.

I waited for her to speak again, but rather she hesitated and pushed her half-moon glasses back up her nose. Probably in her early forties, her mousey hair was escaping from a loose ponytail clamped under a helmet, and her soap-scrubbed skin was completely devoid of any make-up. The top of a button-down shirt was just visible under a long, heavy tweed coat and a tightly wound woollen scarf. She looked like an eminently sensible librarian. Still, I waited respectfully. Although – was she going to say *anything*?

Just as the silence we were locked in became actively uncomfortable, and I had opened my mouth to ask, 'Can I help you?' she suddenly blurted: 'I have the strongest feeling I need to tell you how much God loves your little girl.'

I froze, before recovering myself enough to quickly glance round at Beth – bent over, peering at something on the ground, safe and completely oblivious to what was going on. I turned back to the woman.

'I don't know why, but it felt very important that you know.' She appeared horribly embarrassed – as if she was not in the habit of making outlandish announcements to strangers. 'That's all, really.'

There was another pause, before I managed to say: 'Thank you'.

She looked relieved, and smiled, before pushing down with one foot on the pedal, and lifting the other from the ground. Wobbling slightly she steered the bike round the car, calling out behind her: 'Goodbye, then'.

I stared after her in astonishment, not sure if I should be expecting to see a delicate pair of snow-white angel wings poking out of the back of her coat, or if it was actually rather creepy the way it was now streaming out behind her like a dark cape. She cycled off up the street, and headed over the crossroads – onto the cobbled private road that led to the cathedral. Possibly she was a volunteer there.

'Who was that?' Beth appeared at my side, and we watched together as the woman took the left fork of the path, across the heavily frosted green, disappearing round the corner and out of sight.

'I don't know. Did you recognise her?' We began to walk up towards the crossroads ourselves.

'No.' Beth shook her head. 'Can we go and light a candle after school?'

'Of course.' Taking Beth to light prayer candles in the cathedral was about the extent of my religious practice. I certainly didn't consider myself in any way pious, although I very much wanted to believe in God, and there being more beyond this life. We reached the top of the road and I held out my hand to her again. This time, she took it.

'Wow,' I remarked. 'You've got toasty little mitts today. Warm hands, warm heart!' I looked carefully left and right, scanning the road as completely out of nowhere, an image suddenly flashed into my mind of answering the phone and discovering something awful had happened to Beth, having *not* told her God loved her. I gripped her hand more tightly. Beth didn't notice; we were about to cross, after all.

'Can you see anything coming?' I said, managing to smile, and she shook her head.

'OK, over we go then!'

It wasn't the first time this had happened. While there was probably a logical explanation rather than my having a 'gift', I'd imagined plenty of events only for them to actually come to pass; little things like picturing a glass shattering seconds before someone dropping a tumbler in front of me in a restaurant… right through to driving on a motorway and 'seeing' a car in front of me swerving violently around the carriageway – so I slowed right down, only for minutes later a BMW, several vehicles up, to have a blowout in the fast lane. But these visualisations had never involved Beth.

'Do you know what, Beth?' I said quickly, 'that lady said a nice thing actually. She told me God loves you very much. And so do I.' There. I exhaled. It was now impossible that the future could unfold exactly as I'd just imagined it. I'd prevented it from coming true.

'I love you too,' she replied.

I didn't feel any better though; was just telling her enough? I suddenly had an overwhelming urge to turn around and take her home.

'Mattie's waving!' Beth tugged on my hand and then pointed at one of the girls in her class a bit further ahead, before looking up at me hopefully, a pink flush in her pale cheeks. 'Can I go and see her, please?'

'Hang on a second.' I reached out and touched her skin. It wasn't just her hands, her face felt warm too, despite the chill in the air, but I was rubbish without using an actual thermometer.

I wasn't ever really sure what a temperature felt like the way the other mums seemed to just *know*. 'Sweetheart, are you feeling alright?'

'Yes!' Beth said impatiently. '*Please* can I go and see Mattie now?'

'OK,' I agreed, reluctantly. 'But don't run.'

Our hands slipped apart as she set off. All the same, she wasn't properly hot. Was I just looking for any excuse to take her home because of what that woman had said? Ben would think I'd gone mad if I did that, and probably he would be right. No, he was definitely right! She couldn't miss a whole day of school just because of something I'd imagined happening. Plus, it'd look really weird to Mattie's mum if we did an about-turn now, and then I'd have to phone in sick to work to look after her. I took a deep breath. It was all going to be fine. I'd told Beth God loved her; that was good enough. I made an enormous effort to suppress my anxiety before it inflated out of control and I wasn't able to hold onto it. This was how full-blown obsessive-compulsive disorder began. I didn't have a gift, I just needed to get a grip.

'Hi, Jess!' called out Mattie's mum, who had kindly stopped to wait for me.

'Hi.' I waved shyly, suddenly conscious of my slightly too-short skirt in comparison with her much more sophisticated suit. 'You look nice.'

She glanced down at herself in surprise. 'Oh thanks, I'm due in court later. You working today, too?'

'Yes, but just on the phones, so...' I trailed off, not sure where I was going with that.

She smiled gently. 'Beautiful morning, isn't it? So cold though! It was hideous crawling out from under the duvet this morning – I'm badly in need of caffeine!'

'Me too,' I agreed eagerly, despite hating coffee. 'Intravenously, preferably.'

'God yes,' she agreed, and I smiled, relieved. I was still learning the shorthand for pick up and drop off chats. Safe subjects included: being exhausted, juggling work and the kids, husbands (doing frustrating/irritating things), and needing either coffee or alcohol (wine/gin, not shots), or both.

We followed the girls through the heavy wooden door set back in the red-brick wall that led into their school playground. Mattie's mother waved to the two members of staff on duty, clutching steaming cups of tea as children ran about them. The old-fashioned building in front of us, with its worn flagstone floors, small classrooms and corridors, just about coped with the twenty-four pupils in each year group. A bustling state school would have burst at the seams long before, but here it was the limited numbers and the 'family friendly' ethos that professional, local parents – and my in-laws – uncomplainingly paid for.

Beth disappeared off into the chattering throng of children to hang up her coat, while I made my way to the desk in the reception area outside her classroom, pretending not to notice a couple of other mums staring at me. I tried to pull my skirt down a bit, feeling every inch the incongruous 24-year-old. Thankfully, Beth returned, just in time for the door to her classroom to open, revealing the new head of pre-prep.

'Good morning, Beth.' He smiled down at her.

Beth said nothing, just twirled shyly on the spot, clutching onto the edge of my coat with one hand.

'Can you say "Hello, Mr Strallen"?' I could hear the tension in my too-quick prompt, but he laughed kindly as she stayed silent.

'Don't worry. You go on in, Beth.'

He stood to one side to let her pass, and she went straight over to join Cara – his daughter and Beth's new best friend – on the reading mat. Cara was looking unusually downcast, with slightly puffy red eyes.

'We're a little out of sorts this morning,' Mr Strallen confirmed.

'I'm sorry to hear that,' I said quietly.

'Thank you. Good morning, Olivia! What a nice hat. I like the woolly pom-pom' – another small girl cut through us, followed by her mother, who smiled demurely at Mr Strallen and completely ignored me. I glanced at him, but if the head was aware of the effect he'd had on most of the mums since starting at the school in September, he didn't let it show and cheerily continued: 'everyone gets a little overtired at this time of year. Short days, lots of bugs whizzing around. We all ought to be hibernating really. I wonder, actually, Mrs Davies, if I might have a moment? Could we step into my office?'

My heart gave an extra thud. 'Now?' I said quickly.

'If you wouldn't mind. It really won't take long.' He gestured to the small flight of stairs leading down to the lower corridor, and I looked worriedly back at Beth, sat alongside Cara – who was just staring at me.

'I've got to get to work, but… OK. If you could just give me a second.'

'Of course.'

I shoved Beth's water bottle alongside all the others, and her book bag in the box, before hurrying over to the girls. 'Beth, I need to say goodbye.' She held up her arms for a hug, but distracted, I blew her a kiss instead. 'Sorry, sweetheart, I've got to rush a bit, but have a lovely day, and I'll see you later.'

I briefly paused once I was in the doorway and glanced back at Beth, now holding Cara's hand, both of them chattering busily to each other, before stepping across to where the head was waiting. He held an arm out courteously, gesturing the way. I led with my head down, feeling very self-conscious as he followed behind.

I stood to one side as he opened the door to his compact but neatly ordered office. 'Do please sit down.' He offered me one of the rather battered red velvet armchairs on the nearside of his desk, but I stayed standing and waited until he'd carefully closed the door and turned to face me.

'What the fuck, Simon?' I said.

'Shhh!' He tried to smile, but his hands were held up defensively.

'Two and a half months you've not said a word, but you choose *now* to do this?' I exclaimed. 'The moment's passed, hasn't it? I'd actually rather we just carry on with no contact, no compromising situations – no nothing. I have to be just another parent at the school. That's it. No us on our own. At all. Ever. In fact, I'm going to go now.'

He took off his glasses, blinking slightly as he did so, and placed them on the desk. 'Jess, I ask parents into my office all the time; this is totally normal. No one is going to suspect anything out of the ordinary.'

'OK – firstly, your wife is up on playground duty *right now*; I just walked past her, and secondly, if you even knew half of what most of the women here will gossip about, you wouldn't—'

'Jessica, please.' He stepped forward and put a hand on my arm. In spite of myself, my stupid heart gave another excited thump. 'I haven't engineered this to get you alone. Not like that anyway. We need to talk.'

'Well, I wasn't lying, I really do have to get to work and I'm already having a crap morning – some random on a bike came up to me and said she wanted Beth to know how much God loved her, which really freaked me out. Have there been any reports of strange people hanging around the school?'

He frowned. 'No? She was probably just a God-botherer on her way to the cathedral. I'll check into it for you though, if you like.' He gave my arm a comforting squeeze.

'Please don't do that.' I shook off his hand.

'OK. I'm sorry. I do need to speak with you though.'

'No, this isn't fair, Simon! It's putting me in a situation where you're forcing me to go behind Ben's back, and I—'

'I think Louise knows.'

A cold shiver ran through me. I stepped back. 'Why? What's happened?' My voice dropped to a whisper. 'I haven't told anyone and surely neither have you, so how does your wife know?'

'I've not told a soul, I give you my word. It was when we were going to bed.' He shifted uncomfortably. 'Louise started talking about Beth, saying what a lovely little girl she is, how much Cara adores her, and she's glad Cara's made such a sweet friend. I said nothing to that, obviously, then she started to tell me the plot of some TV drama she'd been watching about this seriously ill child who needed a bone marrow transplant and the husband suddenly confessed he had a secret love child who might be able to donate to their daughter—'

He paused for a moment and waited for me to react. I stayed completely still.

'Only it turns out they're not a match, and the arrival of this child in their lives tears the family apart. *Then* Louise asked me what would *we* do in that situation if Cara was ever seriously ill, given she's almost certainly an only child…' He stopped and looked at me expectantly.

'And?' I managed.

'Oh, come on!' Simon exclaimed. '"*Almost certainly* an only child"?'

'Sounds like she just wants another baby to me.'

'You don't feel the least bit concerned about the direction of that conversation?' Simon continued, incredulously. 'Louise was in a foul mood this morning too, banging around everywhere and shouting at Cara.' He paused, then said in a rush: 'The thing is, Beth *is* the spitting image of me, Jessica. Any fool can see it. And my wife is no fool.'

I swallowed. 'I can see why you might be hyper vigilant when it comes to Louise, but I genuinely think you're reading into things that just aren't there. For a start, Beth is 100 per cent Davies. If you were to look back at pictures of Ben's family, Beth is very similar to his mother at her age.'

'She's fair-haired, like me.'

'Ben and I were both blonde as children before we wound up with dark hair as adults.'

'You've also both got brown eyes. Beth's are blue, like mine.'

'This is crazy, Simon! They told me when she was born blue eyes can stay hidden in a family tree for years; both brown-eyed parents hand over the right combination of genes and – bam! You've got a blue-eyed baby.'

'But the timing was right... it all fits.' He fell silent and just looked at me.

I returned his gaze, full on. 'I would say if I believed Beth was your daughter, but she isn't.'

'I'm not raising this because I want to do something about it.' Simon took another step towards me. 'I would never do that to Cara or Beth, but what Louise said last night really frightened me. I've had nearly eleven weeks of seeing Beth close at hand now and I *know* she's mine. It's not just looks, it's mannerisms too, and as I said, given Louise is much, much sharper than me, it's only a matter of time, Jess.' He exhaled, sat down on the edge of his desk and pinched the bridge of his nose, scrunching his eyes shut. 'This is all my fault.'

'It was both of our faults,' I said immediately. 'We knew what we were doing.'

This time there was a much longer pause. I looked at the responsible teacher in his mid-thirties sat in front of me, and remembered exactly how it had felt five years ago when – a be-suited stranger with an easy smile and confident chat – he'd kissed me for the first time... hidden away in a corner of the bar I was working at, having dropped out of my third year at university only two months after Mum had died. He'd made me feel like I might somehow survive after all. Maybe even be happy again – if I could experience a kiss like that.

'I should have told you I was married to Louise when we met.'

'Yes, you should. But I ought to have told you about Ben too,' I added quietly. 'And I shouldn't have told you I was 22 when I wasn't.'

He snorted gently. 'That's the kind of thing 19-year-olds do, Jess – lie about their age, mess around. Teenage relationships aren't meant to last. You didn't do anything wrong. But I did. The way I treated you *and* Louise was unforgivable.'

I opened my mouth to correct him. Ben had been – and was – so much more to me than a teenage relationship. He and his family had kept me going, supported me through everything; but somehow the thought of discussing them with Simon, of all people, while tucked away in his office, only made me feel more disloyal. 'I don't think either of us come out of what happened particularly well.'

'I don't want you to blame yourself, Jess. You were going through a very difficult time.'

I caught my breath. I could only cope by not opening this box completely. I didn't want to unpack it all again. We were starting to tread on very dangerous ground. 'We both should have known better – but what's done is done,' I tried resolutely to get us back on track, 'and Beth is not your daughter. Given Louise doesn't know anything about us, I don't understand why she would have any reason to suddenly and randomly think Beth looks like you? It's just… pretty paranoid, to be honest. I think what you really need to try and do is find a way to live alongside the knowledge that you cheated on Louise, because that's obviously what's still troubling you, but maybe bear in mind it was a long time ago now; you're both happy, and you have Cara. We're *both* happily married.'

Simon looked at me in disbelief for a moment, and laughed. 'So says the worldly-wise 24-year-old.'

'Don't be unkind,' I said, colouring. 'It doesn't suit you.'

His face fell instantly. 'I'm not trying to be unkind – I promise. I'm sorry.' He paused, before continuing in a rush: 'I mean it – I really am sorry, Jessica; for all of it. It actually makes me so sad to hear you talking like this. Don't get me wrong, it's one of the many things that make you very unusual, but when most girls your age are completely responsibility-free… I hate it. I wish I could wave a wand and change everything for you.'

'Well, given a choice, of course I'd have rather not had Mum die,' my voice wobbled, and I cleared my throat hurriedly, 'but that's just the way it goes, and in any case, everything has led me to Beth.' I smiled, although I could feel my eyes were now shining with unshed tears. 'So don't pity me.'

'You know I felt I was making the right decision at the time, don't you?' Simon said. 'It wasn't that I didn't want to be with you. I will *always* want to be with you—'

'Oh, please don't do this,' I whispered. 'It isn't fair.'

'It's true, Jess. You know it is.'

I took a deep breath. 'The thing is, Simon, when you say that sort of thing five years after the event, actually, it can't help but sound anything other than flat, and insincere.'

'I take your point, but it doesn't change the fact that it's true. Our feelings for each other weren't ever the bit that was in doubt.'

That really was too much to take. 'Maybe not for you,' I tried to keep my voice steady, 'but then I never blanked you in the street.'

Simon flushed with shame. I knew, like me, he could picture the scene perfectly; Louise's long, auburn hair bouncing as she walked up the hill from the train station, holding Simon's hand and chatting excitedly, as he wheeled her suitcase. Her free hand was resting on her tummy in that self-conscious manner first-time pregnant women adopt because they're desperate for people to notice their completely non-existent bump. I noticed it though

— and her wedding ring glinting in the hard March sunshine. I stopped dead in the middle of the pavement, dumbfounded. She was laughing at something Simon had said, and he'd only looked up at the last minute to realise it was me. Horrified, he carefully steered her past me, and carried on walking. It was the smooth pretence that we were complete strangers, and I hadn't in fact woken up next to him earlier that same morning, that caused me what felt like actual physical pain.

'I had pretty serious doubts about your feelings, after that,' I said. 'I thought everything you'd said had been a huge lie to get me to sleep with you.'

'It wasn't a lie. I'd planned to tell Louise about us that very night, but that's when she told me she was pregnant with Cara. It was my responsibilities that changed, not my feelings.'

'And that's why I never heard from you again.' I could have slapped myself the second the words were out of my mouth. So much time had passed that his confirmation or denial shouldn't matter to me any more. I'd just proved it did.

He looked up quickly. 'I thought you'd find it easier to get over everything if you hated me. Even if I had left Louise knowing she was pregnant — which would in itself have made me about the lowest of the low, in my opinion — how could I have also asked *you* to accept my having a baby with someone else? You were just on the brink of becoming the person you were meant to be. Your mother's death had already… altered things… and I didn't want to take anything else away from you. I didn't want to be responsible for fucking up your life further.'

'Only, that's exactly what you did anyway.'

He winced, but I didn't apologise. I wasn't actually saying it to hurt him, it was just a statement of fact. 'Is that actually why,' I continued, now unable to stop myself and having given up on any façade of mature, cool detachment, 'you moved away from here, because of what happened with you and me?'

'Yes,' he said. 'It seemed like the best thing to do. This is a small city. I knew I'd inevitably bump into you one day.'

I winced. That hurt. 'And yet you came back again?'

'Five years is a long time. I imagined you living it up in London or abroad by now, building a career, having the time of your life. Plus Louise still has family here. It was getting harder to come up with good reasons why we shouldn't come back. Jess, in my defence, I had no idea about Beth. If at the time I had known—'

'You'd *definitely* have left your pregnant wife, instead?' I shrugged helplessly. We just stared at each other in the long silence.

I stood up. 'Well, it would have been pretty annoying for you, back then, if you had confessed to Louise about me, only for me to tell you that, ironically, I was also pregnant with *Ben*'s child and I was staying with him. So at least you made the right call.'

'Annoying?' Simon said slowly. 'Jess, the way I felt about you was—'

'No! Don't.' I held up a hand. 'I've got to go now, Simon. Neither Beth nor I are your responsibility. That's all that's important.' I turned away and reached for the door handle.

'Jess, how do you think it felt at the start of term to be settling my little girl in – only for *you* to suddenly appear.'

I closed my eyes. Ben had been so proud to be an old boy, now returning with his daughter for her first day at school – Beth nervously looking around her as we entered the classroom and tightly holding my hand as I shyly smiled at other new parents... the friendly form mistress coming over and welcoming us, explaining practicalities, then saying that she wanted us to meet the newly appointed Head of Prep. He and his teacher wife had just moved back to the area from Yorkshire with *their* little girl! Would Beth like to meet her?

All of us turning around – and my heart stopping as I came face to face with an equally stunned Simon... introductions... watching, horrified, as Simon and Ben shook hands. Shaking hands with a cheerful Louise, chattily introducing herself as Cara's mum first and foremost, new teaching assistant second. Shaking hands with Simon. Our skin touching and eyes meeting in desperate silence as the lively classroom chatter buzzed around us. A million panicked thoughts cascading through my mind. I was going to have to pull Beth out and send her to a new school somewhere else, but how to explain that to Ben and my in-laws after *one day* of attendance when I'd done nothing but happily agree with all of them that Ben's old school was the perfect fit for Beth?

'And then,' Simon continued, 'for the penny to gradually begin to drop that not only by some hideous coincidence are our daughters in the same class at the school I now teach at, they are also in fact *both* my daughters.'

I gripped the door handle a little more tightly. 'Beth is just another pupil to you. That's all. You and I had a two-week fling – barely a relationship – a long time ago. There's nothing more to say.'

'Someone's told me about a job at Grove House that's coming up,' Simon said quickly. 'I'd have to do this post for at least six months first, but then I could apply. Louise knows I've always wanted to work there, so she wouldn't be suspicious. Cara could become a day pupil – no one would be surprised about that because obviously I'd lose my staff discount here. There would probably be a housemistress role for Louise looking after the boarders too. You might have a point about Louise; that I read too much into what she said last night, but I also know you're right about what school life is like, and that what happened between you and me will come out somehow. The best idea is for us to transfer away from here.'

Us.

Hearing him say that one inclusive word, and yet not mean me, hit home. I couldn't help it.

'You're going to leave again?' I said lightly, glad that he couldn't see my face.

'Please understand how much I don't want to be separated from you and Beth for a second time.'

I made a huge effort to get myself under control. 'Beth isn't your responsibility,' I repeated. 'If moving is what you believe would be right for your family, you should do it.'

'It's too close for comfort here, Jess. I'm finding it increasingly difficult seeing you. I—'

'*Please* don't do this, Simon!' I begged, spinning round. 'I've worked so hard to get to where I am now, and I was happy.' To my huge frustration, I felt the tears start to spill down my cheeks.

'Don't cry,' he begged. 'Please don't cry. I never, ever wanted to hurt you. You of all people.' He stood up and in two steps he was right next to me. The distance between our bodies wasn't even enough to call a space. I knew exactly what was a beat away from happening – if we let it. I knew how it would feel; my body waking up again as if long, cold years without him hadn't happened. It had never been about an embarrassing teenage lust – rather an all-consuming force that even at age 19 hadn't frightened or overwhelmed me. I'd willingly given myself over to it.

He lifted his hand as I stared back at him, anticipating his touch… but then I thought of Beth and Cara, and Ben and Louise, and I realised this time it *was* different. I shook my head instinctively. 'No. We can't.'

He hesitated and the next few seconds seemed to last an eternity, before we both jumped as a loud voice called: 'Hello? Can I come in?'

We leapt apart, like someone had swung two magnets around, and the door juddered open to reveal a ruddy-cheeked Louise. She'd shoved it with her foot as she had a fur-lined Parka in one hand and a mug in which some unappetising brown liquid was slopping around in the other.

'Oh! I'm so sorry, do excuse me, Mrs Davies, I didn't think anyone was in here. I was just illicitly dumping my stuff, but now look,' she nodded at her husband as she stepped over the threshold, 'I've been caught red-handed.' She laughed good-naturedly, and plonked her cup down on the desk next to Simon, before tucking a stray piece of her curly bob behind her ear, not a hint of the bad mood Simon had mentioned. She peered at me more closely and said with surprise: 'You're crying. Is everything alright?'

'It's fine.' Simon smartly walked round his wife, and hurriedly closed the door again. 'Mrs Davies was upset by a stranger in the street coming up to her outside school this morning and announcing that God loves Beth.'

Louise raised an eyebrow.

'She's also concerned about some classroom difficulties Beth is having,' Simon blurted.

I tensed immediately. I didn't want Beth labelled in some way when there was nothing wrong with her at all. That was completely unfair.

'Oh no! I'm very sorry to hear *that*,' Louise said.

'Yes, Beth's being bullied.' Simon continued, immediately falling into the out-of-practice liar trap of volunteering too much information.

'Bullied?' Louise looked astonished. 'What – here? You're kidding! By who?'

'Oh, someone in her form,' Simon said evasively, as I looked down at the floor.

'Well, I have to say, I'm amazed,' Louise said, after an uncomfortable moment's pause where she waited for a name, which was then not forthcoming. 'I would have thought Sandra Fey would have nipped it in the bud.' She turned to me. 'You took it to her straight away, of course?' Her face was set with earnest, professional concern. 'She's such an excellent teacher, apart from anything, I'm sure she'd be devastated to think of Beth unhappy. What did she say about it?'

'We're going to monitor the situation carefully.' Simon cut in, adding quickly, 'you won't discuss this with Mrs Fey though,

Louise, will you? I don't want her to feel *she's* on the radar too. It's one of those less said soonest mended situations, I think.'

I silently begged him to stop talking.

'Of course,' Louise said, slowly. 'It's odd that Cara didn't mention any of this, though. She's so fond of Beth that I'm surprised she didn't – oh no…' she paused. 'It isn't *Cara* you're talking about, is it?' She looked at me, worriedly. 'Has she been smothering Beth, or trying to stop her from playing with other people and you've just been too embarrassed to talk to me about it? She does get quite jealous. Not because she's a little horror or anything,' she added quickly, 'she isn't. She's just – like me, I suppose: passionate. When she falls, she falls hard and fast, and she does adore Beth.'

'It's not Cara at all,' I said. 'I promise. Beth is very fond of her too.'

'You're absolutely sure?' Louise said. 'Sorry, I don't want to put you on the spot here or anything, Jessica, but – is it OK if I call you that, by the way?'

'Of course,' I said quickly.

'Thank you. I can see I'm making you uncomfortable – but it's just probably better we get it all out there if Cara's gone a bit… off-piste.'

'It's nothing, honestly.' I smiled.

'Well, it's clearly something, or you wouldn't be crying,' Louise said reasonably.

'What I mean is, it's nothing I'm sure hasn't been dealt with now.' I looked at Simon. 'I won't be taking it any further.'

'Well, I think perhaps *I* ought to talk to Cara. I appreciate you're trying to be discreet and avoid any embarrassment, but honestly, I'm not one to—'

'For God's sake, Louise!' Simon exploded suddenly. 'Mrs Davies and I are dealing with this situation. You can go now.'

Horrified, I watched Louise stare at her husband in amazement. Then she recovered herself, and said: 'Well, I apologise unreservedly, Jessica. I've evidentially misjudged the situation, and overstepped the mark. Please do excuse me. I hope neither myself nor my husband have caused you any offence.'

'None at all,' I managed.

Again, Louise shot an incredulous look at Simon, reached out for the door handle, but then hesitated, turned back and blurted: 'Sorry, but why do I feel like the child being told to let the grown-ups get on with it, all of a sudden? What am I missing here? When do you *ever* speak to me like that?' She addressed her last question directly to Simon, and his eyes widened.

He shot me a frightened look, which I saw Louise register immediately. If she didn't have any suspicions before, she certainly would now.

Her gaze slowly alighted on me. I held it as steadfastly as I could, my pulse starting to pound. Just open the door and walk away, Louise. *Please.* There is nothing for any of us here. We can all just walk away. But I could see something in her expression beginning to change; I was morphing in front of her very eyes: a green, shy and eager-to-please school mum transforming into a woman some ten years younger than her, standing in her attractive husband's office, weeping... and an uneasy energy in the air that she couldn't entirely place.

She wasn't the type to hold back. 'What's really going on?'

Oh God. My head began to swim. I should never have let this happen. Why did I let Beth continue to come here? How could I have been so stupid?

'Nothing!' Simon turned to face me properly. 'It's my turn to apologise, Mrs Davies. My wife is not quite herself this morning. I do hope that—'

'Is it something between you two?' Louise cut across, ignoring him. 'Do you know each other?' Simon was right. His wife was no fool. There was a pause where Simon should have leapt in immediately and denied everything – if he was going to. We all heard it. I closed my eyes as he said, far too late: 'No, of course not. I'm not sure what you're implying, exactly?'

'I'd like a moment alone with my husband now, please,' Louise said, looking straight at Simon.

Now *I* was the out-of-place teenager. I said nothing; just shamefully put my head down – to think that when I'd met him I had been naïve enough to think that falling in love and knowing exactly how I felt meant everything would be simple.

Yes, Louise, there has been something between us. There will always be something between us. We do know each other.

I didn't say that, of course. Dismissed, I stumbled out of the office and clattered back up the stone steps, before hurrying out into the freezing playground, my face burning with humiliation. Finally reaching the door in the wall, I properly escaped onto the safety of the main street and – letting it slam shut behind me – exhaled shakily.

'*Shit!*'

I surprised myself by violently exclaiming aloud. How on earth had that all just happened? What was he going to tell Louise? If he did crumble and confess, Louise wouldn't shy away from confrontation – but would she come after me, or go straight to Ben with her news? And most importantly, what about Beth and Cara? What of them?

I shoved my icy hands into my pockets, only to discover Beth's gloves. I let out a little cry as I pulled them out – the lecture I'd given her when I'd had them all along! It somehow felt vital that I go back and give them to Beth; to get at least something right. But at the thought of coming face to face with Louise, I replaced them and carried on walking.

My eyes filled again as the guilt suddenly overwhelmed me – the whole bloody mess of the hideous situation. I started to walk faster, cursing repeatedly under my breath. I reached the car, and climbed in. Would Simon call me and at least let me know what had been said? Surely, he would?

I was going to have to talk to Ben. That much was clear. But tell him *everything*? I couldn't. I just couldn't do that to him, or Beth. I should have just removed her from school while I had the chance. Of course Ben would have been confused, but I could have made it work somehow. It would have been better than this.

My hands shaking wildly, I started the car engine, looking behind me as I reversed, and was immediately reminded of the lady librarian on her bike. In comparison with what had just happened back in Simon's office, her bizarre intervention didn't seem so extraordinary now.

And why hadn't I heeded it? Why hadn't I just turned around and taken Beth home, after all? This whole thing could have been avoided. I wouldn't have gone into Simon's office, Louise wouldn't have caught me crying… but then it *wasn't* a message… Not from God – not from anyone.

Only at that, I suddenly burst into proper sobs, and had to slam to a stop because I actually couldn't see. I put my head in my hands as I rested my elbows on the steering wheel and tried to force the image of Mum's face from my mind, but it was too late… the stupid radio DJ with his bloody suicide pop trivia. There was a honk of a horn behind me, and I snatched up my head to see another car waiting for my space, indicator on. 'You going?' the man mouthed, then looked taken aback at the wild expression on my face.

I didn't even bother to nod. Wiping my eyes furiously with the back of my hand, the gears grated as I tried to find first, and eventually managing it, I jerked out of the space and onto the road, clutching the cold steering wheel tightly. I took a few deep, calming breaths and visualised myself closing the lid on a box, turning a key in the lock, placing the key in my pocket, shutting the box away in a cupboard, leaving the room, walking out of the house… feeling marginally better I allowed my thoughts to return to Simon. Please God he wouldn't tell Louise everything. Please. Let him have the strength to not offload his guilt and fear onto his capable wife.

Mercifully, I didn't have long to wait to find out what had been said. It was ten twenty-five – not even two hours later – when the phone began to ring, and one of the other girls on reception of the advertising company I worked for leant round her pink iMac, her hand over the receiver and said: 'It's for you, Jess. Personal apparently.'

'Thanks.' I braced myself, and picked up the phone. 'Hello?'

It *was* the school – but it wasn't Simon. I realised it was actually the headmistress I was speaking to, on what I thought was a badly crackling line, but in fact it was her struggling to speak.

I was to please go to the hospital, immediately.

There had been an accident.

Then she said Beth's name and she started to cry. My heart began to thump as the delicate white wings of the librarian angel began to beat faster too – unfurling, growing dark and muscular, blocking out the light and turning the air cold.

God loves your little girl.

No! NO! I'd told Beth! This wasn't right – this couldn't be happening.

And yet it already had.

Beth had died, just twenty minutes earlier, at five minutes past ten in the morning… lying on the icy playground floor, staring up at the bright, blue sky.

CHAPTER TWO

I wasn't told that immediately, of course. The headmistress only said that Beth had fallen – from a climbing frame during morning play – and had been taken by ambulance to our local hospital. A member of staff had accompanied Beth, and would meet me there.

'But Beth's OK?' I asked, trying not to panic because obviously it was serious if they'd called an ambulance. 'Has she broken anything?'

'I don't know yet, Mrs Davies.'

'It sounds as if you're crying,' I said. 'Beth *is* alright, isn't she?'

There was a pause. 'I'm so sorry, Mrs Davies. I certainly don't want to alarm you. I'm just a little shaken up, that's all, but I really don't have any more information at this stage.'

I hung up and got to my feet. 'I've got to go,' I said to the other girls. 'My little girl has had an accident. Can you tell HR?'

'Of course,' one of them said immediately. 'Hope she's OK.'

Hope she's OK.

The words echoed around me as, grabbing my bag, I hastened across the reception area, my heels clicking on the cold marble floor. I swung the heavy glass door open and rushed across to the staff car park, fumbling in my bag for the new mobile telephone that Ben had bought me only three days before. I struggled to open the address book, but thankfully he was the only contact I had in it, so selecting the right number was easy.

'Hello!' Ben said, picking up after five rings. 'You're using it! I told you it would—'

'Ben, stop.' I said. 'Beth's been in some kind of accident. The school have just rung. They want me to go to the hospital; they called an ambulance for her.'

'Where are you now?' he asked immediately.

'Just leaving work. Can you come, please?'

'I'll meet you there.' He didn't ask questions; he didn't say goodbye. He just hung up, and I knew he'd already be on his way.

Reaching the car, I climbed in, and as I reversed out of the tight space – fumbling with my staff pass to activate the barrier – I tried to calm down. They were with Beth, they would be looking after her, she would be safe, but despite my repeating it to myself over and over again, I put my foot to the floor and sped through a light that had already turned red. She would be calling for me.

When I arrived at the hospital, there was nowhere to park and, after driving around in an increasing state of panic, I eventually dumped it in a disabled space. 'I'm so sorry,' I shouted breathlessly, as an elderly man pulled up alongside the car, pointing crossly at the blue badge on his dashboard, 'my daughter needs me.'

Once I was inside A&E, I ran up to the desk. 'My name is Jessica Davies. I'm the mother of Beth Davies, who was admitted by ambulance.'

The nurse only briefly looked up. 'Please take a seat. Someone will be with you in a moment.'

Oddly, her indifference was hugely reassuring. Starting to calm down a little, now I had arrived, I did as I was told, even noticing the sign asking for all mobile phones to be switched off. I was obediently reaching into my bag when someone said: 'Mrs Davies?'

I looked up into the face of an older male doctor, who gave me the small, sad smile, at which my heart seized with panic. I knew that smile. It was the same one the nurses and doctors had given me the last time Mum was admitted.

'Could you come with me?'

I stood up, starting to feel light-headed with fear, and followed him through a set of swinging doors. He stopped in front of what was clearly a relative's room, and politely gestured for me to go in. There was a nurse sitting in there, and two other empty chairs.

No. He should be taking me straight to Beth.

'Please, Mrs Davies.' He motioned again, not unkindly, but as I slowly stepped over the threshold, I turned round wildly as he closed the door behind him.

'What's happened to my daughter? Why have you brought me in here?'

'Please could you sit down, Mrs Davies?'

'No.' I shook my head; my heart was now thumping uncontrollably. 'Where is Beth?'

He took a deep breath. 'I'm so sorry, Mrs Davies, but I have to tell you that—'

Oh

my

God

I closed my eyes; it was as if I was tumbling through the air, but he kept on talking anyway, and then I heard him say it: 'there was nothing we could do, and I have to tell you that Beth died from her injuries.' I plunged into icy water, gasping in shock as it closed in over my head. The nurse jumped up – both of them took my arms and guided me to a chair.

I looked up desperately into the doctor's face, and I realised he had tears in his eyes. I would later discover he had a little girl Beth's age too. He gently explained that yes, Beth had indeed fallen from a wooden cube climbing frame at playtime – a distance of little more than four feet – but she had hit her head on a concrete path that the frame had, for some reason, temporarily been moved over. She never regained consciousness and had been pronounced dead on arrival at the hospital.

A freak accident.

'She didn't have her gloves,' I said, foolishly, punch-drunk.

There was a moment's confused silence before the nurse asked. 'Is there someone coming to be with you, Mrs Davies?'

'My husband.'

'Good – that's good.'

'Can I see Beth, please?'

'Of course. I'll just let them know we're on our way.' The doctor took a step towards the door.

'Is the teacher who was with Beth still here?' I couldn't think straight. 'Can I speak to her?'

'Yes – and of course. One moment.' He opened the door, stuck his head round and called out to a colleague. 'The teacher with Beth Davies, could you just – oh, thank you. That's great. Yes, we will be.'

He came back in, closed the door and sat down again. 'Mrs Davies, I think you should know that Beth would not have suffered in any way. She wouldn't at any point have been aware of what was happening, and—'

'Thank you,' I interrupted, unable to hear him say another word. I knew he was trying to be kind, and I must be sounding horribly calm, and measured. For a moment I wondered what they must think of me, but then found I couldn't care less. It was as if I was watching this happen to myself. 'It's very nice of you to reassure me.'

'Is there anything you would like to ask me about?—'

We were interrupted by a knock at the door, and the nurse got up to open it. 'Mrs Davies? Yes, she's in here.'

She opened the door wider, and in walked Simon.

I simply stared at him for a moment. 'You?' I managed eventually. 'It was *you* that came in the ambulance with her?'

He nodded.

'Could we have a moment's privacy, please?' I asked the nurse and doctor. I heard the door close behind them, and then we were alone.

'I am so sorry, Jess,' Simon said, his voice breaking as he moved towards me.

'Don't,' I said, scrambling to my feet, the chair scraping on the floor as I leapt back instantly, 'don't touch me.'

Bewildered, he let his arms drop. 'I didn't mean to—'

'Were you there when it happened?' I asked.

He shook his head. 'No. Mrs Fey and Mrs Mottram were on duty. One of the children in Mrs Mottram's class was sick everywhere, and they moved the climbing cube so they could clear it up. Several of the kids started climbing on the frame while they were sorting the mess out; Cara, Beth, two of the boys from Mrs Mottram's class. Beth fell. The children called to Sandra Fey, she turned around and Beth was already lying on the ground.

'I arrived a couple of minutes later; by then someone had called an ambulance. Sandra, and Julie Mottram got the children inside, and I stayed with Beth. I held her hand and I talked to her.' His eyes started to fill with tears. 'I told her you were coming and that you loved her, and she wasn't to be frightened, she was going to be alright, but she'd already gone. I'm absolutely certain she died instantly, Jess; there's no doubt about it.' He wiped his eyes, and I realised I was also crying. 'I'm so very, very sorry. I came in the ambulance with her. I had to. You understand that, don't you? I couldn't let someone else take her.'

There was a pause, and then I nodded, slowly, unable to speak.

He reached out again. This time I let him take my hand. We just stood there, holding onto each other in stunned, naked grief.

'I want to stay with you,' he said a moment later, 'but I expect your husband is coming?'

'Yes, he is.' I was barely able to get the words out. 'He'll be here any minute.'

'OK. I'll get back to Cara then. She was hysterical when I left. She saw it all. Louise is there obviously, but...' he trailed off for a moment. 'Listen, I also need to tell you that Louise knows everything – I told her after you left my office. She's devastated, naturally – but then when this happened... She's not going to breathe a word, Jess, I promise you that. Not now.'

And just like that, the wind changed direction again, re-covering everything I'd just unguardedly exposed with stinging sand. I lifted my gaze to his face slowly, took my hand back and looked at him in astonishment. 'What did you just say?'

'Louise is not going to tell anyone about you and me, about Beth being mine. She—'

'You think I give a *fuck* about that, about Louise, about any of it? My daughter – MY daughter – just died, Simon!'

'Oh, Jess, please! That's exactly my point. I was trying to reas-sure you that you didn't need to worry about anything coming out *now*, of all times, when—'

'Didn't you hear me? She's dead,' I cried. '*She's dead.*' I started to shake violently, and Simon moved towards me again, just as Ben burst in.

'Jess?' he said, frightened and confused. 'Where's Beth? No one will show me where she is; they just said you were in here. Why are you crying?'

Simon didn't say anything, just quietly stepped back, respect-fully turned, and left the room, closing the door behind him.

'Jessica?' Ben asked again, his voice starting to tremble. 'Where is she?'

I looked at my husband, the last to know – again – and I walked over to him before taking both of his hands in mine, as if trying to physically brace him. 'I'm so sorry, Ben—'

'No,' he said instantly, starting to shake his head. 'NO!'

'But Beth died at school this morning.'

I will never forget the sound of the cry he made as I told him. It will haunt me forever.

CHAPTER THREE

I stood outside the cathedral, looking up at the sharp spires spiking the heavy, grey sky, as the gargoyles peered down at me.

'Jess?' Ben reached out and gently turned me to face him. 'It's time.' He pulled me to him, and kissed my forehead. 'I'll see you in there, OK?'

The second he let go of me, Laurel, my closest friend and Beth's Godmother, immediately stepped forward and took my hand in his place, as I turned to watch Ben walk over to the hearse that was parked on the cathedral square.

The undertakers were carefully attending to the flowers around the small coffin – only mine and Ben's arrangement of white roses were going to remain on top of it – as they prepared to hoist it onto the shoulders of my father, Ben, his brother, and my father-in-law. Glancing up again, in an attempt to stop my tears from spilling over – I turned away, and blurrily looked around me in disbelief at our familiar surroundings, now punctuated by this black car carrying my little girl. I did not see the faces of passers-by who had stopped with their shopping bags to stare, some of the more elderly among them making the sign of the cross and whispering silent prayers. Instead I focused on the paths that lined the edge of the cathedral – the ones Beth loved to run round after school. I pictured her; hair streaming out behind her, feet lifting as she ran, the sound of my voice calling after her to slow down and to stay where I could see her.

The tears began to fall as desperately I traced the empty paths.

'Jess, we have to go in now,' Laurel said.

∗

They'd opened the main double doors for us, rather than the side entrances that were normally in use for visiting tourists, and as we reached the threshold, all I could see was a large central aisle gaping in front of me. Gripping Laurel's hand, I forced myself to look up and smile with thanks for everyone coming to honour Beth, but just as outside, I didn't register individual faces in among the congregation. It was a blur of bodies. The first sounds of 'Morning has Broken' began to swell around us, and I knew they were carrying her down behind me, but as I took my place in the front pew, and suddenly there the coffin was, just feet away from me, the shock was still unbearable.

I stared at it, numb with horror. She had held up her arms to me, to hold her when I was leaving in a rush to go and speak to Simon, and I didn't hug her. *I didn't hug her.* WHY didn't I hug her?

God loves your little girl.

I felt Laurel let go of my hand so that Dad could come and stand on one side of me, and Ben on the other. Still I stared at the coffin.

Ben looked sideways at me, and quickly put his arm around my shoulders, took my other hand in his and, pulling me to him tightly, whispered: 'Remember what we said, sweetheart. She isn't there any more, Jess. What was Beth has gone. Listen to me!'

I nodded silently, and he gently let go as I tried not to think that I knew she was wearing her pjs and dressing gown, and Rabbit – which she'd taken to bed with her every night since she was ten months old – was tucked carefully in the crook of her arm. In that box.

It's not her. She's not there. I repeated it over and over in my head, mantra-like. *She's gone. She has gone…*

I closed my eyes and swallowed, but was unable to stop myself imagining her falling, in slow motion, from the top of the wooden frame in the school playground. For just a brief moment, her small body in mid-air after her stiff, cold fingers lost their grip. The coroner had ruled Accidental Death. The post-mortem had confirmed Simon was right; Beth had died instantly.

Why didn't I go back and give her the gloves?

Never mind the gloves, why didn't I take her home when I knew Louise and Simon were in his office talking about *us*?

And I'd wanted to take her home after that woman told me God loved her, and I saw, I SAW what was going to happen! Why didn't I just do it then?

The priest kindly welcomed us and began to talk about Beth, but as he'd never met her, he started using platitudes like 'the sound of water over stones being the everlasting voice of our children, who will live on for ever'. I tried to concentrate instead on the fact that Beth had loved this building. I'd once remarked to her, while we were lighting a candle for Mum, that being in the cathedral made me feel peaceful. She had turned to me and said simply: 'It makes me feel beautiful in my heart.'

I smiled suddenly, through tears. What an amazing thing for a child of five to say. She was so perfect.

I must have zoned out then, or my brain simply couldn't process what was actually happening because, although I was dimly aware of more singing, and talking, somehow the next moment I looked up, Dad was bravely getting to his feet, clutching a piece of paper, and the service was almost over. I tried to send him silent encouragement. What man should have to speak at his granddaughter's funeral?

He stood in front of what I would later be told was some three hundred people, and addressed my question immediately. 'When someone dies at such a young age, and so suddenly, it's hard to see how a service like this might be in any way a celebration of a life well lived, but in the short time Beth was with us, she blessed every day with her love. She was a very kind little girl, sensitive to the well-being of others. She loved her mummy and daddy with her whole heart. She had recently settled well into school life, and looked forward to going every day. Beth loved drawing – as you will see from the front of your order of service; she did that beautiful rainbow – and some of her other favourite things were cake, hot chocolate, fairies, playing with her friends, her grand-parents, balloons and bubbles, coming home after being away, her bedroom, dressing up and playing in her garden. She *didn't* like wearing trousers, hand dryers, mashed potato, or swimming without goggles – but that's genuinely about it. How fantastic is that? What a happy girl she was, and what a wonderful life she had. She was a blessing in the truest sense, and our hearts are breaking that she is gone.'

The sound of sobs and sniffing was growing louder, and I had to stare at the floor intently to try and drown it out. I looked up and blinked, and Ben placed a hand on my arm to steady me.

'I consider myself fortunate to have a strong sense of faith,' continued Dad, 'but while I have no doubt that God has Beth in his loving arms, we, of course, only long for her still to be in ours. How painful the inadequacy of only being able to hold someone in your heart can be.' Dad folded his scrap of paper. 'Good night, my darling. Sleep tight, and God bless you.'

Then it was Ben's turn. I swallowed as he walked slowly towards the lectern, and then turned to face everyone. I had tried to dis-suade him from speaking, but he had been insistent.

He coughed, and stared at the card in his hands in front of him. He said nothing, and as I, along with everyone else, waited, my heart began to thump. He couldn't do it – of course he couldn't. Oh, Ben… I turned to look pleadingly at his father, who hesitated, and began to stand, but then Ben lifted his gaze, and said simply: 'Thank you so much for coming today for Beth. Jess and I are very grateful for your kindness. Some people have said to me that they can't imagine what it must be like to lose a child. I think what they really mean is that they *can* imagine it, and they don't want to. It's just too painful. Beth was five. Our beautiful, sweet, girl was *five*. It's nothing – and she was everything.' He paused for a moment, and tried to steady his voice. 'I'm not the best with words and I could never say anything that could make sense of this anyway. Instead, I want to talk about Beth herself. I want to think about the sound of her laughing, her smile, how happy she was at the end of every day as she snuggled into bed, how kind and gentle she was, how generous she was with her love. I want to say how lucky I feel to have been her dad. She was, and always will be, our inspiration. Jess and I are so privileged to have been her parents, and every single day that we had with her was a blessing.' I heard the tremble in his voice, and I couldn't look at him. 'Thank you. Beth, for being ours. And for being you. As you would say, I love you billions and billions, and that's a *very* big number. I have a notebook at home of all the things that Beth said as she was growing up – the kind of stuff you write down about your kids because you don't want to forget they said it… funny comments, words they mispronounced… you know the sort of thing. It doesn't feel real that the entries have stopped, and that she won't create more pages, but for now, I want to tell you one of them.

'Jess and I had taken Beth to the seaside on holiday last year, and we'd had an awesome day of her riding her bike on the front and having a picnic on the beach. I said to Beth at bedtime: "My best bit of today was eating ice cream." And she said: "My best bit was having fun with you."' Ben's voice finally cracked. 'That's it. Everything, right there. My best bit has been having fun with you too, my sweetheart. It will be my best bit forever.'

The priest said a blessing, the bells started ringing, and we turned to walk out. I wasn't aware that I was crying until Laurel gently reached across and wiped my eyes. I briefly faced everyone and was suddenly overwhelmed by the sea of purple in front of me. They had all taken up our invitation to wear something in Beth's favourite colour, and she would have loved it; purple hats, purple flowers... purple shirts and coats. Even a purple feather boa around the neck of one of my bewildered and shocked university friends. The parents of Beth's school friends were openly in tears, as were most of our work colleagues. Many of them kindly met my numb stare with gentle, sad smiles, and blew kisses.

And then I saw Simon, towards the back, right at the end of the pew. He was hard to miss in any case because of the purple velvet smoking jacket he was wearing. God knows where he'd found it. As I drew closer I saw he was seated with the headmistress, her husband, and Louise – all attending in their official capacity. Louise's strained face was white and streaked wet. As I walked towards them, I noticed she had his hand tightly gripped in hers. Neither of them looked at me until right at the last moment; just as I was about to pass, Simon lifted his gaze and our eyes briefly met. I saw my own devastation and grief mirrored back to me in our second deeply private moment of shared parental loss – only this time Ben was walking *right next to me* – and I suddenly hated Simon with a fury I didn't know I was capable of feeling. I didn't *want* to be conspiratorial with him like this. It was Ben who had been there from the moment Beth had taken her first breath, not him; Ben who had got up to her in the night, bathed her, fed her, loved her. My anger must have shown on my face, however fleetingly, because Simon's eyes widened with shock, and he visibly shrank back before looking away. This was not the place! This was not the fucking place for him to look at me like that!

But just as instantly, as I stepped into the cold outside air, my strength of feeling seeped away again and the strange emptiness of my new reality returned. I didn't want to wear it. It didn't fit. I wanted to wake up wrapped in the cosy blanket of my life of just two weeks ago.

It was at the burial itself – just me, Ben, Dad, my in-laws, and Ben's brother and wife, plus Laurel, and Gav, Ben's best man from our wedding – that it really began to hit me. Unlike at Mum's funeral, it wasn't because of the physical act of interment itself. I kept telling myself over and over and *over* again – as Ben had reminded me – that what was Beth had gone. It wasn't her in there, and that's how I coped with throwing a handful of earth on the coffin; I couldn't have borne it otherwise – but moments later I violently realised that this was nearly it. We were nearly done; it was – bar the wake – nearly over – and I wasn't ready to be finished.

So it was once everyone had finally gone, and we were alone at home, that I finally began to sob, uncontrollably. Ben had come into the sitting room and sat down next to me as I huddled on the sofa, staring at the flames flickering behind the glass of the wood burner. He held me while I cried because I didn't want to have said a last goodbye to Beth. When my tears began to subside through sheer exhaustion, he said simply: 'You need to eat something. There are about a million sandwiches out there. Shall I make you up a plate?'

I blew my nose. 'No thank you, I'll get something in a minute. I promise.' We lapsed into silence. The house was silent at half past four on a Wednesday afternoon. No sound of children's BBC, no rushing around getting tea on the go. No calling upstairs to Beth when it was ready and on the table only to discover *that* was when she'd finally decided to go up to get changed into home clothes. No hearing her shout that she was just coming.

Ben's parents had already removed all of her toys from the room, as well as the small table that she liked to do her drawing at, and it looked too neat and sterile without all of her bits and pieces strewn everywhere, stuffed into corners because we never had enough storage to tidy it all away. I suddenly jumped to a stand, unable to bear it. 'Sorry, the sofa cushions are slipping, can you just get up a minute?' I asked Ben.

'Leave it,' he said, bewildered, 'it doesn't matter. Does it?'

'I can't get comfy.'

He hauled himself up, and moved across to the chair as I ripped them all off, stripping the sofa down to its frame. He watched silently as I started to whack and kick the cushions furiously into shape on the floor.

'There,' I said breathlessly, 'that's better. Let's just tuck the sofa cover in properly too before I put them back on. It drives me crazy the way it drapes over the floor like this.' I shoved my fingers violently right down the side, burying my hand painfully up to the wrist, but I immediately came across something plastic. I pulled it out, and uncurled my fist, only to discover a tiny pair of plastic wings in my hand. They belonged with a fairy that had come in a Kinder Egg; Beth had recently been looking for them.

'Oh!' I said, and tears sprang again to my eyes as I stared at them on my palm. 'I'm sure Beth and I checked there. I can't have done it properly.' Suddenly, I made an animalistic noise, somewhere between a moan, a cry and a shout of sheer desperation and pain, as I doubled over, wrapping my arms around myself. Ben jumped up and caught me as I collapsed onto the cushions, sobbing again, and this time we cried together for our little girl.

Later, as we sat next to each other in the dark room, lit only by the fire and some candles on the mantelpiece, I watched the reflections of the flames dance on the windowpane, as we'd left the curtain open on the dark. I was still clutching the fairy wings tightly in my fist.

'She'll be pleased that you've found them,' Ben said eventually, and reached out. 'Shall I take them and put them on the mantelpiece?'

But my grip only tightened, and I glanced up over the fireplace at one of the pictures of the three of us hanging on the wall, all of us smiling on our first ever family holiday in Cornwall: my laughing, handsome and happy husband, Beth an absurdly fat eight-month-old baby, slightly squished into the corner of the shot, but beaming delightedly. How could this be happening? How?

'OK,' Ben said. 'No problem. You hold onto them for a bit then.'

I have the strongest feeling God needs your daughter to know how much he loves her.

'You know, I keep thinking about what that woman said to you in the street about God loving Beth.'

I looked at him, startled. 'I was literally just thinking about that.'

'Really?' he said, carefully. 'I mean, she was mad – but I'm actually pleased she said it, because it made you tell Beth you loved her. You would have done that anyway probably, I know,' he added quickly, 'but Beth got to say it back to you as well, which is a big deal.'

There was a silence.

I caught my breath, then blurted. 'I feel like it was a prophecy, Ben. Someone was warning me that it was going to happen.'

He frowned. 'If that woman had told you God loved Beth any other day you'd have written it off as a stranger being a bit weird, and forgotten about the whole thing.'

'But it didn't happen any other day, did it?'

'You told Beth God loved her; you told her *you* loved her. What else could you have done?'

'Taken her home,' I whispered.

'Jess, you spent Beth's whole life protecting her. You were an amazing Mum, but you can't stay with someone twenty-four hours a day to stop them getting hurt. You couldn't do it with your mum, and you couldn't do it with Beth either. What your mum did to herself wasn't your fault for not being there to stop her, and what happened to Beth was an accident.'

'Well then if it wasn't a message, that woman should have kept her comments to herself!' I said desperately. 'If she had, I wouldn't have doubted myself when I realised Beth had a temperature, and I would have just taken her home.'

'It was an accident,' he insisted. 'I don't blame the school for moving the frame while they cleared up some sick; I don't blame them for not watching the frame, but for trying to keep the children away from the pile of puke. I don't blame them for putting it over a path that was no more than half a foot wide with grass either side of it, and I don't blame *you* for not taking Beth home that morning because some random nutter came up to you in the street and told you God loves children. Please look at me!' he begged, and I did as I was told. 'I don't blame you,' he repeated. 'You have been the best mother anyone could have asked for, and you can't punish yourself. We couldn't have done anything to stop this from happening.'

If I had told you about Simon, you would never have kept Beth at that school and she would be alive now.

The confession burned silently in my mind. I closed my eyes; I was unable to look at him.

'We've lost our daughter—'
She's almost certainly not your child.

'And we need to support each other now.' He cleared his throat. 'I've started reading a book Mum gave me on how to cope when your child dies, and it says this is an "individual journey only you and your partner can understand, and go on together". We'll—'

Oh God. I leapt up – and went to stand by the window. 'Ben, I know you mean well, but it's a bit early for mapping out objectives as part of a strategy for coping with Beth dying, don't you think?'

Ben looked shocked, and understandably very hurt. 'I was just trying to say…' He petered out. 'Actually, I don't know what I was trying to say really.' He swallowed. 'I just don't want you to blame yourself, and I don't want this to be like when your mum died, but a million times worse because it's Beth.'

I looked at my childhood sweetheart who knew me so well, had loyally stayed with me, phoning diligently from the phone box up the road from his student house so that we could talk privately without his housemates listening in, regularly coming home with me when Mum was particularly bad. Ben was the one who had taken my hand tightly at Mum's funeral, and held me together immediately afterwards when I fell apart. He and his kind parents had been amazing. They must have wanted more for their son, but they never once said it. Because of me, Ben didn't have the student life of most of his friends; he would never have split up with me while Mum was so ill. I overheard two of his female housemates discussing us in the kitchen once, when they didn't know I could hear: 'But he's so insanely fit, and nice, and he fixed the sink like immediately because he's also so *good with his hands*…' they both sniggered, 'and she's so… intense, miserable and up herself. I don't get it.'

If I'd have ended it with him after Mum's death – which, ironically, had it not been for my dropping out and meeting Simon, I *know* would have happened – Ben would have got together with one of those much less complicated and more fun girls, and probably been very happy.

But I did meet Simon, and I cheated on Ben. I fell pregnant and, heartbroken over another man, scared and guilty, I blindly reached out for my rock. Being a decent person – and because of course he assumed it was his child – Ben immediately proposed.

And now my lies have cost my daughter her life, while Ben is in all probability mourning someone else's child.

So yes, Ben, I AM to blame. I am to blame for everything. I had so many opportunities to save Beth. And I didn't. I didn't save her!

'Beth was so lucky to have you, Jess.'

It wasn't even as if I could tell him the truth by offering him absolute fact either way. There was a very small chance Beth might be his; although, purely on the basis of the last two years of us trying unsuccessfully for another baby, it would appear unlikely.

'And you've been the best father anyone could have asked for.' I meant that with all my heart. Regardless of biology, he was at least her dad. Beth adored him, and he, her. Knowing the truth wouldn't free him from the pain of loss – he wouldn't stop loving her – I would just rip what was left of his world apart.

'It was such a beautiful service this afternoon, wasn't it?' Ben tried to smile at me, his eyes shining. 'Do you think I did alright when I spoke?'

He wasn't fishing; he was really asking. I went and sat down next to him again, and took his hand silently. 'It was perfect,' I said sincerely.

'Thanks. There were just so many people there…' he paused, before saying, 'it was good of the headmistress to come – and Mr Strallen. I didn't get to speak to him, did you? I wanted to thank him again for going with Beth.'

'No, I didn't speak to him either.' I thought about glaring at Simon in the cathedral – the first time I'd seen him since we'd spoken at the hospital. Then I thought about Louise gripping

Simon's hand like she was never going to let go, and deliberately not meeting my eye… but then I didn't want to think any of that. Not tonight.

Ben reached out and gently took the wings from me, twisting them between finger and thumb in the firelight. 'She should be upstairs, in bed, while we're down here watching TV, just like normal. She could be – it feels *just* like she could be. All this shit everyone keeps saying about taking things day by day… I don't even know how to get from second to second.'

Tears started to stream down his cheeks again, and he wiped them away with the back of his hand in disbelief. I was suddenly reminded of seeing him cry like that, years ago, when I'd told him after going out with him for six months that I'd kissed someone else at a party. He'd done that exact same thing – wiped his eyes with the back of his hand. I'd been horrified and guiltily told him I'd never do it again.

Feeling the weight of my decisions and regrets bearing down on me so heavily I could hardly breathe, I pulled my hand back. I didn't even know how to tell him I loved him. You're not supposed to hurt someone you love so badly. Suddenly unable to be in the same room as his grief any longer, I got to my feet. 'I think I might go up. Do you mind?'

He shook his head. 'I won't be long.'

I quietly climbed the stairs, managing to walk past the door to her bedroom, and went into the bathroom. There was no make-up left to take off. Instead I rinsed my face, brushed my teeth, and went to the loo. I walked back to our room, got changed, and climbed into bed, before turning to the bedside table for the sleeping tablets the doctor had given me. I hadn't been using them every day, but there was no question I wanted one now. I needed to fall asleep without any nightmares or dreams to follow.

They weren't where I'd left them on the bedside cabinet, however. I got back out of bed, and was about to go down to the sitting room when I realised I could just shout – there was no sleeping Beth to wake up.

'Ben – have you moved my pills?' I called down loudly.

Surprised, he appeared at the bottom of the stairs. 'Yes, I put them in the bathroom cabinet. Sorry.'

'No problem.'

I turned and walked back to the bathroom. Force of habit for him too. Safely away in the cabinet; out of the reach of children.

I opened the cupboard, and sure enough, there was the packet in front of me, but my eyes actually alighted on the Calpol bottle on the shelf below, and the clean spoon sitting next to it, ready and waiting.

I choked down a fresh surge of shock as I picked it up and turned to put it in the bin... only I couldn't do it. I spun round and immediately returned it to the shelf, before hurriedly pushing a pill out of the blister pack instead, gulping it down and switching the bathroom light off – again, no need to leave it on all night now – and hastened across the hall into Beth's room.

'At least let me wash the covers, Jess,' my mother-in-law had pleaded. 'We don't have to clear it out, but let's make a bit of a start, don't you think?'

At least wash the covers – that was the *last* bit I wanted anyone to touch. I pulled back the duvet and quickly climbed into the three-quarter-size bed. We'd bought her an extendable one, but hadn't yet put it up to a full single. I looked around the room briefly. Her stuffed full bookcase, the princess castle in the corner, her wardrobe with a dress hung on the front, her chest of drawers on which sat some of her various treasures: a box of plastic bugs, a torch, a china duck that had belonged to me when I was little, a music box Laurel had given her... a picture of her and me on a mini rollercoaster the last summer, both shrieking with laughter.

I buried my face in her pillow as the tears came again and, crying silently, I deeply breathed in the scent of my child, and waited for the tablet to work – for the merciful release of a chemically induced loss of consciousness to come.

CHAPTER FOUR

'Are you getting up?' Ben appeared in the doorway, dressed in his work jeans, Timberlands and sweatshirt.

'I'm not going in today, no.' I tried to smile at him from the bed, but turned my gaze back to the window, where I'd already opened the curtains on the morning and was staring out at the blank, grey sky.

'That's over a week you've been off, now.' He paused. 'Although to be fair, not many people will be going anywhere today, so you'll probably get away with it.'

I winced at his unwitting choice of words.

'Please don't stay in here all day though, Jess.' He gestured around Beth's room helplessly. 'It's not healthy.'

I didn't say anything to that, just kept looking past him, trying to pretend he wasn't still watching me.

'We need to decide about next week, too, when I get home tonight?' he said, after a pause. 'Mum's said she'll book it for all of us; we just have to tell her where we want to go. She's suggested Barbados, which sounds a bit much.' He shrugged. 'I don't know what you think. I mean, obviously it's really kind of her and Dad… and probably everyone's right that we should do something completely different for Christmas this year. Mum's not hassling, she just wants us to get something nice I think. If we want it, that is. She just needs to know then she'll go to the travel agents and sort it.'

'Yes, alright.' I was exhausted just listening to him.

'I'm sorry that I have to go in today,' he said quietly. 'Dad did say he could manage, but we've got two flats to finish off by the end of this week for the new tenants at the weekend. I've got to do all the coving and skirting, and there's an auction of a six-bed house on West Strand in West Wittering this afternoon that Dad really fancies. He reckons we'll get it for about £200k. Should be a nice profit on it if we tart it up, add it to the portfolio and bide our time.' He looked at me and waited.

'Sure, it's not a problem.'

'To be honest, Jess, I'm finding it easier if I stay busy. That's not a criticism of you though,' he added quickly. 'So you'll get up in a bit then?'

I screamed inside, but managed to stay silent. He would go in a minute.

'OK, well… I'll see you later then. At the least, please promise me you'll eat something? Jess?'

'Yes. I promise.'

'Good. Well, keep your phone on and I'll check in with you at lunchtime. I've lit the fire; you could get dressed and go and sit down there for a bit. Your dad rang and said he's really sorry but he's woken up with a shocking cold; so I've asked Laurel to pop over instead, assuming she can get here, of course; although, the main roads are all still open, I think. Right – back in a bit then.' He paused in the doorway. 'You're sure you're going to be alright?'

I still didn't answer. Just nodded. I was trying not to cry again and I didn't want to put that on him just before he left. It wasn't fair.

Sighing, he left the room, and a few moments later, I heard the front door close behind him. He didn't call out goodbye.

I closed my eyes in relief as silence descended on the house. When I opened them, it had started to snow again. Fat flakes were tumbling past the window. She would have been so excited. I lay still and watched as the world began to quietly white out into welcome stillness, but then next doors' children suddenly shrieked with delight, obviously having rushed out into the garden to make footprints in the fresh fall that was settling over the last few days' myriad of trampled paths. How could Beth be lying beneath the same snow other children were playing in?

I threw back her duvet, and as the cold air hit my skin, I got stiffly to my feet, my body hunched over from another night squashed into her small bed. I couldn't lie there and listen to their happy shouts. It was too much. I looked down, briefly, into our untouched back garden – drifts still covering the bushes and the bird table, which looked like an oversized chess piece. Ben was crazy to go in to work with it like this. He must really not want to stay at home.

Shivering, I bent to pick up my dressing gown from the floor. I doubted Laurel was going to be coming over with the snow this heavy, so I didn't need to get dressed. Not that she'd mind about that anyway.

I pulled the robe on, and paused again for a minute by the window. The flurry had stopped as suddenly as it had started, with only tiny isolated flakes now wisping through the air. The branches of our oak tree were weighed down with snow once more, making it look like a set of tired, drooping lungs; bronchial twigs reaching out into nothingness.

I leant my head against the pale blue wall of Beth's room, feeling the cold leech into my warm skin.

Come back.

Beth.

I turned her name over again in my mind, and then hesitated. 'Beth,' I whispered, aloud.

But instantly, I wished I hadn't because, of course, there was no answer. There would never be any answer again.

No 'yes Mummy?' I closed my eyes and imagined the sound of her voice, and her small arms around me. It had been so recently that it had last happened that I knew exactly how it would feel. 'Oh!' I gasped, winded with the pain of longing. 'How am I ever going to do this, Mum? Please tell me that she's with you, and you're both safe. Please!'

I opened my eyes and stared out into the garden, desperately, for something/anything: a floating feather, a small robin, a burst of sunlight… I would work with any cliché at all right now, and seize it with both hands willingly… but there was nothing. No sign of afterlife.

But then, where had 'signs' got me last time?

I pulled the cord a little too tightly around my middle; I could feel it digging painfully into the flesh, but not loosening it, I started to make my way downstairs. I padded into the kitchen to get a glass of water, and noticed instantly that Ben had laid the table for me – a cereal bowl, spoon and a packet of muesli, a toast plate, knife, butter in a dish and a small pot of jam. It was both such a kind and worriedly sad gesture all in one that I couldn't bear it. I picked up the box and put it back in the larder, then replaced the cutlery into the drawer too, before feeling suddenly drained and collapsing onto a chair, putting my head in my hands. This was so *wrong*. I shouldn't be the focus of Ben's attention. He had every right to be as bereft as me; he needed looking after too. Why did I keep letting him down like this? Ben was a good man; he didn't deserve this, *any* of it! He didn't deserve me.

My deceit – locked down for so long – bobbed up again, from where it now sat, just below the surface where anyone might see it floating there, barely hidden. My *not* telling Ben the truth was making a mockery of his bereavement; I knew it – but no matter how many circles I turned in, I was equally certain there was no way at all I could now confess, not now Beth was gone. I felt another wave of rage, and I didn't WANT to be distracted by this. I ought to be concentrating simply on Beth – but then whose fault was that, that I couldn't?

Mine. All mine.

Louise was probably still out there thinking that too. I imagined her suddenly, stood in this kitchen, telling Ben everything; how they'd both been betrayed… and Ben's face as he learnt the truth. I shivered. Ben would never, ever recover.

There was a loud knock at the front door, and I jumped, before feeling my heart sink. Laurel. I just wanted to go back to bed and sleep – to shut everything out. There was a second insistent rap, and I hesitated. She would have made a huge effort to walk from the other side of town to see me, and she'd be worried if I didn't answer.

I got to my feet and made my way into the sitting room, before opening the front door, but the woman standing on the doorstep with her back to me – about to walk down the path – wasn't my best friend. As she turned around at the sound of the door opening after all, I realised it was Louise Strallen.

'You?' I gasped in shock. Having just literally imagined her here, to suddenly be confronted by her in the flesh, was completely overwhelming.

'There are some things we need to discuss,' she said abruptly 'Are you alone? It won't take long, and don't worry, I'm not here to make a scene.'

I hesitated, but stood to one side.

She stepped out of the snow, past me, and walked into my house.

CHAPTER FIVE

I closed the door, and turned to face Louise. She'd lost a lot of weight; her face looked gaunt. She sniffed, having stepped in from the cold, and stared openly at me. The only colour to her skin was the violet shadows under her eyes. 'I want to start by saying I am sorry for your loss.' She spoke clearly. 'Since Simon confessed to me in his office, the only thing that's kept me going has been Cara. You must be in hell right now without Beth.'

I simply wasn't able to respond to that.

'Obviously, I'm aware that Simon has told you I know everything, and just so we're both clear, that is *everything*. He explained you both met after your mother's suicide when you were 19. I can only assume he told me that detail to make me feel sorry for you, or in an attempt to justify why, two months after she died, you met my husband and fucked him.'

I stayed silent. I knew she wanted me to react, but I had nothing left to give.

'I gather Simon fell very much in love with you, although you also had a boyfriend at the time – now your husband? It wasn't about sex apparently; neither you nor he were drunk. Simon was planning to be honest about you, and leave me, but I told him I was pregnant with Cara before he had the chance and he decided to honour his responsibilities. He didn't know you'd also fallen pregnant. Am I right so far?'

I just wanted her to leave. 'He never knew I was pregnant, no. Just as I didn't know he was married.'

'So,' she continued, 'you then have no contact. You marry your boyfriend and have Beth. We have Cara. Five years pass. We now reach the part that Simon insists is pure coincidence. Somehow, Cara and Beth randomly wind up in the same tiny class, you supposedly having no idea that Simon is a new teacher at the school you've enrolled Beth at, and Simon equally as devastated by the discovery as you, allegedly. Fate, no doubt,' her voice wobbled dangerously, 'as you're meant to be together. Around this time, Simon also begins to suspect Beth is his daughter. I don't suppose you'll answer this question honestly, but is he right? Was Beth his?'

'No.'

'You said that extremely quickly.'

'I don't want to talk with you about Beth. Would you mind leaving now, please?'

'I don't *want* to be here; and I meant it, I'm genuinely sorry for your loss, as any mother would be.' She cleared her throat. 'You say you didn't know Simon was married when you met him. Let's suppose for one moment I believe that. I'm having considerably more trouble with you being completely unaware this man you'd had a child with – and then abruptly ended it with you – was a teacher at your daughter's first school? You didn't, in fact, think it might be the perfect way to engineer a relationship with her real father and half-sister by sending her there?'

'Please leave me alone.'

She ignored me. 'Did you send Beth there deliberately?'

I shook my head, exhausted. 'No. I didn't.'

'So why the tears in my husband's office, Jessica, and the implausible reasons for needing to speak to him alone if you don't have an agenda any more? That scene told me everything I needed to know.' She paused, and shoved her hands deep in her pockets, starting to rock on her heels. 'Since then, I've thought about everything a lot, and I suppose it shouldn't hurt like this given it all happened so long ago. The thing is, to me, because I've just found out, it *does* feel like it's only just happened. It's been nearly three weeks since he told me and I still feel as if I discovered you and my husband had sex yesterday. I mean, I get it – you're very beautiful. You're young, slim, trendy. *I* can't stop thinking about you – I can see why he couldn't either. I cannot stop thinking about you,' she repeated, closing her eyes tightly and clenching her jaw. 'And then I think about the two of you. Him touching you, kissing you. You fucking him. You're driving me mad.' She paused. 'And it does hurt. It *really* hurts.' The last few words escaped from her in a weirdly high-pitched wail, and I thought for a moment she was about to start crying.

Instead she exhaled deeply, stopped moving, dropped her head down and muttered something under her breath that I couldn't quite make out. The fire Ben had expertly lit had made the room claustrophobically warm, and Louise's coat was thick, but I realised the pinpricks of colour starting to appear on her pale cheeks wasn't the heat, but a rising excitement. She yanked one hand free from her pocket and began to drum her fingers lightly on her leg in agitation, the other staying buried. She seemed to be preparing for something. 'I know you don't know *me* very well, but I'm actually a nice person, Jessica. I'm certainly not in the habit of going around making threats. So this is probably going to sound ridiculous, but after I caught you both in Simon's office and he confessed everything, I wanted to kill you.' She looked up again, her eyes now so wide open she appeared to be sleepwalking. Even her voice had taken on a dreamy quality. 'I went straight to the school records, got your address and started thinking about how I'd do it. I was going to come round here – bring a knife, hide it in my coat and – *stab you.*'

She snapped off the last two words so unexpectedly I jumped. She didn't even notice.

'It would be so easy. I don't want you in my head any more.'

I caught my breath. She meant it. She wanted me dead. It could die with me. 'Do it then,' I begged. 'It'll all be over.'

I watched her tense, before she rushed right up to me – so close to my face I flinched again. We were practically touching. I shut my eyes and waited, sensing the movement of her arm slowly drawing up, the crinkle of her coat sleeve, before a press of cold metal on my neck. My heart began to thump, and I dropped my head back, further exposing my throat... but nothing happened – and the next moment, her lips were right next to my ear, hot breath on my skin.

'Believe me, I'd watch you bleed out right here on the floor,' she whispered, her voice quivering, 'but I have a little girl to think about. Someone who depends on *me*.' As tears began to slip down my face, the flat of the blade pushed a little harder onto my skin. 'They'd lock me up, and then you'd have everything. You know, even though she saw it all happen – Beth falling – Simon still left Cara in the ambulance rather than stay with her. What have you done to him?' She sounded almost incredulous. 'He's her *father*. She needs him. I need him. I know you came looking for my husband, I'm sure of it, but you ought to know, he's not yours to take.'

'That's not true. I didn't—'

'You can insist otherwise until you're blue in the face.' She pushed harder still with the knife, and I coughed at the pressure; only, just as suddenly, she stepped back. 'He can't even look at us because of you.'

I gazed at her, stunned. Her hands were back in her coat. It was almost as if the last few moments hadn't happened.

'Cara's at home today; all of the schools are closed because of the weather. She's asked Simon several times to make a snowdog with her, or to have a snowball fight, and all he keeps saying again and again, is "maybe later". I just want to scream at him: "SHE'S here. SHE'S alive. Just notice her! She's five!" He should be doing whatever it takes to make sure he's not going to lose her, or me. Only he's not – because of YOU.'

She shouted so loudly I shrank back. 'But Louise, I—'

'Shut up.' She didn't miss a beat. 'Just shut up! You are to leave us alone to rebuild our lives, and *this* is what you're going to do.' She started to draw her hand from her pocket again but between her fingers was nothing more than a small scrap of paper. 'Our phone number at home, in case you don't already have it.' She flicked it at me. 'Ring it this afternoon at 3 p.m. I'll know it's you so I'll leave it for Simon to answer. Tell him to meet you at The Armoury tonight at 6 p.m. When you meet, you're to tell him you want nothing more to do with him, ever again. You tell him you've never loved him – no matter what you may have said at the time – it was nothing more than a teenage crush. You reiterate Beth was not his daughter – whatever impression to the contrary you gave him at the hospital after she died. Then you tell him you're moving away from the area.' Her voice was much calmer now, as if she'd practised this bit.

'But my husband's family business is here… they're all very close. He will never leave.'

'Then you'll have to go without him.' She started walking back towards the door. 'Because if you don't move, I will tell your husband the daughter he is grieving for was never his, and that you lied. I'll destroy everything he has left.' She shrugged. 'Or kill yourself if you like, and I won't say anything.'

I sank to my knees, no strength left to stay standing, as she saw right inside my head. For the hundredth time, I thought of my poor father. A wife *and* daughter. I could never do that to him. I shook my head mutely.

'Then call our house at 3 p.m. I want you to be the mistake my husband and I never, ever talk about.'

'Louise – Ben is such a good man. He's done nothing wrong.'

She walked over and crouched down alongside me. 'Well, if he's really such a nice person, he doesn't deserve to have what's left of his heart broken, does he? You're clearly never going to tell him the truth yourself, or you would have done it already. So do the one decent thing you can for the poor bastard – leave him. He'd be better off without you. We all would. Now,' she straightened up, 'we have nothing more to say to each other beyond, again, my sympathies for your loss. Beth was a lovely little girl.'

I stood still as she opened the door and walked out into the snow, leaving it deliberately wide open behind her. She stopped briefly at the gate, and for a wild moment I pictured her changing her mind, spinning round, running back and lunging the knife into me after all – but she carried on resolutely putting one foot in front of the other. I waited for a moment or two more, as the heat leeched from the room and I began to shiver, but she was gone.

I thought about Ben – trying so hard to keep going – and Louise reappearing to tell him the truth. I saw Cara tugging at Simon's sleeve, begging him to play with her, but being ignored… I heard Louise's wail in my mind. How desperate did a woman have to be to do what she'd just done? And then, of course, I saw Beth holding up her arms to me, and my head began to swim.

He'd be better off without you, we all would.

Louise was right. I'd caused such suffering and pain.

There was nothing left to do but slowly get to my feet and close the door after her as the house returned to deathly silence.

CHAPTER SIX

When Laurel actually did arrive, at half past one, she was delighted to find me up and dressed.

'Well done, Jess,' she said encouragingly, as she sat down on the sofa next to me. 'Hey, shall we go out for a little walk? We could pop into town and get a hot chocolate, or something?'

I shook my head. 'I'm fine thanks.'

'No problem, and no rush. I understand completely.'

You really don't. I have somewhere else I have to be soon. 'Laurel—' I blurted.

'Yes?' She looked at me, concerned. 'What's up? You seem a little... agitated.'

I hesitated. How could I even begin to explain? 'Nothing. I might get a tea, or something. Do you want one?'

'I'll make it.' She jumped up quickly and disappeared into the kitchen.

I leant my head back on the sofa, and closed my eyes, but I could almost feel the scrap of paper Louise had given me burning in the back pocket of my jeans.

'Lau, you know how Ben and I were trying for another baby for ages before Beth died, and it just kept not happening?' I called out desperately.

She reappeared instantly in the doorway holding a teaspoon, eyes wide. 'Yes?'

'Oh, no, no!' I shook my head. 'I'm not pregnant. Sorry, that wasn't what I was going to tell you.'

She looked very relieved. 'Go on then, what?'

I cleared my throat and said carefully: 'Well, a few months ago, I told Ben that I'd been to the doctor, had a test, and it turns out to be my fault, but that given my age, they weren't worried, and we just had to try a little bit longer before they intervened with any treatment.'

'OK,' Laurel said, confused. 'And?'

'I lied. I didn't go anywhere or see anyone – there's nothing wrong with *me* at all.'

'Right…' Laurel came over and sank down again. We sat in silence as I waited for her to think it through, my heart starting to thud at finally being on the brink of someone else knowing the truth after all this time; someone who might help me. Louise was almost certainly right. I owed it to them all to leave. But if I walked out and Ben met someone else, and they then tried to have children, they would eventually discover – as I had realised about a year ago – that it didn't appear Ben *could* have children…

At which point he was going to wonder how on earth we'd had Beth.

And the house of cards would come tumbling down anyway.

I felt annihilated, suddenly. I just wanted to sleep. Forever.

'Oh, Jess!' Laurel said, and I jolted slightly, bracing myself. 'You've been taking the pill all this time, and Ben doesn't know?'

I stared at her, realising that, of course, that was a far more obvious conclusion for her to reach.

She took my silence for confirmation. 'It's OK.' She moved closer and put an arm round my shoulder. 'I don't blame you for one second, and you shouldn't blame yourself either. You're only 24! Just because you'd already had… Beth,' she said her name hesitantly, 'wouldn't have meant you'd have automatically been up for having more kids.'

'Laurel,' I cut in, 'I like hearing Beth's name. It helps. You don't need to worry about saying it. It's people *not* saying it that's hard.'

She coloured. 'Sorry. It's just, I don't like to make you think about her, if you're not, and—'

'I am thinking about her every second, every minute. It's really OK to say her name.'

Laurel bit her lip, and I felt bad for picking her up. 'Carry on.'

'Well, I know Ben really wanted a brother or sister for Beth, but...' she paused, 'please, *please* don't tell me Ben has suggested you start trying again NOW?'

'No, of course not. Not at all,' I said quickly.

She looked relieved. 'I didn't think that sounded much like him.'

Although, of course, if I were to stay, he would undoubtedly suggest that, at some point in the not too distant future, and what then? I shifted uncomfortably. 'Can I ask you something? Do you believe in "the one"?'

Laurel looked at me carefully. 'You know I do. But that doesn't mean I'm right.' She hesitated. 'Jess, what you and Ben have is really amazing. You're the best of friends – you have a lot of history together, he's been there for you through thick and thin, and you were incredible parents to Beth. If that's not love, I don't know what is. Please don't start questioning everything in your life; you're going through such a devastating time. Now is not when you should be making any major decisions that you might regret later.' She looked at me pleadingly, and I fell silent. Everything she'd just said about Ben was true; she had long been a fervent supporter of his: one of the reasons why I'd never told her about Simon.

'I think I might need to leave Ben.' I felt dazed hearing myself say it aloud.

She looked devastated. 'Oh, Jess, but he loves you so much! I know things haven't always been what you might have chosen them to be, but please don't do anything now. Genuinely, I don't think you're in your right mind. Not that you need lessons in how grief works, of course.'

I sighed and leant my head sideways, resting it briefly on hers. I couldn't even begin to explain to her how Beth dying and Mum's death were so completely different. How much I wished with my whole heart that it could have been me, and not Beth – that I would have given my life for her to live.

'I'm not trying to tell you something you don't already know,' she said awkwardly. 'I know when my grandmother died, I felt as if—'

'The thing is, I do love Ben,' I cut across her rudely, my goodwill vanishing instantly. I literally couldn't bear another person's well-meaning comparison of Beth dying to their having lost one of their relatives. It made me insanely angry. They had no idea, and they should thank God for it. 'But there have already been lots of times when I should have ended it, and I didn't. He deserves to be happy. It was different when we had Beth, there was a reason for us to make it work, but now… like you said, we're only 24.' I was deeply unsettled to realise I actually wasn't sure if everything I'd just said was driven by Louise's blackmail and the overwhelming guilt she'd triggered or if I was finally acting on long-held, genuine feelings.

'It's just so sad.' Laurel was near to tears. 'Could you not wait until after Christmas? It was always going to be a really, really shit time for you both. Just go away, like he wants you to, and see how you feel about it in January. Don't you think?'

I exhaled deeply.

'Please? For me?' she begged. 'Don't do anything just yet. Why don't you come out tonight? There's just a few of us from school having a couple of pre-Christmas drinks. Nothing big. Everyone would love to see you both.'

I just stared at her for a moment, blankly. *Christmas drinks?* She was trying. It wasn't her fault. I shook my head. 'Thank you, but I think I'll pass. What time is it now though?' I glanced past her anxiously at the clock. The hands were creeping closer to two o'clock. One hour left to make my decision.

'Jess, there really is no rush to do anything about Ben, you know? Not when you've been thinking about this for such a long time, really. A week or two more won't make any difference at all.'

Even that wasn't true any more.

I finally managed to pack her off at twenty to three, insisting that I would be fine, I wouldn't do anything rash, and I just wanted to rest. As she unwittingly stepped into Louise's footprints in the snow, and turned to blow me a kiss, I blew one back and, shutting the front door, pulled Louise's piece of paper from my pocket, and went to find the phone.

I lifted it down onto the carpet, and stared at it for a moment before stretching out on the floor, holding the number tightly in my hand as I looked up at the white paper lampshade, and tried to calm my thoughts. It made me think of lying on Mum's bed next to her after she'd come out of hospital the first time, just after my sixteenth birthday, both of us staring up, like this. She'd remarked how she wished she could live on the ceiling – it all looked so empty and simple. I knew what she meant now. I wanted very much to be somewhere away from all of this.

'Mum,' I said slowly, aloud, 'I know it wasn't that you didn't love me enough to stay. Or that you gave no thought to how you leaving would affect me. If you had been able to think, or control it, you would never, ever have done it, but I miss you, Mum – and I need your advice. I know I don't love Ben. Not in the way I should. Not like I love Simon.' I completely caught myself by surprise with the last few words I said aloud, and then properly jumped as the phone suddenly sprang into life, and began to ring. I twisted my head in amazement to look at it, then laughed at my own absurdity. 'That better not *actually* be you, Mum,' I said aloud, reaching out to pick up, but I dropped the receiver clumsily.

When I finally got it up to my ear and said, 'Hello?', Ben was already repeating, worriedly: 'Jess? Jessica? Can you hear me? Are you there?'

'Yes, I am.'

'Oh, good.' He sounded very relieved. 'For a minute I thought you weren't in, and I was going to have to try your mobile, but I bet you haven't even got it switched on, have you?' He tried to sound light and as if he was teasing, but I knew he wasn't; he was actually asking. 'Anyway, I just wanted to call and make sure you're OK?'

'What time is it, Ben?' I asked.

'Um, it's ten to three? Why?'

'No reason.' I felt sick.

'Laurel called and said you're struggling today.'

I breathed out slowly. 'A bit, yes.'

'Before you say it, *I* know every day is a struggle, but you know what I mean. She's especially worried about you. That's all.'

'I'm fine. Really.'

'You'd tell me if you needed me to come home?'

I closed my eyes. He was such a good man, and I was such a burden to him. 'Yes. I would. What time will you be back tonight?'

'About half six. Why?'

'No reason,' I lied. 'I might pop out, that's all. I didn't want you to worry if I wasn't here when you got home.'

'That's great!' He sounded so delighted I couldn't have felt more disgusted with myself. 'Where are you going?'

'Just into town.'

'Would you like me to come and find you when I'm done?' he asked eagerly. 'We could maybe get something to eat?'

'No!' I said quickly. 'Thank you. I'll come back.'

'OK,' he said, not entirely masking his disappointment. 'I'll stop and pick up some food on my way home, then. I might make a curry! How about that?'

'Sounds great.' I couldn't bear it any more. 'I'd better let you get on with some more work. See you later.' I went to hang up, just as he said: 'Jess? Dress up warm. It's really cold out. And Jess?'

'Yes, Ben?'

'I love you.'

There was another, much longer, pause while fresh guilt punched me in the stomach. 'I love you too.'

He hung up, and I slowly pressed down on the receiver to clear the line; the dialling tone sounding in my ear. After Mum died, I used to call home when I knew Dad wasn't there just so I could hear her voice on the answerphone message: 'I'm sorry we can't take your call at the moment, please do leave any message you'd like to.'

I let the receiver momentarily fall from my hands and, still holding Louise's bit of paper, I reached into my front pocket and pulled out the Dictaphone Ben had bought me. For the millionth time, I rewound the tiny tape to the beginning, and pressed play.

'Go on! Say – "Mummy! Answer your phone!"' Ben's voice was distant. There had been a lot of feedback when I'd held the Dictaphone up to my mobile to record Beth's first and last voice message before it was automatically erased.

I scrunched my eyes tightly shut, as I heard the faint giggle I'd listened to over and over again, and then her voice: 'Mummy! Answer your phone!' I swallowed, and rewound it.

'Mummy! Answer your phone!'

Click – rewind.

'Mummy! Answer your phone!'

I let it slip from my fingers because the insistent whirring tone coming from the landline telling me I hadn't hung up the receiver properly was growing louder. I sat myself up.

Now was the time. Louise had said three o'clock.

I stared at the phone. I should remove myself from everyone's lives. It was the right thing to do, and I now wanted to do it.

I exhaled, darted a hand out, snatched it up... and began to dial.

CHAPTER SEVEN

The ringing echoed in my ear; it seemed to be growing louder and louder... I was actually doing this. There was a click as someone picked up, and I shivered, preparing to speak to Simon.

But instead, a breathless little voice said: 'Hello?'

It was like jumping into a bath of scalding water unawares. I gasped in shock.

'Hello?' the voice repeated, more uncertainly.

The pain was so exquisitely white hot that, for a second or two, I was unable to speak. She sounded so exactly like Beth. Louise had said it would be *him* that answered. She must realise how this would make me feel? Surely? Was that the point?

'Hello, Cara,' I managed eventually. 'Can I speak to Daddy, please?'

'Daddy!' she called out. 'It's for you... I don't know.'

There was a muffled sound of the receiver being passed over, and then Simon's clear voice. 'Hello?'

'It's me,' I said.

There was a stunned silence, and then Simon said cheerfully: 'Hello, David. How are you?'

I thought of Louise in the background, knowing he was lying – and badly. How was he going to explain it if Cara asked afterwards why the lady was called David? But then he probably wasn't thinking straight.

'I'm sorry to ring you at home.'

'That's OK,' he said brightly. 'How can I help?'

'I take it Louise is there with you by the way you're talking?' I tried to keep my voice calm and controlled.

'Yes – absolutely!'

'I need to see you. Today. At 6 p.m.'

There was another pause. 'That might be tricky, David.'

No, it'll be fine. Trust me. 'I'll be at The Armoury at 6 p.m. tonight. I wouldn't ask unless it was important.'

'I'll see what I can do.'

'Did you hear where I said I'll be?'

'Yes, The Armoury,' he said, confused.

Good – he'd said it aloud. Louise would at least be certain now that I had done as I was told, and that it was me he was speaking to.

'I'll see you there.' I hung up, my hands shaking.

I got to my feet stiffly, feeling cold – and went upstairs to run a bath.

I winced as I climbed in, watching my skin turn sugar-prawn pink in the too-hot water. Staring at the blank, white tiles in front of me, I glanced right, at Beth's plastic teapot, still sat in the corner of the bath. Cara's innocent voice calling her daddy echoed in my head.

Standing up suddenly, I let the water out; I needed to get this over with. I wanted to get on a plane and just disappear. Quickly washing my hair in the shower, I went through to our bedroom, drew the curtains to shut out the dark and pulled on jeans and a black jumper. I hadn't worn make-up since the funeral, and I hated myself for being vain enough to bother, but I applied some anyway, and dried my hair. Glancing at myself in the hall mirror by the front door however, having shoved my feet into boots, found my hat and buttoned up my coat, I reached up and roughly wiped off my lipstick. It was wrong to be wearing it. Totally wrong.

Yanking open the front door, I breathed in the sharp, cold air of early evening as I stepped onto the path, crunching the snow that was already icing over. It was very strange to be outside again after three weeks of being almost exclusively in the house. I dug my hands into my pockets and put my head down. There was woodsmoke in the air and people were hurrying home to warm houses rather than heading out, like me. Normally I loved this time of year, when people left their curtains open because their Christmas trees were in the front windows. I found the glimpses into strangers' lives fascinating, but this time I only saw wreaths on doors, and families all cosy, eating tea, the TV on in the background, children rushing around excitedly. I stared down at the compacted snow, lit up orange by the street lights, as I trudged past rows of identical terraces, getting closer to the city centre.

In the precinct, late-night shopping was in full swing and, despite the weather, plenty of people were grappling with bulky shopping bags and rolls of wrapping paper as they struggled over slippery pavements. I put a few coins in the collection box of the Salvation Army who were playing 'Away in a Manger' as I passed – Beth had sung it solo at her playschool nativity the previous year – and then, arriving at The Armoury, I stamped my feet and swung open the door.

A hot fug of booze, fags and food hit me, making my empty tummy rumble involuntarily. I took off my hat and looked around the busy bar, but he wasn't there, so I walked through to the much quieter restaurant section and immediately saw Simon sat in the middle of the room with his back to me. There was already a bottle of red wine and two glasses on the table.

I took a deep breath and walked slowly over. 'Hi.'

He turned at the sound of my voice, and looked visibly shaken as I took the chair opposite him.

'What?' I asked warily.

'Nothing! You just look… you've lost a lot of weight, that's all. And you didn't exactly have any to lose.'

I made no comment, just unzipped my coat, took it off and put it over the back of the chair. 'I'm sorry about earlier, calling the house.'

'It's OK. I know you wouldn't have unless it was really important. What's happened?'

I couldn't answer at first; I just lifted my gaze and looked at him desperately.

'Tell me,' he said softly. 'I can't help unless you tell me.'

I gave a strange, strangulated laugh. 'You can't help anyway. No one can.'

He didn't say anything to that, just reached out and clasped my hand in his. Our fingers automatically intertwined, and my eyes filled with tears at his touch as I blurrily stared down at us for a moment, just holding onto each other. I sighed shakily, and pulled away, reaching into my jeans pocket for a tissue. Then as if I'd always known it, I suddenly announced: 'I'm leaving Ben.'

He looked shocked, almost as much as I was to hear myself repeat it. 'Where are you going? To your dad's?'

'I don't know. I think I'm probably moving away from here, leaving in the morning. I haven't told Ben yet.' I dutifully spoke Louise's words, and yet they felt strangely true, even if I couldn't believe I'd just said them.

Simon sat back in his chair. 'Moving away?' he said blankly. 'Another country, moving away? Or just to the other end of this one, moving away?'

'I really have no idea, Simon,' I answered truthfully.

'Don't. Please,' he said suddenly. 'I don't want you to go.'

I swayed slightly and briefly closed my eyes. A handful of the right words? I would never be that weak again.

'I have no right to say that to you, but—'

'You have a daughter, Simon.'

'I know,' he said quietly, 'and you're right, Cara needs more time. It would destroy her if I left right now. But once she's stronger, and I'm certain she can cope – with my help, with all of our help – I will move out. I'll divorce Louise and we can be together. Me and you. If we make it OK for Cara, it will be. You don't need to threaten to leave to try and shock me into action, Jess. I've been waiting for you to be ready, but I've wanted this to be on your terms; it *had* to be something you decided.'

He spoke calmly, as if it was an obvious truth.

I stared at him, astounded. That's what he thought this was about? *Us?* He hadn't even mentioned Beth. It was as if she'd never existed.

He stood up quickly. 'You've gone completely white, hang on.' He marched off towards the bar, and finding it unmanned, looked irritated and pushed through the door into the main pub.

I exhaled, and leant my head back, looking up at the ceiling. He had *not* just said all of that? Had he?

'When he comes back, tell him he's wrong, you've never loved him. Make him understand that when you move away, he's not to come looking for you, ever again. It's over and you want nothing more to do with him.'

I jerked my head up in astonishment at the sound of a voice to my right, and peered round the corner of the booth it seemed to be coming from. Louise was huddled in the corner, eyes wide with shock, knees up to her chest and an empty tumbler loosely in one hand.

'What are you doing here?' I was barely able to get the words out. 'Aren't you worried he's going to see you?'

'I don't think he'd notice if I jumped up and sang "Jolene" right there on the tabletop, do you?' Her voice wavered. 'I came to make sure I heard you say it. But now I wish I hadn't been listening. Just tell him it's over between you and stop talking to me, he'll be back any second.'

'But—'

'Just do as you're told!' She squeezed the glass so tightly it shattered, and I gasped. Her fingers were cut; I could see little ribbons of skin on the inside of her knuckles. The now sharply jagged base she was still clutching was decorated with thin swirls of blood, but she didn't let go, just softly moaned with pain. I had no idea if it was physical, but I instinctively stood up to help her.

She instantly twisted the glass in my direction. My first thought was that she was going to shove it at me, but she was actually lowering it threateningly towards her *wrist*. Horrified, I recoiled, my heart crashing in my ears, as Simon reappeared in the doorway clutching a shot of whisky. I collapsed back down onto my seat in shock, and turned back to him.

'You weren't going to leave while I was in the bar?' He half-joked and sat the drink down in front of me. 'You need this, not wine.'

'Simon, I brought you here today to tell you I don't ever want to see you again,' I said loudly and clearly. 'Don't try and find me when I leave. I want to start a new life away from everything that's happened – and you can't be a part of it. I don't *want* you to be a part of it.'

He sank down into his chair, just looked at me and blinked in confusion, before saying eventually: 'I don't believe you.'

But I meant every word. I couldn't bear any more suffering. 'Losing Beth has changed everything. It's changed me forever. I'm not the person I was. I won't be, ever again. You don't know me any more, Simon. You think you do, but you don't. What you and I had was an infatuation. That's all, and it's over.'

He shook his head, resolutely. 'I'll know you for the rest of my life, and you leaving won't stop me from loving you because

I *do* love you, and you know that. But I want you to be happy. If you change your mind, come and find me. I'll still be waiting. It's only you. It's only ever been you. I can't force you to love me, Jess, and I want you to have the freedom to choose.' He stood up. 'I have to go, I'm sorry. My mother-in-law is at ours. I had to make excuses to come out and questions will be asked if I'm not back soon. You know where I am.' He leant across the table and kissed me briefly on the cheek, before grabbing his coat and walking out of the pub without a backwards glance.

I let my head drop for a moment, before reaching for the whisky, downing it and getting to my feet. I hesitated and returned to Louise.

Tears were freely flowing down her cheeks which she was about to brush away with her sleeve – she'd pulled it right down so I couldn't see her wrist.

'Please don't hurt yourself,' I begged, worried that there might also be bits of glass caught up in the fabric and she might cut her face as well as her hands. I leant forward to remove the larger pieces from the tabletop, but she sprang into life.

'Get the fuck away from me,' she hissed. 'I swear to God if you touch me, I'll kill you right here.'

I obediently stumbled out of the pub, feeling sick at what she had apparently been about to do to her wrists, and frightened by the strength of her loathing for me. Looking like a drunk about to throw up, I wobbled as the cold air hit me and had to lean on the wall to steady myself, earning some curious glances and knowing wry smiles from passing shoppers. They were right: like Louise, I'd well and truly reached my limit. I simply couldn't take any more.

Straightening up, I put on my coat, and started for home, only on impulse to change my route; heading out instead towards the cathedral green. A group of girls my age passed by in little black dresses and heels, arms crossed over their chests as they shivered without coats, tottering towards the pubs. Plenty of people were around; the cathedral itself was lit up brightly, guests arriving for some sort of concert. I stopped briefly under a street light and watched them; bright, merry smiles and busy chatter as they stepped carefully over the cleared path to the door. Instead, I pictured the scene as it had been in the late hot summer months; people lying on the grass eating ice creams, toddlers running around. Me and Beth walking home chatting happily, holding hands, her proudly swinging the carrier bag containing her new school uniform. I slowly reached out my empty hand, imagining hers slipping into mine. It was so real I could almost feel it. I shut my eyes with desperate longing and *tried* to feel it. I must have looked mad.

But when I opened them, I was still alone. A couple rounded the far side corner of the cathedral, some distance away, arm in arm – they were about the same age as me and Ben, and laughing, very obviously in love. They didn't notice me staring. I was completely struck by their open, easy happiness – as it should be, as they deserved it to be. I wished desperately that I had been able to give Ben that. I had failed him so badly.

I turned, light-headed with a sudden clarity. I would leave in the morning, but for now, it was time to head back for my last night at home.

CHAPTER EIGHT

'It's not properly hot at all,' Ben said, putting the plate of curry down in front of me. 'I promise. You'll be fine with it, it's really mild.'

'Thank you for making this,' I said, picking up my fork, and hesitating before eating a mouthful of rice.

Ben sat down opposite me and began to attack his food hungrily. 'How was town? Busy?'

'Yes,' I said. 'I was surprised really, given the weather.'

'Well,' he said, 'I suppose they grit everything, don't they? People have still got to get to work.'

There was a pause, and he looked up quickly. 'Sorry. That wasn't a pop at you.'

'I know,' I said truthfully.

He cleared his throat and resumed eating, more slowly. 'So where did you go?'

'The cathedral.'

He looked up again. 'Really?'

'I didn't go in. I just stood outside. There was a carol concert.'

He took another mouthful. 'Had you been planning to go to it?'

'Yes,' I lied. 'But it turned out I couldn't really face it after all.'

'So, what did you do instead? Just walk around a bit?'

'Yes.'

He looked troubled. 'Didn't you even?—'

'So how was your day?' I cut in quickly. 'Did you get that house?'

He brightened. 'Yes, and it turns out next door might be coming on the market too, Dad's tickled pink. Talking of which, when we've had this, shall we make the call on Christmas? Let's face it, we could do a lot worse than Barbados!' He gave me a brave smile, and my heart ached for him. 'And then I'll go to Blockbuster and get us a vid if you like? What about that *Notting Hill*? You like Hugh Grant.'

'Actually, I'd really like to go and check on Dad, if that's OK?' I forced down another mouthful, trying not to gag. The sauce was incredibly rich. 'I'm a bit worried about him being in on his own, and feeling under the weather.'

'How are you going to get there?'

'I'll drive.'

'But Jess, the roads really aren't great. Look, I'll take you, OK?'

'Ben,' I said gently, 'I'd like to go on my own, please.'

He carried on eating in silence for a moment. 'Tell you what, I'll drop you at your dad's and I'll go and see my parents, then come back to get you. How about that?'

I sighed. 'If that's what you'd prefer.'

'I would. Yes.' He watched me forking up more food. 'Just don't eat it if you don't want it, Jess.'

'No, no,' I insisted, 'it's delicious. Thank you.'

We ate in silence for a few more minutes, until he scraped his chair back suddenly, making me jump, and put his empty plate in the sink. 'I'll go and make sure the car doesn't need de-icing, and get my shoes on.'

I managed a few more mouthfuls, but once I was certain he'd gone, I stood up and quietly tipped the rest of it into the bin, covering the evidence with an empty crisp packet and a pizza delivery leaflet. I didn't want to hurt his feelings, but I simply couldn't face it.

We drove to Dad's in silence too, Ben concentrating on the road. We slipped at least twice; it was a good job he had driven.

'I'll be back to get you in an hour then.' He twisted to face me when we arrived. 'Does that give you enough time?'

'Yes, thank you.' I opened the passenger door, then turned and kissed him briefly on the cheek before climbing out. I heard the car pull away as I picked my way carefully down Dad's path and knocked on the door.

The light flicked on in the hall, and through the stained-glass panels at the top, I saw the blurred outline of my father coming down the stairs and felt immediately guilty. He'd clearly been in bed.

'I'm so sorry, Dad,' I said, the second he opened the door. 'I've got you up when you should be resting.'

'Don't be silly.' He smiled at the sight of me, but was looking pretty dreadful. In pyjamas and his dressing gown, his nose was streaming, he was clutching a handful of tissues and his hair was uncombed. 'Come in,' he said, standing to one side, 'but don't kiss me. I don't want you to get this.'

'You look pants, Dad.'

'I feel it, rather,' he agreed, closing the door behind me.

'Have you eaten anything today?'

'I'm fine, Jess. Don't worry. You really didn't need to come and check on me. I'm OK.'

'Let me make you a drink. Would you like a hot toddy?'

'Well, you could, but I haven't got any honey, or lemon, so it'd just be a whisky.'

'Sounds good to me.'

'Ah,' he said, following me as I turned and made my way down into the kitchen. 'You're up and dressed and you've got make-up on, but... how are you today, Jess?'

'Oh, you know. Wishing it could have been me that died and not Beth. Aching for my baby with every fibre of my being, an overwhelming guilt that makes me feel physically sick that I wasn't there when she fell.'

'One of the better days, then?' Dad said.

'Yup.' Tears had already started to leak down my cheeks, and I wiped them away as I reached up to the cupboard for a couple of mugs. 'It's starting to get worse, not better. And in other news – I've decided to leave Ben.'

Dad sat down heavily on a stool. 'Right. I see. Does he know?'

I shook my head. 'Tea or coffee?'

'Neither. Let's actually have that whisky. It's in the larder.'

I took a few steps across the room and found the bottle. I didn't bother to get glasses though, just slopped a measure into one of the mugs.

'Jessica,' Dad rebuked, gently.

'I'll have that one then. Here.' I reached for a wine glass, upside down on the draining board, and poured another shot into it, then offered it to him.

He raised a reproving eyebrow, but took it anyway. 'Cheers.'

'Cheers.' I took a large gulp of mine as I leant against the work surfaces. My empty stomach immediately contorted in protest at my second shot of the day, and my throat scorched.

'So, you're leaving Ben because?...'

A woman whose husband I slept with put a knife to my throat, then threatened to tell Ben he's not Beth's father, and finally – half deranged – almost glassed herself in front of me.

'Because it's the right thing to do.'

Dad took a mouthful of whisky. 'So you *want* to leave him?'

'It's not that simple.' I coughed and took another sip. 'I'm not going to go into the reasons behind my decision, because then, when he asks you, you'll be able to honestly say that you don't know. But I've no doubt it's the best thing for him.'

'Hmmm. I'm not sure it's ever a good idea to try and make decisions for other people.'

'Trust me, Dad. This is different. I want to protect him from being hurt… and this way, I will.'

Dad looked at me carefully. 'Has something happened to prompt this decision?'

I shook my head. 'No. I just can't face Christmas and then starting a new year knowing how I feel, and not doing anything about it.'

'Are you leaving him to be with someone else?'

'No!'

He held up a defensive hand. 'So you'll be coming here, then. That's all I meant.'

'Oh, I see. I'm not actually coming here, no. I'm leaving tomorrow… I'm moving away.'

'What? But Jess, this is crazy! Moving away to where?'

'I'll call you when I arrive, and I promise I'll let Ben know too.'

Dad gave a sharp intake of breath. 'Oh, Jessica – you're just going to walk out on him?'

'The house is his – or his parents' – in any case. I'd almost rather be able to just leave and keep it fixed in my mind as it is. It would break my heart to have to dismantle her room. I couldn't do it.'

'Who says you have to?'

'Dad. Please.' I looked up at the ceiling, my eyes clouding with tears again. 'This is hard enough as it is.'

'OK,' he said determinedly, putting his glass down. 'I'm going to have to break one of the golden rules of talking to a bereaved person, and give you some advice. Sometimes after you've had too much to drink, you nonetheless feel like you could get in the car and drive. You are every bit as impaired by your grief right now as if you really were drunk. You are not in control, even though you feel as if you are, and you are not making good choices. You don't *have* to make this decision now, so don't.'

'I've already made it.'

'Your mother died in truly tragic circumstances that I wish, I *wish*, I could have protected you from, and now so has your daughter. This is more than anyone should ever have to bear. My already broken heart aches to make this okay for you all the time.' Dad reached across the kitchen bar and gripped my hand fiercely, his eyes watering. 'But I can't. I can't walk this walk for you, my dearest child. I can tell you though, that trying to run like this, leaving everything behind, may feel like the answer, but it isn't.'

'I know,' I whispered. 'And I'm not leaving *you*, Dad, or Laurel, or cutting anyone out of my life. I will actually miss Ben very much. I'm not *in* love with him, but I do love him. I just have to go away for a bit.'

Dad sighed.

'I want to get on a plane,' I said truthfully. 'I've made so many mistakes, and I can't make them right. I don't know how to make them right. It's too much. I can't do it.' The tears began to spill over again.

Dad got up, came over and hugged me to him as I sobbed into his sleeve.

'I understand, but you still take yourself with you, Jess. Wherever you go.' He exhaled deeply. 'Twenty-four is too young for all of this.' He released me and walked stiffly over to the sideboard. Pulling open one of the drawers, he removed his wallet, and handed me a bank card. 'Use this one. The pin is 3476. I'll top it up in the morning – and I'll keep it topped up. I also need to know that you're safe, OK? Please don't just disappear.'

I hesitated, then took it. 'Thank you. I'll pay you back. I'm going to get a job as soon as I can. I'm not going to take my mobile phone. It wouldn't be fair to Ben, but I promise I'll stay in touch.'

'And do you also promise there's nothing you want to tell me that I could help with?'

I thought of Louise, trying to protect her child and keep her safe. Dad was right. You do anything for your children. Anything at all. I shook my head. 'There's honestly nothing more to say.'

❧

'Jess?' Ben called across the landing, and I jolted in the darkness. 'Are you still awake?'

I blinked, sleepy and confused. 'Yes. Why?'

There was a creak of floorboards, the door to Beth's room pushed open and Ben stood there in his boxers and a T-shirt, shivering. He folded his muscular arms across his chest and said: 'Please will you sleep with me tonight? Not like that… I just really need the company. I'm sorry to wake you, and to ask.'

'Sure,' I said, still half asleep. 'I'll be right there, just give me a minute.'

He disappeared, and I sat up, rubbing my eyes, before automatically grabbing the pillow and shuffling out into the hall. It was only when I arrived at the threshold of our room, I realised the significance of this; getting into bed with him for the last time. I hesitated. I hadn't slept in here since before the funeral, and he hadn't asked me to. Would it be better to refuse now, knowing what I was going to do in the morning?

He turned to see me. 'Thank you,' he whispered. 'I had a bad dream.'

I went in, and sat on the end of the bed. 'Do you want to talk about it?'

'No. Can you just hug me?'

I put my pillow down and climbed in next to him. He wriggled awkwardly into my arms, and I realised he was quietly crying. I held him, stroking his head, like I had done so often with Beth when she woke in the night, and once I was sure he was asleep, I gently slid free, moving to my side of the bed, to wait for the morning to come.

I must have finally fallen asleep myself in the early hours because, when I woke, Ben was standing over me, donkey jacket already on, holding a cup of tea which he carefully put down on my bedside table.

'Thank you for last night,' he said. He straightened up and cleared his throat. 'Can I talk to you about something quickly, before I go?'

'Yup.' I blinked a few times, and tried to focus. 'I'm listening.'

'Yesterday my mum told me that a friend of hers mentioned it might be helpful for us to write things down to each other – when we're finding it hard to talk, or we can sense that the other doesn't really want to, but might need to. You won't need to do this because you always know what to say, but I'm so rubbish, I thought I might try it.' He shrugged uncertainly. 'I don't know exactly what you're supposed to do, if you write letters, or your thoughts or what. But anyway. I've had a go. Here.' He passed me a note and then bent and kissed me. 'I'll see you later.'

I held the small piece of paper in my hand until I'd heard the front door slam, and then I unfolded it.

I didn't know what a broken heart was until now.

Beth not being here hits me like an actual punch in the face, sometimes when I've not even got up from the last one.

I don't know how we make this work. But I want to.

I don't really want to go away this Christmas. I know we should, but part of me actually would rather stay here, if I'm being honest.

I love you.

I let my hand fall to the bed covers, still holding the piece of paper, and stared at the pattern on our curtains for what felt like an age before I let go of the note, slowly got up and went to the bathroom to shower. Once I was dressed, I came back into the bedroom, reached under the bed and pulled out one of our hold-alls. Placing it on the bed, I looked at Ben's note again, hesitated, and picked it up. Reading it afresh made me want to cry, but I couldn't – there was nothing left; just as my leaving was going to break what remained of Ben's heart.

But if I didn't…

Louise would tell him everything.

Could I tell Ben the truth myself after all? Stay, and tell him? I couldn't think straight. I was beginning to believe Dad was right, I wasn't capable of making this decision.

I thought then, about what Ben had said; I should write my feelings down. Fetching my notepaper and pen from the cupboard in the sitting room, I sank down on the sofa, curled my legs up and under me, and began.

Dearest Ben, I wrote.

There's something I need to tell you

But I didn't know what to say next. I sat there for so long my legs went stiff before I put the pad and pen down, and went up Beth's room instead. I sat down on the carpet, leant back on the wall and looked around me, fixing it all in my mind. I gently touched her bedspread, smoothing the wrinkles. I reached under the bed and pulled out the last three books we had read together the night before she died, and carefully slotted them back into place on the bookshelves with all the others.

I knew then how the rest of the letter was going to run.

I got to my feet and left the room, gently closing the door tightly behind me.

PART 2

Seventeen Years Later

CHAPTER NINE

Sunday, 20th November 2016

'Happy Birthday to you!
   Happy Birthday to you!
   Happy Birthday, dear Ed!
   Happy Birthday to you!'

We all cheer and pull party poppers as my husband leans forward to blow his candles out.

'Mind your hat!' His sister Kate jumps up and snatches the paper party crown off his head. 'You'll set what's left of your hair on fire.'

'Hey!' says Ed, pretending to be offended, and pats the back of his head. 'Less of that, thanks very much.'

'You're right, there is,' Kate agrees. 'That's my point. You want to hold on to what you've got.'

'Steady, Katie.' Ed's dad puts a hand on his daughter's arm. 'He can't help it – there's that many candles on the cake, the whole pub's going to go up if we're not careful.'

'Except, sorry to point out the obvious, Dad,' Ed turns to Bob, 'but if *I'm* now old as God's dog – that makes you…'

'Peter Pan,' Bob says decisively. 'I don't age, me.'

'That's true, actually,' I agree. 'You've not changed in the eight years I've known you.'

Bob puts his hands wide and smiles beatifically. 'Jessica, I've always said you're a lovely girl. I'll tell you what it is.' He leans forward in his seat as if he's about to tell me a secret. 'Good genes – and that's just luck of the draw – but it's all that golf too, you see. You've got to keep on the move, get plenty of fresh air – lovely! Plus it keeps me out of Sheila's hair.'

'Yes, it does,' Ed's mother agrees from the other side of the table, where she has Kate's son and daughter sat on either knee, happily watching CBeebies on her phone, 'but it's having these little ones around,' she nods down at the four-year-old twins and then over at our two-year-old son, James – sitting in a high chair, absorbed in fishing raisins out of a small box – 'that really keep us young. We're very lucky.'

'We certainly are. It's everything I ever dreamt of, actually,' Bob says. 'Everyone sat round this table right now means the world to me and Sheila. We couldn't be prouder of all of you, and what you've done for yourselves. And your mother's right; as for these little kiddies,' he gestures at his grandchildren, 'to say we feel blessed…' His eyes well up, and he reaches into his pocket for a hanky as we all chorus 'Ahhh!', and Sheila says gently: 'You soppy old thing.'

'How much have you had, Dad?' Ed laughs, and pats his father's arm affectionately.

'Enough to feel happy, not enough to need a nap,' Bob shoots back. 'It's like old John Lennon says.' He blows his nose. 'Love's like a boomerang: if you chuck it at people, it'll come right back to you.'

Kate looks puzzled. 'John Lennon never said that?'

'Yes, he did,' Bob insists. 'Daniel will know.' He turns in his seat to address Kate's husband, returning from the bar carefully carrying three pints. 'Didn't John Lennon say love is like a boomerang, Daniel?'

'Um.' Dan sets the drinks down. 'I think he said it was like a precious plant, actually. Are you thinking of Forrest Gump, perhaps?'

We all laugh, and Bob gives him a dismissive wave. 'Ah – what do lawyers know anyway?'

'Very little,' agrees Daniel. 'Luckily, I'm a barrister.'

'Wwwooooo!' we all chorus teasingly, and Daniel grins as he raises his glass. 'Anyway, to the man of the moment. Happy birthday, Ed. Sorry, I just missed the candles.'

We all chink glasses, and Ed clears his throat. 'Well on the occasion of my forty-second birthday, I would like to thank you all for helping me celebrate. I'd like to thank my son, James, for – by some miracle – sleeping in until half past seven this morning… and last but not least, I'd like to thank my beautiful wife, Jess, for agreeing to marry me exactly seven years ago today, which was only bettered by the wedding day itself, and then in turn by the day James was born. I couldn't love you more than I do, and I can't wait to move into our new house after Christmas, and start the next lot of adventures.' He leans forward to kiss me, as the rest of his family chime in with 'Hear, hear!'

A couple of waiters appear to clear the pudding bowls and ask if we'd all like fresh plates, and coffees? I decline, tell Ed I'm just popping to the loo, and remind him to keep an eye on James who is tucking into an enormous slice of cake.

❦

I'm happily fluffing up my hair in the mirror, before returning back to the table, when suddenly a very pretty twenty-something girl bursts in, clutching her mobile, tears streaming down her face.

'Are you alright?' I ask instantly.

'My boyfriend's just finished with me!'

'Oh! I'm so sorry!' I say, thinking she means by phone. 'Can I go and get someone for you?'

She shakes her head. 'No, thank you. He's waiting out in the car to drive me home. I've just tried to call my mum and dad, but they're not answering.' She looks in the mirror despairingly.

'And now he's going to know I've been crying. He said he's met someone else.' More tears well up, and I reach into a cubicle for some tissue to pass her.

'Thank you,' she sobs, trying to get herself under control. 'I'm sorry.'

'Please don't worry. You've just had a nasty shock.' I hesitate. 'You know, the person who *is* right for you is out there somewhere now. Probably just having his lunch, wondering what to do with the rest of his afternoon. You will meet him one day, I promise.'

She tries to smile but can't. She looks heartbroken.

'It's true,' I insist, emboldened by my lunchtime glass of Prosecco and her poor, sad little face. 'You will be happy again.' I suddenly see myself at her age; carefully propping Ben's 'Dear John' letter on the kitchen table, grabbing my bag and getting into the taxi – and my smile fades slightly. 'You can't see how it'll ever happen, but somehow it does. Trust me.' I reach for the door, and brighten again. 'Usually when you're not looking for it, and in the most ordinary of places. You take care of yourself.'

'Thank you,' she says gratefully as I give her a final smile of encouragement, and leave.

❧

I sit back down next to Ed, and he gives my leg a friendly pat. 'Hello. I was beginning to think you'd fallen in.'

'I was busy dispensing relationship advice to strangers. Hello, darling.' I lean forward and kiss James. 'Who's my best boy?'

James grins, points at himself and says: 'JAMES!'

'Yes, you are! And what's your favourite food, James?'

James considers that for a moment and announces delightedly 'CAKE!', holding a sticky handful of sponge aloft.

'Yes, it is!' I agree, before reaching under the table to get a wipe from my bag. 'There was a young girl crying in the loos because her boyfriend had just finished with her for someone else.'

Ed pulls a sympathetic face. 'Poor kid. Still, s-h-i-t', he spells out, 'happens.'

I laugh. 'Yes, that's not *exactly* what I told her. I said she'll probably meet the person who's right for her when she's not even looking.'

Ed sits back, interested, and crosses his arms. 'Like – I don't know – when she's on a train?'

I glance at him, and grin. 'Yes. Probably when she's minding her own business, trying to read her book after work and doesn't want to talk to anyone.'

He raises an eyebrow. 'So this *very* good-looking bloke will keep trying to engage her in conversation, but fail totally – so he'll have to try again once they've got off the train, and confess to her that he only got on it in the first place because he'd seen her standing on the platform... he'd actually been intending to go in the opposite direction. And then he might persuade her he wasn't a nutter... they'd go for dinner a week later – and be engaged within the year. Something *very* romantic like that you mean?' He leans forward.

I kiss him. 'Not that he'd go on about it, or anything. Come on – let's get the bill before your dad tries to pay for everyone, shall we?'

Once we've said goodbye to the rest of the family, and begin a slow amble home, my mind drifts back to Chichester – and Ben. I remember exactly how it felt closing the door to the house, knowing I would never return. I literally walked out on my life. We stroll a little further in easy silence, Ed's arm companionably round my shoulder while James sleeps in the pushchair – before I remark aloud: 'I can't actually believe it's seventeen years on Tuesday.'

Ed glances at me. 'Did you ask Mum if she can have James for the afternoon so you can go down to Chichester and do the flowers?'

'Yes, and she said that's fine, which is very kind of her.' I hesitate. 'Ed – does it honestly not bother you that Ben still sends me a white rose every year on Beth's anniversary?'

He looks surprised. 'No. Of course not.'

'It would bother a lot of people, I think.'

'It's nothing to do with me,' he says. 'I don't mean that rudely, just that it's a part of your life that's private to you and Ben. It's a flower once a year, it's not like you're both chatting to each other all the time. I don't feel threatened by it any more than I should think Ben's wife does. She's got two kids of her own; I've got James. We understand about Beth. I actually think it's very special what you and Ben do.'

I take a deep breath. 'I really meant because *you* know the truth, you know everything – and Ben doesn't.'

'I know that's what you meant, and that's why I said what you both do is very special. I have a lot of respect for him making the effort to let you know that Beth will never be forgotten, and that someone who knows exactly how incredible she was is out there feeling exactly the way you are too, on that day every year, in particular. And I think the kindness you've shown him all this time in protecting his memories of his little girl – because you'll never have irrefutable proof that he *wasn't* Beth's father – is one of the very many reasons that I love you.'

My eyes shine suddenly with tears. 'I love you too.'

He kisses the top of my head. 'Now, the big question is: when we get home, do we really have to do more sorting out? Because I can't be arsed. I say we just let the removals people pack everything and we'll sort it all once we're in the new place. Plus I don't want to be the sad Dad who spends his birthday doing a tip run.'

'Fair enough.' I recover myself. 'We do need to get rid of all of the old rubbish so we don't take it with us to the new place, and this is the perfect opportunity to declutter, but you're right, we don't have to do it today. We'll probably jinx everything if we're too organised anyway.'

'Nah – it's going to be fine,' Ed said confidently. 'Our cash buyer is raring to go – we're at the point of exchange all the way up the chain. I bet you it's gone through by Tuesday, you watch.'

'You can take the boy out of sales, but you can't take sales out of the boy,' I tease. 'Is this how you deal with all of your clients' concerns when they're about to sign on the dotted line?'

'If you can't make it, fake it,' Ed says cheerfully. 'But in this case, I don't have to. Hold onto your hat, Mrs Casson – because things are about to get very exciting indeed. Trust me. Nothing is going to go wrong, I promise.'

CHAPTER TEN

'I can't believe this has all gone so wrong. In ONE week,' Ed says loudly, while I try hard to keep a hold of a furiously wriggling James in my arms who is shouting: 'James get down!' – just in case I hadn't got the point. 'How can we be back to square *sodding* one, again?'

'Ed! Not in front of James! – I'm sorry about this.' I turn to the estate agent, an older man in his late fifties, who is eying James with a wary respect. 'Normally we wouldn't bring him, but our au pair left two days ago; we've no replacement yet and no one else could have him for us at such short notice.'

He smiles blandly and I can see him thinking that I'm just another forty-something mother unable to control her only child and her first world problems. He's seen it all before.

'It's just, we weren't expecting to be house-hunting today at all, obviously,' I continue, 'but as you know, our sellers pulled out because they got a bigger offer—'

'The unethical mother flippers,' Ed interjects.

'Ed!' I say despairingly.

'What? What's wrong with that? He's two; he doesn't know!'

'If he goes to playgroup and says mother flipper, you really don't think the other mums will know exactly what that means?'

'OK, OK! Sorry, princess.'

I narrow my eyes at that too, and my husband groans. 'Ah come on, what now?'

He knows perfectly well what. For ages after he started calling me princess, I genuinely thought it was a term of endearment, which, although flying against every feminist bone in my body, I secretly liked. Until I realised it meant I was high-maintenance.

'I can see why you're both feeling frustrated,' the agent says soothingly. 'It *is* unethical of your seller's agents to have continued to market the property while it was under offer to you. Not behaviour we ever adopt at Grantly-Brocken. You can rest assured your buyer through us is still keen as mustard, and if *you* find a property to buy through us too, we'll do all we can to keep things on track this time.'

'Well that's why we really wanted to see this house and the next one, especially as they only came on yesterday… and you're right, we don't want to lose our buyer. Ordinarily we wouldn't ever attempt to do viewings with our two-year-old, though.' I shrug apologetically.

'It's no problem at all.' He smiles, smoothly. 'I've got three boys of my own. All grown up now, but I remember them at that age like it was yesterday. You won't believe me, but you'll miss this one day. They don't stay your babies for long.'

Ed and I exchange a look, and in the moment of silence that follows, my husband steps in and reaches out for our son. 'Come here you.' He swings James up onto his shoulders to James's shriek of delight, and turns to me again. 'This place isn't for us, is it?'

I shake my head, regretfully. 'It's a very nice house,' I explain to the agent, 'but the garden isn't going to work. It's a grown-up, outdoor space with all that paving and the sunken pond… Al fresco entertaining when we're going to need football nets and space to let off steam.'

The agent nods. 'I hear you.' He checks his watch. 'Well, we've finished a little earlier than I'd anticipated, but I think let's just crack on to Thrent Avenue, shall we? Before someone,' he nods at James, 'needs a nap. You see?' he says smugly, and taps the side of his head knowingly, 'you never forget this stuff. Far be it from me to mess with a nap schedule.'

We laugh politely.

'Right, I'll meet you there.' He steps down the hall smartly and holds open the front door so we can make our way back down the path to the car. Ed straps James in as I sit in the passenger seat watching the agent lock up the house, before leaping into his black Audi and roaring off.

'That's a shame,' I say, as Ed climbs into the driver's seat and starts the engine. 'I really had high hopes for that one.'

'Me too.' Ed pulls the seatbelt across his body and clicks it in. 'I loved the house, and I could tell you did, but that garden was rubbish, Jess. He'd be like a caged bear.'

'I know,' I say wistfully as we pull away. 'But it had a magnolia tree in the garden and everything. I always imagined I'd live somewhere with a magnolia tree.'

Ed snorts. 'I'm sure you did.'

'Shut up. It's not the most important of criteria, I agree, but still. Anyway,' I sigh, 'onwards and upwards. Thrent Avenue. I'm trying not to get too excited about this one. It needs a bit of work; it's very reasonably priced; we could go up in the loft... so there has to be a catch.'

Ed nods. 'There definitely will be – I just haven't been able to work out what it is yet – and even if there isn't, if we feel this way about it, so will a million other people, so I think you're right, let's not get our hopes up, OK?'

'Agreed.' I start scanning Rightmove again on my phone. 'I feel like I live on this blasted site at the moment. I just want us to be able to stay around here so badly. I like being this close to your parents; I really want James to still have that cousins on tap thing, which we also get if we stay near your sister, but Jesus, a bigger garden and more downstairs space is coming in at one hell of a price, isn't it?' I keep scrolling. 'I'm just so frightened of leaping at the wrong place though, just so we don't lose our buyer. This has to be the last one we view before we just bite the bullet and rent instead, Ed.'

'I know, I know. Fingers crossed.'

'*Why* didn't we have a smaller wedding four years ago and spend it on a more sensible house with some storage? We would have saved so much money now. I can't even bear to think about it.'

'Well, we didn't actually know we were going to need somewhere to store a million plastic toys, did we?' Ed jerks his head in James's direction. 'God bless surprises.'

I twist to look at James in his car seat, who smiles back at me and, sensing an opportunity, says hopefully: 'iPad?'

'No, James. No iPad now.' I turn back to Ed. 'We've really got to cut back his screen time you know, he's becoming obsessed.'

'He only watches CBeebies, Jess,'

'He's still going to grow up with a deformed neck at this rate. Ooh! A nice one's just come on in Weald. I know we wanted to stay in Tunbridge Wells, and not be in a village, but it's really sweet – and a nice garden, close to the primary school. Let's phone the agent now!'

'Hang on, let's do this Bent Avenue one first, then we will. We need to stop for lunch anyway. We could pop into their offices after that.'

'But Ed, this one in Weald looks really nice, and let's face it – you're right, we're never going to get *Thrent* Avenue. It'll go to sealed bids – we won't get a look-in. James isn't in the mood anyway, and he actually *is* going to need a nap soon. Let's just sack it off and make the Weald one the last one we view.'

'Sweetheart, I *know* it's Thrent, and not Bent,' Ed says gently. 'When we were kids, it used to be one of those roads in town you didn't really hang around in, partly because there used to be a really dodgy pub nearby where loads of fights used to kick off. I still struggle with the fact you now have to pay well over half a million quid for the privilege of living there when you used not to be able to sell a house on that street for love nor money.'

'Oh, I see.' I manage a smile. 'Sorry.'

'It's OK. It was already on the up by the time you moved here; you weren't to know. Jess, are you alright?' Ed reaches for my hand. 'You seem a bit niggly. It was what that bloke said back at the last house, wasn't it? About children growing up quickly.'

I sigh, more deeply this time as Beth runs around the cathedral paths in my mind, laughing happily. The agent couldn't have been more wrong. They stay your babies forever. 'A bit, but don't worry – I'm OK.'

Ed lifts my hand and kisses it, before letting me go. 'James is going to fall asleep about two minutes before we get there, isn't he?'

'Probably. If he does, you go in and I'll stay in the car with him.'

Ed shoots me a look.

'I can't pretend I've not gone off this place now,' I explain. 'Sorry.'

'We're nearly there now, Jess. We might as well. What's the harm in looking?'

James manages to stay awake, but also does something that makes him completely incompatible with going into someone else's house. Ed insists on changing him so that I can make a head start however, probably in an attempt to re-enthuse me. I climb out, scanning the slightly neglected – in comparison with its neighbours – Edwardian end terrace in front of me, but all I feel is confused. I don't understand. This should be crawling with eager potential purchasers lined up in back-to-back ten-minute slots. Where is everyone else?

'Hello, hello!' the agent grins from the doorstep. 'A moment of respite, eh? Now, I'll just double-check first before we crash in.' He knocks loudly, and waits. 'I probably should say, this is a divorce,' he whispers. 'He's looking for a quick sale – although I didn't say that – and she doesn't want to go. We advised an open house; she refused. The compromise was to do a couple of "gentle" viewings to get things underway, which is ridiculous given the level of enquiries we've had already. You are one of the lucky two selected applicants. I'm not actually making this up,' he insists at my expression of disbelief. 'If you play your cards right, you might be about to get the early Christmas present of your life. Right, I think we're safe. In we go!'

He slides the key confidently into the lock, and shoves the door open. It judders slightly, catching on the ground, having swollen over the years with damp and not been rectified; the kind of noise the family no longer notice any more because it's become part of the fabric of their lives.

The agent rolls his eyes. 'Easy to fix though,' he says. 'After you. I'll leave it ajar for your husband so he can just let himself in.'

I step into a very dark hall. The stairs are right in front of me, with two doors side by side to my left leading off to different rooms. Further down the passage is a closed, stripped pine door, which must lead to the kitchen. Everything is closed off and unwelcoming, not helped by it being freezing cold, and painted an oppressive royal blue. There's a sad, out of control palm tree in an earthenware pot in the corner next to the cupboard under the stairs, twisting around trying to find the light, and lots of African prints and tribal masks on the wall. I glance at the coat hooks immediately to my right, crammed full of various sage-coloured macs, brown jackets and faded cotton fringed scarves that smell very similar to a heavy, cloying Body Shop perfume I used to hate in my teens – Ananya, I think it was called? I step away, also to avoid tripping over the jumble of mud-encrusted walking boots and faded trainers cascading off a wooden rack.

'Interestingly, of course, with this one, the owners haven't done the obvious – despite being here nine years – which is to knock the sitting room into what is listed as the study, although it's much larger than that description suggests. They've kept them separate, but if you have a look at the floor plan here,' the agent shoves it under my nose, 'you can see the solution is to make it all one downstairs space, even going into the side return and extending out what's currently the dining room. It would flow beautifully and make it all much, much lighter. It's almost unheard of now to find a property like this not done up within an inch of its life. Do you want to start in the sitting room?' He gestures to the first door on my left.

I look around me. I actually don't want to start anywhere. I don't know why, but I don't like this house. 'No, the kitchen, please, so I can see the garden.'

'Of course.' He opens the door, and we walk into a dining room. Stripped wooden floorboards are contained by the gunmetal grey walls, and a small chandelier hangs from the low ceiling. A vase of faded roses with drooping heads sit on the scrubbed table, and one chair is pulled out, as if someone left in a hurry. It reminds me of the private dining room of a wannabe gastro pub that doesn't get used very much.

'Very Miss Havisham,' the agent remarks drily, nodding at the roses.

Perhaps that's how you know you're in an overpriced area: the estate agents make literary references. I walk uncertainly across the room and glance into a small kitchen that definitely needs updating, with a sink full of dirty breakfast things.

'While the presentation leaves a lot to be desired, set it right, give it back to me next year, and you'll more than double that investment. Easily… plus, you could be in by Christmas!' He turns to me, suddenly serious. 'I honestly think if you make an asking price offer this morning you'll get it. You must have one hell of a guardian angel, that's all I can say.'

I smile blandly and say nothing as I move on. I trust only my own instinct these days. Glancing through the back window into a surprisingly nice garden however, I spy a mature apple tree and a nice long strip of grass, wet tufts blowing in the wind.

'So have you lived in Tunbridge Wells for long?' the agent asks conversationally.

'My husband has lived here all his life. I moved here for work, um – nine years ago, which is when we met. Wow. I didn't realise it had been that long.'

'Practically a local yourself now,' he says warmly. 'I don't need to sell the area to you in that case, you know exactly how desirable it is. What work is it you both do, then?'

'My husband works in London in sales. I'm a freelance copy editor. When I first moved here I was editing a local magazine. Well,' I correct myself, 'what I mean was I spent all day wading through hundreds of emails and selling advertising space, with the occasional feature thrown in.'

He smiles sympathetically. 'So now you stick to correcting punctuation, that sort of thing? Don't all copy editors secretly want to be writers themselves?'

'Nope,' I say firmly. 'They don't. I'm happy to leave made-up worlds to the authors. I prefer dealing in facts and reality.'

'Well, if you work from home now you must need a nice office space? Or at least the potential to build one?' he adds slyly.

'It would be helpful,' I agree. 'I'd like to have a room I could shut the door on at the end of the day.'

The kitchen is at least a bit brighter than the rest of it. And the agent's right – it could easily be extended. I tussle with myself for a moment. 'Let's have a look at the rest of the downstairs, then,' I say, uncertainly.

The agent nods smugly and we walk back through the dining room, our heels echoing on the boards, into the hall.

'It might be a push, but you could try squeezing a downstairs loo in here.' The agent pulls open the door to the understairs space, blocking my path, as I stare at a tangle of hoover tubes, a mop and bucket, a condenser dryer, a precariously balanced ironing board, tennis rackets, a rugby ball and shelves of various tins and half full plastic bottles, all fighting for space. It's like the forest around Sleeping Beauty's castle, only constructed entirely of domestic items. Bizarrely, it makes my mind up. Someone else can take this project on. I just don't like this place. I *really* don't like it, and it's as simple as that. It might be deal of the decade, I still don't want to live here. I hope Ed hasn't bothered getting James into his coat and hat.

The agent closes the door and shuts it all away. 'So, shall we wait for your husband,' he asks, facing me, 'or go straight on up and?—'

'No,' I interrupt. 'I've seen enough. I think I'm just going to—'

'It *is* you… I knew it was.' A low voice sounds behind the agent, making him jump and turn to look over his shoulder in surprise. We both stare in confusion into the gloom of the apparently empty hall towards the light coming in through the glass panels at the top of the front door that's now been pushed to. There is a slight movement in the jumble of coats, and as my gaze leaps left, I realise two unblinking eyes are watching me. A woman slowly peels away from where she has been leaning on the jackets, almost as if she'd quietly hung herself up. Her arms are crossed, and her hands appear to be buried inside the sleeves of a man's grubby Barbour. She's wearing black leggings tucked into heavy lace-up boots that only accentuate her too-thin, fifty-something frame. Dyed, dark red curls are escaping wildly from a low, careless ponytail at the nape of her neck.

Louise Strallen.

The temperature plummets, and I'm aware of my breathing instantly speeding up.

She steps forward properly into the light as the front door blows slightly open in the wind, and faces me full on, staring incredulously as if she can't believe I'm stood in front of her. 'I knew Simon was lying, that this sudden desire for divorce had to have come from somewhere. He promised me it wasn't anything to do with you, and yet here you are, in my house.' She blanches suddenly; I watch the colour literally drain from her face. 'Oh shit. I've just worked it out. He's planning to sell the house to *you*, deliberately cheaply – then you'll move in here together once I'm gone.' She puts both hands up to her mouth as she shakes her head in disbelief, like *The Scream*. 'No. No! I won't let you!'

Her hands fall away and she flies up the hall towards me. The agent steps back in shock as she passes, and I shriek, instinctively holding up my arms to protect myself because she's suddenly flapping around me like a crow, a pointing finger becoming more vicious, jabbing at my raised arm like a sharp beak, as she shouts: 'I won't let you do this to me! Do you hear me? *Do you hear me?*'

I'm cowering, and all I can smell is a mixture of the sickly perfume, garlic and stale booze pouring from her hot, angry skin. Her hands twist into fists, and she starts to hail sharp hits down on me that become harder and harder – but in a flurry of arms and shouts, the agent begins to pull her off, trying to restrain her as she kicks out and writhes furiously while he drags her backwards down the hall. She manages to break free, spins round on the spot and glares at him. 'Don't you touch me, you cunt.'

Somehow the profanity is all the more shocking because she enunciates it so smartly in her well-spoken voice. This dishevelled woman is completely at odds with the one I remember from Simon's office all those years ago, even the one that came to my house and threatened me. What has happened to her?

The agent stares at Louise in disbelief, his tie pulled out and his hair askance. I can see this will be his 'for the first time in thirty years as an agent…' story back at the office later, but neither is he entirely sure it's over, and she isn't about to attack *him*.

The front door judders properly open, breaking the stand-off – to reveal James straining at his reins and Ed right behind him.

'Knock, knock!' my husband says cheerily. 'Sorry I took so long, I tried to put him across my lap, but that didn't work, then I had to strap him back in his seat while I cleared a space in the boot instead, because it's the only big enough flat space to change him. And I couldn't find the reins after that. Anyway. We're done now.' He pauses, looks between us all, and then quickly reaches out and grabs James safely to him. 'What's going on?'

'Wait,' Louise is thrown, 'you're still married? And,' she stares at James, then turns to me in surprise. Her eyes look almost yellow. 'You had *another* baby?'

I flush. 'I had an *additional* baby. Not a replacement.'

She ignores that. 'He must be – what, two?'

'Yes. He is.' I'm so stunned by what just happened, I actually continue to converse with her.

'I'm sorry, but do we know you?' Ed is confused.

'Darling, you might not remember,' I say, dazed, 'but this is Louise Strallen, Simon Strallen's wife, who was head teacher at Beth's school.'

I watch Ed freeze for a moment. 'Ah,' he says softly. 'Yes, I know exactly who you are, now. This is your house? Well, what a very small world.'

Louise hesitates, and stares at him again, puzzled, and I realise she's trying to decide if she recognises him or not. It's been seventeen years since she actually saw Ben, perhaps she doesn't remember what he looks like. Especially as both of my husbands do in fact share a similar colouring. Louise bites her lip. Not anxiously, but as if she's testing her teeth. 'Well now, forgive me, but I thought that you'd both separated. I'm *delighted* to see that's not the case, or that, at least, you got back together. How nice for you.'

'Thank you,' says Ed, frowning. 'So, you're selling up? Moving far? Hang on, love. You can't get down yet.' He grips James tightly as our son tries another wriggle.

'Well now, Ben, here's the thing,' she says – Ed glances at me, but doesn't correct her – 'I don't want to move at all. But Simon has – out of the blue – asked me for a divorce. My friends all think there's someone else, although he denies it, of course.'

The agent doesn't say anything, just looks uncomfortably at the ground.

'I'm very sorry to hear that,' Ed says. 'Starting again is always difficult and we wish you well, but we won't take up any more of your time, now. Come on, Jess.' He holds out a hand, and I rush past Louise to stand alongside him in the open doorway.

'You're wrong, Ben,' Louise says, looking at the three of us. 'Starting again is impossible. You think everything is mended and normal, but it's never the same. And it's not that small a world. You know, of course, that your wife had an affair with my husband?'

'She wasn't my wife, actually, when she had a relationship with your husband,' Ed says. 'But, for the record, yes, I do know.'

Louise looks slightly taken aback, but continues: 'You'll also know then, that after my husband ended their affair, your wife came looking for him after quite an extended time apart. Almost as if she couldn't let him go.'

James wriggles again. 'Get down. *Please,* Daddy?'

'No, bub, we're going now,' Ed says firmly. 'Come on, Jess.' He takes my hand. 'Thanks for your time,' he nods at the agent, who faintly waves back in acknowledgment as we turn to leave.

'Don't you see what I'm saying, Ben?' Louise raises her voice, calling after him. 'Despite *promises* to the contrary, she keeps coming back. I don't think you know your precious wife at all.'

Ed pauses and turns around. 'Can I save you some time? Is this the bit where you tell me I'm not Beth's biological father?'

Louise's eyes widen.

'Because you're right. I'm not. You know something else, Louise?' He challenges her. 'I have a real problem with married men having affairs, and somehow it's always the *woman* who gets all of the blame. Why are you directing all of this hate at Jessica, and not Simon? She was *19* when your 30-year-old husband met her – and *this* is the man you've fought to keep for seventeen-odd years? I mean, really?' He looks disgusted. 'Your friends are probably right; I expect he is asking for a divorce because he's met someone else. But it's not *my* wife.'

'Except, Ben, they *love* each other!' she taunts, calling after us, but for the first time I can also hear desperation in her voice. 'He's waiting for her. He told her he'd wait forever! Why won't you just leave us alone, you little whore?'

We drive in horrified silence to the end of the road – even James is quiet – and Ed continues through the centre of the town without stopping.

'I think we'll go somewhere a bit further out for lunch,' he says eventually, 'maybe towards Weald. We could drive by that other place and have a look?'

I nod, wordlessly.

'Well, turns out I wasn't wrong; it is still Bent Avenue, after all.' He pauses, then adds 'All this time, Jess? He's been living in the *same town as us* and you never knew?'

'Of course I didn't know. The agent said they've been in that place for nine years. Not once have I seen either of them.'

'"Nine years"?' Ed says quickly. '*You* moved here nine years ago.'

'Yes, because I was offered my job here. I was living in London and there was no point whatsoever in doing a reverse commute to the rest of the world. You know this, Simon.'

'Ed,' he corrects me instantly. 'I'm Ed, *he's* Simon.'

'God – I'm sorry! I'm so sorry,' I say horrified. 'I think I'm just overwhelmed. I didn't mean—'

'It's alright. I know you didn't. Look, we hadn't even met then. If you did move here because you were following him, or something like that, it's OK. You can tell me. But now would be a really good time to be honest about it, if that *is* what happened.'

I stare at him. 'I was *not* following him! Ed, this is a massive town – pretty much a suburb of London these days. I had no idea he lived here. I swear, I've never seen him, or his family. Not once.'

He glances sideways at me. 'OK, I believe you. Apart from anything else, no one could be that good an actress. You look like you're about to be sick. Are you alright?'

'Um, I don't honestly know,' I say truthfully. 'I can't believe that all actually just happened. It was very quick-thinking on your part though, pretending to be Ben.'

He looks surprised. 'It was your idea. I just played along. You said "Darling, I'm not sure if you remember Louise", or whatever it was – like I'd already met her. I assumed that was what you meant me to do.'

'No. I was just asking if you remembered who she was from what I'd already told you?' I look out of the window. 'I'm not smart enough to lie on the spot like that.'

He doesn't say anything for a moment, before asking. 'It's not true, is it, Jess? What she said? I accept that you didn't move here on purpose to follow Simon nine years ago, but you haven't deliberately tracked him down again now, have you? It is one hell of a coincidence that we wound up in their house today when, like you said, it's a massive town.'

I actually laugh in disbelief. 'You're not serious?'

'Perhaps it's just fate then, the universe drawing you back together.'

'It's nothing of the kind,' I say immediately. 'It was a tragic coincidence that we wound up at the same school as him and his family seventeen years ago, and an unfortunate one that we unwittingly went into his house today. But I'd hardly call them frequent occurrences. Would you?'

'Jess, calm down. You're getting all icy and acerbic.'

'Because you just accused me of tracking down my ex behind your back. You didn't see, but Louise actually just went for me back then. The agent had to pull her off me.'

'She attacked you?' He's appalled. 'Why didn't you say something? We should have called the police. We still could – do you want to press charges?'

'No! No, I don't, she's ill, Ed. Anyone could see that. She tried to sort of slap me, that was all – but it was extremely distressing – as was having her say "You had another baby?" implying I'd simply replaced Beth. As if she didn't matter.' My voice begins to tremble.

'I'm so sorry. You're right.' Ed puts his hand out on mine. 'And I'm sorry I made that pissy remark about fate, too.'

'Although, actually, the second I set foot in that house, I wanted out,' I say. 'I could feel it; something was badly wrong. I wish we'd just sacked it off, like I said.'

We fall silent for a moment.

'James has gone to sleep, hasn't he?' Ed says.

I twist to look at our son in his seat. 'Yup. He's out for the count.'

'I'll drive us to Weald then, give him half an hour or so more. We can spin past that other place then head back into Sevenoaks for lunch, if you like?'

'OK.' I actually just want to go home, but conversely, I also want to get away from here. Where is Simon? Walking around, mere streets away, as he has been for the last *nine years?* Ed's right. It makes me feel sick.

'She definitely wasn't a well woman, I don't think. She reeked,' Ed remarks. 'It was coming off her in waves.'

'I know. I thought that too.' I stare out of the window at the blur of plush, manicured countryside. 'She certainly looked... very different to the last time I saw her.'

'Do you think it's her that's tracked *you* down? The way she let rip like that, it was like it had happened yesterday, not seventeen years ago. Never mind her husband, *she* seemed pretty obsessed with you.' Ed looks momentarily troubled. 'You haven't noticed anyone – I don't know – hanging around?'

I look at him, frightened. 'No? Although that estate agent did say something weird to me. He said we were "selected" to view the house… but then you heard what Louise shouted, she wants me as far away from them as possible. It doesn't make any sense that she'd track me down. It must just be a random freak occurrence. That's the only logical explanation.'

'Hmmm,' Ed says doubtfully. 'Although Simon's a teacher, isn't he? You can't move for elite schools in Kent. It's not really surprising he ended up here, I suppose.' We drive in silence for a moment. 'So, still want to live in Tunbridge Wells?'

'No. Funnily enough, not so much,' I say. 'But then they're obviously moving, and with a bit of luck, about a million miles away. I don't ever want to see either of them again, as long as I live.'

CHAPTER ELEVEN

As I come down from settling James, at 7 p.m., Ed is looking for the car keys to go and pick up the takeaway we've ordered.

'I might stop and pick up a bottle of something too? I thought we could watch a movie when I get back. Nothing heavy – a comedy, I think. Are you alright?' He reaches for my hand. 'It's been a shocker of a day, but it's over now. Try not to think about it any more, ok?'

'I'll do my best.'

Once the front door quietly closes behind him, and I hear our car pull off the drive, I pick up my mobile and head into the kitchen for a glass of water. Sitting down at the table, I begin to sip it slowly, looking at the single white rose in the vase in front of me; it has shed two petals since this morning. I pick one of them up carefully. Seventeen years and four days since I last held Beth.

What would my 22-year-old girl be doing, this Saturday night? Teasing me for staying in with a takeaway and thinking *that* was the main part of the evening, when hers was just getting started? Would she be going out around here with her friends, or heading into London and getting the last train home? Would she even still be at home – maybe she'd be working in another country, having not been out of university long and keen to explore the world; I would have encouraged that. But then, would I have been allowed to be her friend on Facebook, or might I have had to rely on texts and phone calls to make sure she was OK? I wouldn't have liked *that*. Probably though, she wouldn't even be on Facebook: would Snapchat and Instagram be more her style? I think of her beautiful smiling 5-year-old face – so open, happy and innocent – and try to picture how that face would look now. She would be beautiful, and I would be so proud of the woman she had become.

Sometimes I find myself staring at young women in the street, wondering if that is what Beth would be wearing, or how she'd do her hair. They probably think I'm jealous of them – wishing I was young again. I suppose, in a way, I am. But ultimately, Beth remains permanently frozen in my mind as a 5-year-old – and the more time that passes, the harder and harder that becomes. I won't ever know what she'd be wearing now, or how her voice would sound, what she'd like or dislike. She is imprisoned in my head, and I will wish forever that I could set her free so she could come back to me.

I place the petal back down, and get up to walk over to the sideboard.

Pulling open the drawer, I take out the small, worn brown photo album that Dad sent me just after I left Ben and went to Australia. I close my eyes briefly at the memory of my own unoriginality. What a poor, messed-up 24-year-old thing to do; thinking that going halfway around the world was going to make anything better.

Sitting back down at the table, I flick through the first pages that are full of Mum and me – in one or two I'm a little girl Beth's age – images carefully selected by Dad because Mum is genuinely smiling, even with her eyes. I stare at the pictures and trace her hair with my finger. She had such wonderful long hair. I remember playing with it while I sat on her lap and she read me stories. At least, I think I do; Dad has told me so often I used to do it, it feels like a memory.

There is another one of me looking incredibly similar to Beth – and then it's on to Beth herself. She was so blonde. Just like James is now; although, unlike her, he's darkening up as he gets older. There's a particularly lovely one of Beth on my lap, with all of our friends from home around us. It was my 21st birthday. Beth is grinning hugely, not fazed at all by being the only child among so many 20-year-olds. I'm laughing and Ben is stood behind me, hands resting on my shoulders, looking proud as punch. Laurel is there too, pulling a party popper. Most of the others, I'm no longer in touch with. Even if I hadn't left, we would have all found it too hard. They wouldn't have known what to say to me, and I wouldn't have been able go back to being one of them; as if having Beth had never happened. I look closely at myself. If Beth had lived, she would now be older than I am in that picture.

Breathing out slowly, I try to steady my thoughts. Seeing Louise today has smashed the two halves of my life into contact, instead of them oscillating alongside each other as they do normally; and this slipstream is not a comfortable place to be. I continue to look through the album; Beth pushing her baby in a pushchair, on her first trike, playing with Play-Doh, at the beach, in the bath, blowing out candles, dressed as Snow White, opening Christmas presents excitedly, as her brother will do in a month's time, and then I reach one of the final pictures: her first day of school, blonde hair in bunches, standing outside the front door clutching her book bag, on a warm, sunny September day.

Feeling the usual familiar tightening of guilt in my gut, I quickly get up to put the album back in the drawer, but instead, on impulse, get out my ancient laptop. I know I shouldn't do this, but...

I start it up, and then once I've signed in, I go straight to iTunes and select the file that Ed put on there for me. I hit play, and after the moment of static, there it is: the distant sound of Ben's voice: 'Go on! Say – "Mummy! Answer your phone!"' Then Beth: the faint giggle and then 'Mummy! Answer your phone!'

But as always, after the brief exquisite hit, is the immediate comedown. Angry with myself when I *know* how it was going to make me feel, I scrabble for my mobile and call Laurel.

'Hey! Hello you!' She sounds breathless.

'Are you able to chat for a moment? I won't be long; I'm really sorry but I'm having a wobble. Can you just anchor me back?'

'Of course.' She understands immediately. 'I was thinking about you this morning. How has your day been? Houses any good?'

'Um, not so much. We're back at home now.'

'Us too. The boys are watching *Star Wars* for the umpteenth time, Chris has gone to get us a Thai takeout, and I'm on countdown until half eight when I can legitimately pack them off to their rooms and have a glass of wine. This bit when they start going to bed later and you lose your evening is hard. I take it the lovely James is in bed?'

'Yes, he is. Ben has gone to get us a takeaway too.'

'Sorry?' she says, astonished. 'Did you just say Ben?'

'Oh Jesus, what's wrong with me?' I put my hand to my forehead. 'I did something similar in the car this afternoon, only to Ed's face. Today can't end soon enough.'

'Oh, sweetheart,' she says, and I hear her start to settle in as if she's sitting down in preparation for a longer five minutes than previously advertised. 'Talk to me. Has something happened in particular?'

I take a deep breath. 'Do you remember after I started my counselling, I told you about the affair I'd been having with Beth's teacher, Simon, and how Simon's wife, Louise, came to the house and confronted me the day before I left Ben?' I tread carefully around the version of events Laurel knows.

'Yes, I do. That was also the day I sensitively came round to ask you if you wanted to come out with all of us for Christmas drinks, less than a month after you'd lost Beth.'

'You were just doing your best, Lau. Don't be hard on yourself. You were there, that's the important thing.'

'Hmmm. You're generous to say so.' She hesitates. 'I actually saw Ben in town today.'

I glance back at his rose on the table. 'How was he?'

'He was good. Christmas shopping.'

I smile. 'That's very organised.'

'I said exactly the same thing. He had a neat little list and everything. Both of his stepsons were with him too; they were going home for lunch then he was taking them to watch Chichester City play. They all looked happy. It was nice.'

'I'm really glad to hear that,' I say sincerely.

She hesitates. 'We've also been invited to his wife, Jo's, 45th party at their house in a couple of weeks. I mean, we see them at lots of things and we're part of the same group, so maybe she felt like they ought to invite us, I don't know, but anyway… Ben said to say hi when I next spoke to you. And that he'd been thinking of you. Bless him,' Laurel sighs. 'Bless you and Beth too.' She pauses, before continuing: 'I'm sorry. I interrupted you. You were saying did I remember that day before you left—'

'Which was also the last time I saw Louise, Simon's wife. Well, Ed and I went to view a house today, here in Tunbridge Wells, and not only did it turn out to belong to Louise and Simon—'

Laurel gasps.

'She was *actually there*. I have been unwittingly living in the same town as them for the last nine years.'

'Oh, Jessica!'

'I know. All this time I've imagined Simon miles away, and they've been on my doorstep – only for me to wind up on theirs today. Worse still, they're getting divorced – which is why they're selling up – and she suddenly appeared in the hallway when I was looking round, told me she knew I was the reason Simon had suddenly decided it was over, then she went for me.'

'What, physically?' Laurel is appalled.

'Yup. Came tearing down the hallway like some sort of banshee, shrieking and poking at me, then started hitting me. The estate agent had to pull her off.' I try to laugh, but realise there are actually tears in my eyes.

'Oh, Jess! That's so horrible. Where was Ed when this was happening?'

'Changing James's nappy in the car. He appeared just after the estate agent had stepped in – at which point, Louise, thinking he was Ben, immediately asked him if he knew I'd shagged her husband.'

'Oh, Jesus…'

'I know. Thank GOD I'd already told him.' And told him *all* of it, I think, privately, to myself.

'She's still holding onto it after all this time?' Laurel is incredulous. 'I mean, OK, I get it – you're probably not the first person she'd want to invite into her house, but it was years ago!'

'I don't think she was in her right mind. She looked terrible; her eyes were all yellow and she smelt horribly hung-over. I couldn't believe how much she'd aged.'

'He wasn't there? Simon, I mean?'

'No, thank God,' I say. 'Nor was their daughter. Just Louise. It completely freaked Ed out, though. He asked me in the car afterwards if I'd been in contact with Simon again as it was a pretty big coincidence that we wound up in their house, of all people.'

There's a moment's silence. 'But it was just a coincidence?'

'Laurel! Of course it was!'

'Sorry – I don't know why I said that. Well, maybe it's time to think about moving further afield after all, then? You don't want to be looking over your shoulder for old loony pants Louise every time you're out and about, especially now you know she lives in the same town as you.'

'True. But then on the flip side, I haven't seen them once in the last nine years, so there's no reason why I should now. I know where she lives, but she doesn't know where *I* live. Shit!' I jump, before the words are barely out of my mouth, and turn around in my seat to look up the dark hallway. 'Just as I said that, someone knocked on the front door.'

'Yikes. Maybe don't open it?' Laurel jokes drily.

'Ha ha. It'll just be Ed with his arms full of food, hang on.' I pad up the hall and, still holding the phone with one hand, release the catch with the other and swing the door wide open with a smile.

But the person stood in front of me is not Ed. The phone almost slips from my fingers in shock and I feel the blood run from my face. I hang up wordlessly and just stand there for a moment. 'It's you,' I say stupidly.

'Hello, Jess,' says Simon, holding out a huge bunch of flowers. 'Long time no see.'

CHAPTER TWELVE

His blond hair is now silver, and his eyes crinkle at the corners as he smiles sadly – Beth's bright blue eyes staring back at me. He's no longer wearing glasses and he certainly doesn't look his 52 years. He's been taking care of himself: there's not a hint of baggy fat straining at the front of his crisp white shirt, or over the waistband of his expensively cut suit trousers. I always did like him in a suit – a fact he well knows. If he was balder, more jowly and plumper perhaps, maybe I'd be disappointed and working a little harder to see if the man I'd once found so hypnotic is still there, but as Simon has only improved with age, it's even more of a surprise to discover I don't find him in the least attractive. I don't feel anything at all – except appalled that he's stood right in front of me.

'What are you doing here?' I whisper.

'It's OK.' He holds up a hand, mistaking my shock for subterfuge. 'I'm going again straight away. I've only come to apologise. I managed to persuade the estate agent to give me your address. I'm so sorry, Jessica. To say that I couldn't believe it when they told me what Louise did this morning…' he trails off, and shakes his head. 'I thought she was having one of her epic moments when I got home and she started ranting at me about you – although she didn't say you'd been to the house – but when the agent called and talked me through the actual events… what it must have been like for you and your husband… and even your son too, I believe?' He smiles painfully. 'I really am so very sorry. Louise is not herself at the moment. Well, she hasn't been for a long time, if truth be told.'

I hesitate. 'No, she didn't appear as I remembered her, at all.'

'She's got severe alcohol issues, as I'm sure you realised. She doesn't normally get drunk, as it were – she's a top-up drinker. It's always in her system. That's why she behaves the way she does. Why she behaved as she did today.'

'I'm sorry to hear that.'

He shrugs tiredly. 'It's also the reason we're finally divorcing, and selling up. Cara recently left home, so… Anyway, you don't need to hear all of this. Here—' He passes me the flowers, which I take automatically, before he takes a step back. 'Do please pass my apologies on to Ben as well. I have to confess I pulled up just as he was getting in the car to leave, and I hope it's OK that I left it five minutes or so, to make sure he'd definitely gone. It wasn't me being a coward as such – although I wasn't particularly keen to get a punch in the face – more just that I didn't want to upset him further. He knows about me now, I gather? Well, us. And my relationship to Beth.'

A punch in the face? I stare at him, and then at the flashy flowers in my arms. I think about the single rose in the kitchen behind me and some instinct makes me stay quiet about Ed's real identity. 'Yes, he knows everything.'

'I'm very pleased you obviously managed to get things back on the right track, despite you leaving him all those years ago. One thing though: your surname is Davies. The agent told me you were Mr and Mrs Casson?'

'Really?' I pretend to be confused. 'How strange!'

He looks at me. 'Perhaps I misheard. Well, apologies again, and if—'

'Simon, I can't take these,' I interrupt, holding the flowers out to him. 'I'll have to explain them otherwise when my husband gets back in a minute, and he won't be OK with you coming here like this. It's better that you just take them away with you. I'm sorry.'

'I didn't really think about that.' He stares at the flowers.

'Take them home for Louise.'

He looks up at me bleakly. 'You're kidding, right?'

'I wasn't actually, no.'

'Well, that's generous of you, considering everything she said to you today.'

'It could have been worse; at least she didn't have a knife in her pocket this time.' I say it without thinking.

'Sorry?' he says immediately. 'When *did* she have a knife in her pocket?'

There is an ugly silence.

'Let's just leave it, Simon,' I try. 'It was all a long time ago, and—'

'No, hang on. Louise threatened you with a *knife*?'

I hesitate. 'That day I met you in the pub and said I was leaving, she'd been to see me at home, earlier. She told me she wanted to kill me; she had a blade in her coat pocket and made me promise to move away and have nothing more to do with you, or she'd tell Ben about us – about Beth not being Ben's daughter. You know all of this by now though, surely?'

Simon is listening intently. 'No,' he says. 'This all definitely comes as news.'

'Seriously? Louise has never told you?' I'm astonished. 'She was in the booth behind us in the pub that afternoon, listening to every word.'

His mouth falls open. 'She was actually there? So I've always thought you ended everything between us because you wanted to, but in fact it was because Louise intimidated you? Blackmailed you, to be more precise?'

'Yes,' I admit simply. What else is there to say? 'Although, I wasn't really myself at the time anyway, of course.'

He stands still for a moment, just looking at me. 'Well. Brava Louise. Mission accomplished.'

'Simon, it's probably best that you go, and don't come back here.' I cross my arms uncomfortably. 'And that *is* me saying it this time. Not anyone else.'

'Of course. I won't disturb you, or Ben, again. I'm selling the house, as you know, and in fact I have a new job in Surrey too, so I won't really be around in any case. It was very nice to see you again though, Jessica,' he concludes politely, starting to walk away, 'and I truly am delighted to see that life has treated you more kindly these last few years. Do take care, won't you?'

'You too.'

It's as if we are complete strangers and, just for the briefest of moments, I consider how much I loved him all those years ago, when he swings back suddenly. 'Jess, when you told me in the pub that you had never loved me, it was all a mistake, was that true, or was that what Louise told you to say?'

'What she told me to say.'

'And that I was never to contact you?'

'Yes. That was her too. She told me she would destroy Ben. There was no doubt in my mind that she meant it.'

He looks momentarily devastated. I glance down at his hand holding the flowers. His knuckles have gone white he's gripping them so hard. 'So all this time, when I thought…'

I hesitate. 'Simon—'

But just as suddenly, he's smiling again. 'It's OK. Let's just not. What's done is done. All the best, Jess. Really, I mean that. Take care.' He gives me an odd little wave and then turns on the spot, making his jacket swing as he strides back towards his car. I've closed the door before he's even reached the bottom of the drive.

Ed arrives back five minutes later to find me sat on the sofa unseeingly watching TV, imagining Simon returning to that dark, oppressive jumble of a house in which he and Louise live. Trying to make sense of what I've just told him.

'Did you put any plates in the oven?'

I shake my head.

'OK,' he shrugs. 'No worries. You alright? You look stressed.'

'I'm fine. Just trying to relax a bit.'

'I'm not surprised, after today. Why don't you stay put and I'll bring it through to you?'

Sure enough, a couple of moments later, he bustles back in and passes me my food.

'All quiet?' He nods at the ceiling, above which James lies sleeping.

'Yes. All fine. He hasn't made a peep.'

We start to eat, Ed flicking around the movie channels as I consider how to tell him that Simon has just been here. He's going to be understandably furious, and have a million questions:

But how did he find us?

What did he want?

What do you mean he waited for me to go before he came to the door?

Do you still believe this is all just a coincidence?

Well if it's nothing to worry about, why didn't you tell him who I really am?

OK, I take your point – because Louise thinks I'm Ben, you want Simon to think that as well, and while I get you're still doing it to protect Ben, what about protecting us?

I can't see what's going to stop her coming here and potentially going for you again, given how obsessed she is with you. Do you?

All of which are very good questions. Louise is evidentially unstable. She attacked me this afternoon. Suppose she followed Simon tonight, she will now know where we live.

How did we really wind up in their house today? HOW?

Ed looks over at me. 'You're not eating.'

'I can't stop thinking about Louise Strallen.'

He sighs and puts down his fork. 'Me too. When you said the estate agent had told you we were "selected" to view the house, what do you think he meant?'

'Well, I put it down to being marketing spiel,' I say slowly. 'Having seen her today, it's perfectly clear she was in no mood to have anyone looking around – what was she even doing there at all? She called the agent a cunt, Ed. I expect they just didn't want to risk an open house in case she lost it and scared everyone off in one fell swoop.'

'Maybe… I don't want to sound dramatic, but this is a woman who very obviously isn't right in the head, and once told you she wanted to kill you. The very first thing she said was "I knew it was you". I know I already asked you this earlier, but you're certain you haven't noticed anything out of the ordinary? No one following you? No odd phone calls? And you've had no contact from Simon?'

I swallow nervously. I have to tell him now. He's asked me outright. 'He came here tonight while you were getting the food. He brought flowers to apologise for Louise's behaviour.'

'Come again?' Ed takes his tray off his lap and sets it on the floor. 'Simon was *here*, tonight? When were you going to tell me?'

'Ed, that's not fair. I just have. You've been back for not even half an hour.'

'How does he know where we live?'

'The estate agent told him.'

'WHAT? But that's outrageous! What about the Data Protection Act? They can't do that! Suppose *she* followed him here or something?'

'That was actually my thought too,' I confess.

'Fucking hell.' He puts his head in his hands for a moment, then looks up. 'What did he say?'

'He just told me Louise has severe alcohol problems. He's taken a job in Surrey, so is leaving imminently. He also thinks you're Ben, and—'

Ed grits his teeth.

'That's it.'

'Nothing else weird, or strange?'

'Not really. He seemed to be on his way somewhere else actually, he was fully suited and booted—'

'Arsehole,' Ed says immediately. 'Dressing to impress, more like. Nothing else happened though, that was it?'

'Oh, apart from he didn't know Louise had threatened me all those years ago.'

'Well, after today that won't exactly come as a shock, will it? I'm going to ring the agents in the morning and give them a verbal kicking. They can't justify giving out our address like that. Better still, I'll go in personally. How am I supposed to protect you and James if they're going to fuck about? And Simon! He had no business coming here, and he knows it!'

I look at Ed, my mouth slightly open. I've never seen him so angry.

'Except, of course, it's Sunday tomorrow,' he realises aloud, 'and they'll be closed. I'll have to do it on Monday instead. It's not that I want to frighten you, Jess, but I saw the way Louise looked at you today.' He takes a deep breath. 'You don't remember that woman Dan prosecuted two months ago, do you?'

I rack my brains, trying to think back through the family conversations over other Sunday lunches out when his brother-in-law might have chatted to us about his latest cases. 'No?'

'She murdered her ex-partner's new wife with a kitchen knife. Daniel said it was a "crime of obsession". She'd planned it all meticulously. She did a practice run of delivering flowers to the woman's house, before she turned up the following week, used a stun gun on her then attacked her in the kitchen.'

'I think I would have remembered that.'

He closes his eyes briefly. 'Yeah – that's because you'd taken James out into the pub garden because he was playing up, and I asked Daniel *not* to mention it to you. I remember now. Jesus, I'm a twat.'

'It's OK.'

'No, it's not. I'm sorry. This is just messing with my head a bit.'

'I can see that.'

'I don't want to scare you, and of course bad things happen to people all the time, and that doesn't mean you should live your life looking round corners, it's just, something about today doesn't smell right. I can feel it. I think I'm going to talk to Daniel about it; ask him if there's anything we can do legally. An injunction or something. We should have called the police earlier today. I'll text Katie and ask her if he's around to chat in the morning.'

He reaches into his pocket for his mobile, fires off a message to his sister and then throws the phone on the sofa and stares back down at his plate. 'We should eat our food.'

'I don't really feel massively hungry any more.'

'Me neither. Do you still want to watch a movie?'

I hesitate. 'I think I might just go to bed and read, actually.'

He nods. 'I won't be long. I'll lock up.'

I opt for a well-thumbed comfort book, but don't really take any of it in; I'm too busy thinking about what Ed said about the woman doing a dummy run to her victim's house before coming back for more… Thankfully, Dad texts me to ask how the viewings went, which is a welcome five second distraction from that deeply disturbing train of thought, although I'm deliberately vague with my reply because I don't want to worry him. I simply say we won't be going back for second viewings, which has got to be understatement of the decade. Laurel texts too, checking if everything is OK after we got cut off earlier? She assumes my battery died, and she didn't want to call back straight away as she knew we were just about to eat. I message her that I'm fine. If I tell her Simon was here, there is no doubt that she'll ring instantly – and I don't want to go through it all again, not right now.

Instead, I turn over to go to sleep, but I still have too much adrenaline in my system: all I can think about is Simon stood on our doorstep, Louise rushing up the hall towards me... and Beth reaching up and asking me to hug her goodbye...

I only manage to doze fitfully until Ed comes to bed, but then later in the night I dream I can hear a child crying and calling 'Mummy!' in a house I don't recognise. I know I have to get to them – they are in danger – but as I burst from room to empty room, the crying by turns becomes louder and then more distant, then louder again... until Ed nudges me and tells me James has woken up and is calling for me. Do I want him to go instead?

Sitting in the dark on the armchair next to my son's cot, rocking his slightly feverish small body in my arms and singing softly as he tries to get back to sleep after some Calpol, I stare at the dark stairwell in front of me, and my mind goes from 0–60 in under five seconds. Suppose Simon *has* foolishly led Louise right to us? I imagine her creeping around the quiet rooms below, only to finally approach the stairs; one foot softly placing onto the step, then another, and another... I tighten my grip on James.

If this is just the start and my unwittingly walking into her house today has unleashed something in Louise, she should know that I am a different woman.

This time, I will not fail to protect my family.

This time, I won't make any mistakes.

James is still unwell in the morning, with enough of a raised temperature for us to reluctantly cancel a planned lunch at Ed's parents. Instead we stay at home and watch an unhealthy amount of *Swashbuckle* and *Justin's House*, in an attempt to get James to stay still and give himself a chance to get better. Ed does speak to his brother-in-law about Louise though. We discover that under the Protection from Harassment Act of 1997, there is a case for a section 4A charge if a course of conduct causes a victim 'serious alarm or distress' and the defendant's behaviour has a 'substantial adverse effect on the day-to-day activities of the victim'. It is disheartening, however, to also learn the Act says I must have experienced at least two incidents, and the claim would have to be made within six years of when the harassment happened.

'Dan did say we could go over this afternoon and talk it through with him if we want?' suggests Ed. 'Although he doesn't think there's much we can do.'

I stroke our son's head as he sits on my lap, lolling against me and concentrating on the TV screen. 'James really isn't well enough to go out, and I certainly don't want to pass on whatever he might have to their kids. Kate won't thank us. I could stay here and you go, if you like?'

Ed shakes his head. 'I don't want you in the house on your own at the moment. I'm sorry if it freaks you out to hear that, but it's true. I can't work from home tomorrow, but I've spoken to Mum and Dad, and they're expecting you at theirs any time from 9 a.m. I've just said you're behind on a book deadline and need them to help with James. So I'm going to leave here at half eight, the same time as you. James will be well enough in the morning for that, I'm sure.'

'That's very kind of you all,' I say slowly. 'But that arrangement isn't going to be practical on a long-term basis, is it? You can't just—'

Ed holds up a hand. 'We *can* do it tomorrow though, and I just need a bit of time to work out how best to play this going forward. I've got a couple of ideas; I just need to mull them over and maybe make a few calls.'

I stare at him confused. 'I have no idea what that means. A "few calls" to who?'

'Don't worry,' he reassures me. 'I'm not going to do anything without talking to you about it first.'

'OK,' I say slowly. 'It'd help if I phoned the estate agents in the morning to talk to them about giving out our address then, would it? You're going to have enough to do by the sound of it.' I absolutely want to make clear to them that they must never do something like this again, but neither do I want Ed ringing and going ballistic at them. They are one of the biggest agents in the town and handling our cash sale. I don't want anything messing that up. Especially not now.

'Yeah, that'd be great, if you don't mind? And don't worry, Jess. I've got things in hand. I promise.'

❧

James hasn't quite finished his breakfast when Ed appears at half eight on the dot. He checks his watch. 'You'll be out of here in the next ten minutes, won't you?'

'Yes, I promise.'

He kisses James goodbye. 'See you later, little man. I'm glad you're feeling better, and look after Mummy for me today, won't you?' He straightens up. 'Sure you're also okay to call the estate agents today, Jess? I really don't mind doing it.'

'I know you don't. But it's no problem. I've got a few admin things to do anyway – I need to email a couple of other au pair agencies for a kick off, so one more call won't make any difference.'

He nods, satisfied, and once I've strapped James in the car six minutes later, I reach for my phone from my bag to quickly get it out of the way before I forget.

'Ah – good morning, Mrs Casson,' says the agent from Saturday, once I'm put through to him.

I hesitate, remembering Simon's query. 'I sometimes use Davies actually – but Casson is fine.'

'OK, right.' The agent sounds slightly confused – as well he might be – but not especially bothered. 'I'm sorry. My mistake. So now, is this about your sale – which is… let me check… going through fine, or are you ringing with some – how shall I put this – feedback – regarding Thrent Avenue?'

'That's one way of putting it, yes. I was very unhappy to learn that—'

'I thought you might be.' He interrupts me before I have a chance to finish my sentence. 'It was a most unfortunate situation. Most unfortunate indeed. Now, you won't be surprised to hear, I'm sure, that after what happened on Saturday morning we've had instructions to remove the property from the market, but I can assure you, we would have terminated our agreement with the vendors in any case. Thankfully, we weren't put in that position, but I do want you to know we take our clients' security very seriously at all times.'

'Well, evidentially not that seriously because—'

'Ah now, they were exceptional circumstances though, Mrs Davies, I think we can agree on that? I can honestly tell you I've never had a vendor become physical with a client like that before, and I hope I never do again. The poor woman was obviously a very disturbed individual, God rest her soul.'

'Well yes, she – hang on,' I stop, confused. 'What do you mean, "God rest her soul?"'

'Oh, you don't know? I'm afraid to say Mrs Strallen died last night.'

CHAPTER THIRTEEN

He's not able to tell me anything more than that. Just that they received a phone call from Mr Strallen first thing, who, given the circumstances, instructed them to temporarily withdraw the property from the market and cancel all viewings.

Stunned, I simply thank him for letting me know, and hang up, forgetting to say a single word about their disclosing our address without permission. Not that it matters any more, of course.

I sit there for a moment or two in the driver's seat, just staring out of the window as James chatters to himself in the back, reading his animal book.

God help me, I feel sheer relief that she is gone, and yet…

Another death.

The woman who burst into Simon's office all those years ago was so vibrant; colour in her cheeks, joking with me about dumping her dirty coffee cup, and even before that, when I had watched her walk up the hill with Simon, she was so happily holding his hand, secretly knowing that she was expecting their first baby, and that she'd be changing his life for ever that very evening.

And what of that baby now?

Oh poor, poor Cara. She's only 22! That's no age to lose a mother, even when I suspect she's not had one for some time. Lord knows I understand what that's like, and what Cara will be going through now. Like a light switching on in a dark room, there is a sudden flash in my mind of the horrific scene I found in Mum's bedroom that afternoon, before I instantly slam it off again. But just as suddenly, another fear slices through me: what if Louise committed suicide too? Oh fuck no. Please, *please* my walking into her house on Saturday didn't trigger something that finally resulted in Cara's mother taking her own life. I never meant for that. I had no idea they lived there!

I start the car, panicked. I have to go and make sure they know that I didn't mean for this: not just for Simon, not *even* for Simon, but for Cara's sake. She was Beth's friend. I can see them now, sitting on the mat in the classroom together, holding hands, the morning Beth died. Just two little innocent girls. Cara had been crying then, I now remember. Simon had said something about Louise being in a foul mood. Has she actually always been like this, then – a difficult woman? But in my heart of hearts, I know that is not true because *I* am partly responsible for her becoming the husk of the woman I saw on Saturday, all of that loathing in her yellow eyes.

James is still ill enough to fall asleep after only five minutes of driving, and as the unusual quiet descends, doubts begin to creep into my undistracted mind; the sensibilities of driving over like this out of the blue, and my motives for doing so. The closer I get, the more anxious I start to feel. Cara is not Beth. Of course I feel a connection, but… I breathe out… she is not my daughter. She was my daughter's friend many, many years ago, for less than a term. I'm not going for Simon – I know that's not true. So really, is this to assuage my own guilt?

I ought to change course now, and simply go straight to my in-laws.

And yet even knowing that I shouldn't be doing this, still I keep on driving, moth to a flame, eventually turning into Thrent Avenue. I cannot stop thinking of the girls sitting together, holding hands.

Pulling up right outside the house, I look at it worriedly. The upstairs curtains are drawn and it all looks every bit as closed off as it did the day before yesterday. I glance in the back at James – who is now snoring gently. Leaving the engine and heater running, I softly open my door, and shivering in my thin jersey top, climb out and push it to – but not completely shut. I quickly rush round to the other side and open the passenger door, before going back to close mine properly. I have a horror of James getting locked in the car. I don't have long before he senses the car motion has stopped and wakes up… I'm only going to be a matter of seconds anyway. I hasten up the short path to the front door and knock hurriedly, before turning back so I can check James is still safe.

The door opens with that juddering thud again, and I half glance behind me so I can at least acknowledge the person who has answered.

'Jess? What on earth are you doing here?' Simon looks astonished – and absolutely terrible. In complete contrast to Saturday, gone is the suave suit and crisp white shirt. He's wearing a pair of old-man jeans with a brown belt, and a button-down bottle green sweatshirt. The skin on his face is saggy with exhaustion, black and grey pepper stubble prickling over his chin. He looks like an exclusive wine club advert gone wrong.

'I called the estate agent,' I blurt. 'And they told me about Louise. I'm so sorry, Simon.'

'Thank you.' His eyes fill with tears. 'Ignore me,' he whispers. 'It's the shock.'

I glance back at the car and then to Simon again. 'Of course it is. You must be devastated. I mean… on Saturday, she seemed… so full of energy.' I trail off lamely, not knowing how to continue.

'It's all my fault, Jess,' he says suddenly. 'She *was* fine. Well, as fine as she ever is… was.' He corrects himself. 'Until I got home after seeing you on Saturday night.'

My heartbeat momentarily slows and I just stare at him. 'What do you mean?'

'She didn't tell me about you coming here, and I didn't let on I knew, but after what you said about her threatening you seventeen years ago…' He takes a deep breath. 'All this time I've thought you left because you didn't love me, and you didn't come back because you didn't want to. I could handle that. I was pleased it meant you were happy again. But to discover that was a lie, and Louise was responsible… I was angry. I was very, very angry. I came home and confronted her with what you'd told me. First she denied it, but then asked how I knew. I told her I'd just seen you. She went crazy at that and said she was glad she'd done it, and she wished she *had* killed you.'

I swallow, starting to feel a bit nauseous.

'That was it. I said I was leaving, immediately. I got a bag out from under the bed and began packing. She was sobbing and begging me not to go. She said she was going to call Cara and tell her everything. I ignored her and she completely switched tack at that, saying she'd change – she would stop drinking, she'd get better and we'd be a proper family again. I told her I'd heard it all before and, this time, it was too late. I got to the bottom of the stairs with my things when she suddenly ran back up, into our en suite, slamming the door and locking it behind her. She went completely quiet, and I fell for it – I started panicking. It's got no windows, you see. You can only get in through the door and it's a heavy, old-fashioned turnkey.

'I went up, called through to her to come out, and she shouted that she was going to prove it to me. She was stopping drinking here and now. She'd be the person I'd fallen in love with again. She was sure she could do it. She was weeping and weeping; it was dreadful. I felt so guilty—'

I glance at James again, to see that he is starting to stir and rub his eyes. Shit. I look back at Simon, as he continues, unaware.

'The thing is though, she *can't* stop. Literally she can't. She's been drinking so long that it's physically dangerous for her to do it like that. She tried once before and collapsed from a seizure. The only time she genuinely quit for a bit was under medical supervision, as part of a rehab programme, when they prescribed her diazepam. We'd been to see our doctor – he's a family friend – last week and he'd prescribed her some more, but she hadn't wanted to start taking it. I told her not to be so stupid, and to come out, or I'd call the police. She told me she had scissors in there and if I phoned anyone she'd hurt herself. OK, I said – fine. You win. I'm not going anywhere. Come out and we'll talk... She didn't, until about eleven o'clock. I promised to stay the night and that we'd discuss everything in the morning. I told her to either have a drink, or take some of her meds. She promised she would. We both went to bed.'

I nod, feeling awful that I wish he'd hurry up a bit. Of course he's in shock, which is why he's going into such detail, but James is going to wake up any minute, and I don't want to be rude and have to cut him off completely, mid-flow.

'She was in the bedroom; I was in the spare room. All yesterday she was very subdued. She said she felt ill and wanted to stay in bed. I tried to get her to eat, but she wouldn't. I couldn't leave her like that, so I just stayed downstairs. Then at about seven o'clock, I walked to the M&S garage to get her some chocolate. Partly I needed to get out of the house, and partly I thought it might be something she'd eat, but I forgot my wallet, so I came back and it was completely quiet in the house. I went up and the bathroom door was wide open—'

James starts to look about him in confusion, and seeing me out of the car, shouts: 'Mummy!'

'Just coming, darling!' I call back.

'You've got to go – it's OK. I understand.' Simon gestures at James. 'Anyway, she was on the floor, dead. I called the police – and our GP friend, who came straight over and said it was another seizure brought on from the sudden withdrawal. Her meds were all still in the bathroom cupboard untouched. She'd got bite marks on her tongue apparently, and there was a graze on her head where they think she hit it when she fell.' He exhales as if he can't believe it himself. 'Cara is on her way home. She's been doing a ski season in Chamonix as a chalet girl. I had to call her and break the news over the phone this morning. As *you* know, when you've had a mother like Louise, you learn to live expecting to get a phone call like this one day, but when it actually happens—'

'Mummy!' James shouts again.

'I'm so sorry, can we just walk down to the car so I can hold James's hand for a minute while I listen to you?' I say desperately.

'Of course. Hang on.' He reaches behind him and puts the door on the latch as I hasten down to my son.

'Hello, Mummy. Nice to see you.' James repeats one of his stock phrases as I appear alongside him, then points at the floor and a copy of a crappy Peppa Pig book. 'Peppa, please.'

'What a good polite boy!' Simon appears behind me, and smiles at him. 'Hello, James.'

James gives a little wave, grins and then goes all shy at his own boldness, burying half his face in the side of his seat.

Simon turns to me. 'He's gorgeous. You must be very proud of him.'

'Yes, I am.'

Simon's smile fades, and suddenly his face is bleak. 'Where did it all go so wrong, Jess? I know I did some things that I shouldn't have, but there was never anyone else; it wasn't something I made a habit of. I didn't intend to fall in love with you and hurt her. I tried my hardest to be a good husband, and a good father. How do I make this OK for Cara, now? She's still so young!'

I hold James's small hand and, stroking it with my thumb, take a deep breath. 'You keep every thought like that to yourself. You tell her how much Louise loved her, and that what happened was an accident. She was trying to detox herself because she wanted you all to be a family together. She never stopped trying, and she was the best mother she knew how to be.' I choke up and try to smile. 'Sorry. Forgive me, I'm really not attempting to make this about me, and what happened to *my* mum. I just feel desperately sad for Cara. I'm also not telling you to say anything that isn't true. But protect her, Si. Don't tell her things she doesn't need to know, or that she has no power to change – things that she now can't ask Louise about. Does she know about me, or Beth? Any of it?'

He shakes his head.

'Then keep it that way. Louise obviously didn't want her to, and that should be respected.'

He closes his eyes briefly. 'I have ruined so many lives.'

'No, you haven't. You're not that powerful.'

He snorts gently.

We stare at each other for a moment. Suddenly, I feel acutely uncomfortable to have slipped back into talking to him like this so easily. Loss is hanging damply in the air all around us, draping over the bare trees.

'Mummy!' James says uncertainly.

'I have to go,' I say, and Simon looks awkwardly at his watch. 'It's probably a good idea, to be honest,' he admits. 'Cara's flight was at 7 a.m. from Geneva. She'll be back any minute.'

'You didn't go and get her from the airport?' I can't help the surprise in my voice.

'I offered, Jess. Of course I offered. She said no, she'd be OK.'

You should have gone anyway, I think privately, but don't say it. What would it achieve? 'We'll go now. I'll be wishing you and Cara all strength.'

'Thank you. And thank you for coming. It means more to me than you'll ever know.'

I hesitate, and rather wish he hadn't just said that, I push aside another twinge of unease as I think about how Ed would feel if he knew I was stood here now. But then I came for Cara's sake. No one else's. Ed would understand that. I let go of James's hand, and close the car door. 'Take care of yourself, Simon. And again, I'm so sorry for your loss. Goodbye.' I turn swiftly on my heels, pre-empting any awkward handshake, or an attempt at a kiss on the cheek, by deliberately walking around the back of the car.

Simon has already turned away however, and is looking up the far end of road. A taxi has just turned the corner and is coming towards us.

'Cara!' he exclaims. 'Jess, can you go, please. Now!'

Understanding his panic, and without another word, I jump in, and start the engine. Looking in my rear mirror as I quickly pull out onto the street and safely away, I see that Simon has already spun on his heels and is walking smartly up the path into the house. My heart is thumping loudly as we safely reach the end of the road and merge into busier traffic. I don't risk another backwards glance.

Ed arrives home an hour later than intended because the trains are delayed. James is already down, and I'm chopping onions when he bursts into the kitchen, red in the face, unwinding his scarf. 'I'm so sorry!' he gasps, out of breath. 'I tried so hard to get back here before you! How long have you been home?'

'About an hour. I gave James his tea and bath at your mum's, but I had to come back after that.'

'An hour? Shit! I'm so sorry, Jess. I'll work from home tomorrow.'

I shake my head. 'You don't need to. Ed, I spoke to the estate agents today.' I reach across the counter for the glass of red wine

I've already poured, and pass it to him. 'Louise Strallen died last night.'

His mouth falls open and he just stands there holding his glass. '*What*?'

'She had a seizure, hit her head and died. She was trying to detox herself. Apparently it's really dangerous to stop suddenly when you've got a chronic, long-standing problem.'

He looks astonished and takes a large slug of wine. 'The agents are unbelievable – they have got to be the gobbiest firm I think I've ever had dealings with.' He pauses. 'I can't believe they told you all of that!'

'They didn't. I went to Thrent Avenue. I saw Simon.'

Ed looks at me steadily, and carefully puts down his glass. 'You went to see him?'

'Yes. But not like that. All I could think about was his daughter – Cara – and Beth. And I know what it is to lose your mother like that, suddenly and yet not suddenly at all, because you've been waiting for it to happen for so long, expecting it almost.' My voice starts to shake. 'And it's partly because of me that Louise had those problems in the first place.'

'No,' he says, 'that's not true. You didn't cheat on Louise, Simon did. You didn't know he was married. Her obsession with you was beyond your control. Her drinking was beyond your control.'

'I couldn't stop thinking about Cara, and Beth.' I try to smile, but my eyes fill with tears.

'Hey!' He steps over and wraps his arms round me. 'I get that you understand Cara's loss today. Of course I do, it's complicated for you on so many levels, but you need to step away now, Jess. You can't help Simon, or Cara. You can't allow yourself to be drawn back to this any more than you have been already.'

'You're right. I know I've messed up,' I confess, pulling back and wiping my eyes. 'Just before I drove off, I gave Simon some advice on how to help Cara through this, and he thanked me for coming. He said it meant more to him than I knew, and just that was enough to unsettle me. I'm sorry, Ed. I'm sorry that I went there this morning. If I were you I'd be feeling really angry, but I promise you, there is absolutely nothing going on. I have no feelings for Simon like *that* at all, I just felt so... so...' I struggle for words. 'I felt so *sad*.'

'It is sad, Jess. What happened to your mum, and Beth – what's happened to Louise. It *is* sad – all of it. Don't worry about going there today. I understand.'

'I won't make the same mistake again.'

'I know you won't. Come here.'

We just stand there in silence and he holds me tightly.

'You know what's really awful?' I say. 'My first thought, when the agent told me she'd died, was one of relief.'

'Well, that's because she was dangerous, Jess,' he says. 'I don't blame you for feeling like that for one minute.'

I hesitate, and I don't know what suddenly makes me say it – an instinct perhaps – but I pull back and look at him. 'You know those calls you were going to make?'

'Yes, what about them?'

'They were nothing to do with Louise, were they?'

He looks confused, and then his eyes widen. 'You think I had something to do with her *death*?'

'I think you love me and James very much indeed. And I think you know a lot of people.'

He laughs in disbelief.

'Ed, look at me. Truth?'

He looks almost angry for a moment. 'Of course that's the truth! I'm in sales, not the Kent mafia. I understand you're very upset, Jess – but keep your feet on the ground, eh? She was a drunk – and a nasty one at that. They never believe it'll get them – they always think they're the exception to the rule – but eventually it does. Every choice you make catches up with you in the end. Just be thankful she's not your problem any more and that we can get on with our lives now.'

*

Three weeks later, I'm on Rightmove again, trawling around absently; although, with it being one week until Christmas, I'm not expecting anything of note to have been added and I'm really only supposed to be looking at places to rent now. Hesitating, I add 'Sold STC' to my search criteria and, as I scroll through, Thrent Avenue *does* appear: 'Under Offer'. So Simon did put it back on, and they are obviously still moving. Well, that's good. I feel a genuine sense of relief for him and Cara. Wherever they are, I hope they manage to have as peaceful a Christmas as possible, and I hope this really is a new year for both of them.

*

During the first week of January, I'm driving through town with James, who is sitting in the back of the car alongside our new French au pair, Sandrine. She's making animal noises with him, and I'm only half concentrating on the responses he's offering. Before I realise I'm even doing it, I've turned into Thrent Avenue. I start slightly, and sit up a little straighter, determined not to look as we approach the house, but I can't help myself – even slowing down as we pass by. The 'Sold' board is lying in the front garden, which has already been brutally hacked back. Despite the time of year, scaffolding has gone up, there's a large plastic tent over the roof and a well-known – and expensive – builder's placard is tied to the railings. The front door is wide open and men are going in and out.

Well, that was quick.

I take one last look before pulling away. Ed's right; it's time we all moved on now.

CHAPTER FOURTEEN

'So tell me how the house stuff is going?' My NCT friend, Natalia, who has come over for an afternoon playdate with her little boy, picks up her mug of coffee and takes a sip.

'All good.' I lift crossed fingers. 'We're set to exchange on Friday this week and we move into the rental place two weeks after that, then complete a week after *that*.'

'Very sensible,' Natalia nods. 'I honestly think renting first is the only way to buy these days. I know it's a faff, but you'll be able to look for somewhere properly once you've sold – and you'll be in a great position. Plus you'd have been crazy to turn down a cash buyer.'

'True,' I agree and take a mouthful of tea just as Sandrine appears in the kitchen doorway clutching a basket of washing, waiting shyly, and tucking her long black hair back behind her ear, as I attempt to swallow quickly. 'Hi, Sandrine,' I cough. 'Sorry, come in. This is my friend, Natalia,' I gesture across the table 'and that's her little boy, Otis.'

'Hello.' Sandrine smiles politely, then turns to me. 'I would like to iron these now, if that's OK?'

'That would be brilliant, thank you,' I say gratefully.

'No problem. Nice to meet you, Natalia!'

'Nice to meet you too.' Natalia smiles, waits until she's out of earshot, then lets her mouth fall open. 'Wow. Her English is good given she's – what – 12?'

'She's 18.'

Natalia wrinkles her nose. 'Really? Well, at least you don't need to worry about Ed getting a crush on the new hot au pair, I suppose.'

'Natalia,' I reprove gently.

'What?' Natalia says. 'Good for her, not feeling like she wants to wear make-up. She's tiny too; it must be like having another child in the house.' She sips her coffee and watches James and Otis busy with toys on opposite sides of our playroom. 'Strange, isn't it, the way kids just don't play *with* each other at this age,' she remarks. 'Just alongside each other. Kind of makes you wonder why we bother killing ourselves to take them to playgroups and classes to "interact" really, doesn't it?' She pauses and shifts on her chair uncomfortably, her face flushing with embarrassment. 'I'm sorry, Jess, that was hugely insensitive of me, what I just said about having another child in the house. I didn't think and then it was out there.'

I look at her in surprise, then realise what she means. 'Don't worry about it. Beth would be 22 now anyway – hardly a child. And do you know, Sandrine has actually been here nearly a month already?' I change the subject. 'I can't believe how January is flying past, can you?'

'I really am sorry,' Natalia repeats, then hesitates. 'Can I ask something I *have* thought before, though? Doesn't it feel really unsettling to have girls living in the house with you who are pretty much around the age Beth would have been? I'd really struggle with that if I were you.'

Would have been… I'm fond of Natalia, but her complicated personality mix of being highly sensitive to the point of fragility, yet also direct and blunt to a fault doesn't always make for a relaxed coffee conversation.

I take a deep breath. 'Well, you remember the first one we had? The Norwegian girl called Berit? If I'm honest: yes, that was tough.'

She was so sweet, very fair-haired, and lovely to James. I completely underestimated how it would affect me, watching her play with him and realising it should have been Beth. It was ridiculous, now I look back on it. We just thought it would be good to have an extra pair of hands, and some company for me in the house. I don't know if you remember but when James was born, Ed's Mum and Dad were busy looking after his sister's kids *a lot* because she had just gone back to work; my dad was recovering from a hip replacement… Anyway, it poleaxed me, watching Berit; half seeing Beth, half knowing it wasn't and couldn't ever be. Although somehow it was even worse when she had to go home. I was gutted.'

'I remember. We were all a bit worried about you, to be honest. Me and the other girls I mean.'

'Were you?' I'm surprised to hear that. 'It wasn't that I felt like I was losing Beth all over again, obviously, more just the sensation of loss itself. I don't know, I'm not explaining it very well, but I know it was a lot easier when we went on to have Mariana and then Milla—'

'Was she the greasy Finnish one who kept cakes in her drawers and started "collecting" your jewellery?'

'Yes,' I sigh, 'and then Haduwig.'

'Ha! Yes. I'd forgotten Headwig. The German one who cried all the time and left after three weeks?'

'Poor thing. She'd not been away from her home town for more than two nights in her whole life. What was she thinking? Anyway, the point is, I realised I liked it. I like having them around, and helping them to have a nice, safe experience of living in this country. It's something I can do for them, and they do for me.'

'And it's much cheaper than a full-time nanny.'

There's another pause.

'Sorry,' Natalia says again. 'I didn't mean to quash that romantic "Heidi goes to England" thing you were building there with my nasty cynical comments. I'll shut up now.'

'On the subject of nannies,' I say firmly, 'tell me how it's going with Liza settling in? James – can you let Otis have a go too? Thank you, darling. Good boy.'

'Great, obviously,' says Natalia drily, 'which is why you have the pleasure of my company this fine Tuesday afternoon. She's back tomorrow, allegedly; although I did almost lose it when she texted to say her osteopath thinks her bad back is exacerbated by *picking up children*. Three days off ill in your first two weeks is pretty rubbish, by anyone's standards. Luckily, she's on a three-month probation – what are we now?' She picks up her phone and checks the date. 'It's January 24th today so I've got until... well, effectively the end of April to bin her if she's still hopeless. That said, she is actually one of the better ones we've had in some ways. Fundamentally she's safe, and she can just about cook. But, my mother-in-law also took great pleasure in telling me that last time she'd seen him, Otis was in a sick-stained T-shirt. He'd puked a bit and Liza hadn't bothered to get him changed, which made me feel awful. She said she hadn't realised. How can you not notice a child's been sick on himself? I suppose that's the benefit of your set-up though, isn't it?' She nods over at my laptop sitting on the side. 'Although you're here working, you can keep an eye on Sandrine all the time.' She hesitates. 'Is that *why* you do it like this, Jess – so you don't ever have to actually leave James on his own?'

I pause. 'Yes and no,' I admit. 'Copy editors always work from home these days anyway, but yes, I like to be around for James in the background. I know it's not very rational, but I don't want him to be looked after away from me when he's still too little to tell me if something's not right. But, I also need to work, obviously. So it's the best compromise. I *do* let them go off to toddler classes, and that sort of thing, on their own, though.'

'I'm not having a go, just asking.' Natalia sighs, leans over and pats my hand. 'I'd go completely mad stuck with Otis 24/7, but I get why you feel you need to do it.'

Beth lingers in the room with us for a moment longer, looking at me with a bright smile, and, as sometimes happens to me – will always happen to me, I think – I find myself randomly on the verge of tears.

'Anyway, Sandrine is great,' I force the shakiness from my voice as Natalia lowers her gaze and concentrates on her mug. 'She just gets on with everything, but that's probably because she's got brothers and sisters back at home in Toulouse. I also think it makes a difference that she's a friend of Helene and a known quantity. I couldn't believe it when she emailed and asked if we were still looking for a replacement.'

'You've had the luck of the devil.' Natalia sips her drink again. 'Plus, of course, no agency fees. So all round, you definitely win. Want to trade my worryingly attractive, back-knackered nanny for your sweet little au pair?'

'Worryingly attractive?' I ask, getting myself back on track. 'You're not serious, are you?'

'Nah.' Natalia shakes her head. 'Adam knows he can't afford to leave me. Least of all for the staff. I'll say one thing for my husband, he has a very acute awareness of the true cost of extramarital flirtations. He had an email from one of his colleagues – a group one to his whole team, mind – and this guy was announcing he'd left his wife and kids. He put "Clare and I remain friends, but will be divorcing, and I'd appreciate it if you'd soft launch this information where appropriate". It then went on to say: "You may also see me with Susie from Accounts in a social setting, but I'd welcome your discretion at this stage".' She snorts derisively. 'Let's leave aside that the scumbag actually said "soft launch". As Adam pointed out, what a—' she glances over at the boys, 'silly old sausage, but needless to say, Susie is barely thirty. It might be all "sausages" now, but I'll bet she's up the duff by the end of the year. Then he's right back to square one, only with two sets of school fees and no more sausages for anyone, because you can guarantee Susie won't be in the mood for so much as a chipolata for the next twenty-odd years. Women like her make me sick. You can't just pretend that a wife and children aren't real, you know?'

'No. You can't.' I sip my tea. Natalia is on form today, although of course this time she has no idea that what she's saying now is so close to the bone it's scraping.

'It's such a cliché. What's wrong with these girls that they even find the older men attractive in the first place? I mean, Adam's alright, but he tucks his shirts in his pants; if he makes a joke once, he makes it a thousand times; he's slightly mooby and incredibly grumpy. Why choose that when you could legitimately have a gym-toned twenty-something? Otis! No! Don't take that too – you can't have everything. Give it back; James was playing with the tractor. Susie's almost a cert to have "daddy issues", isn't she?'

'Maybe she just loves him,' I say quietly, before jumping up to move James out of Otis's hitting range.

Natalia wrinkles her nose.

'I'm not saying that makes it acceptable,' I say quickly, returning to my seat. 'Not if he's married. *Never* if you know he's married. I can't imagine the humiliation of your husband "soft launching" your separation to his work colleagues. It would be excruciating.'

'I'd go and find Susie from Accounts if it were me. I'd take Otis, make her look at him and see the consequences of her actions.'

'Really? It'd be her you'd blame? Not Adam?'

'I'd feel betrayed by him, yes, but it'd be her I'd want to hurt. We all know marriage can be tough and there are moments of weakness – but a single person exploiting that and becoming involved with someone who is married is indefensible, male or female.' She takes a casual sip of her drink. 'The bloke my sister-in-law worked with outright targeted her, even though he knew she had a family, and now my brother is the poor—' she glances at the kids and spells out, 'b-a-s-t-a-r-d visiting his kids every other weekend, and listening to them crying down the phone asking when he's coming back. Yes, I hate her, but if I saw that man who promised her the world and is already cooling off faster than you can say "turns out I don't want family life after all", I wouldn't be responsible for my actions.'

I'm sat at the kitchen table again, only this time with a glass of wine while trying to work, when Ed arrives home.

'Everything alright?' he asks, coming over to me and dropping a kiss on my head. 'Rough day? It's not like you to be drinking on a week night while editing? Shit, there's not a problem with the house, is there?'

'No, that's fine, still on track for Friday. I'm OK. Just tired.'

He looks relieved, but says: 'Sure? You look like it might be more than that?'

'I can't concentrate. I've been thinking about Louise Strallen again.'

He looks dismayed, like he wishes he hadn't asked. 'Really?'

'It was something Natalia said earlier about a bloke Adam knows, who's having an affair with a younger woman.'

Ed sighs, and sits down.

'She said if it were her, she'd go over and have it out with this girl, and I suppose it got me wondering. Was it really that mad of Louise to confront me the way she did, all those years ago? Would I really have behaved any differently in her shoes, given what she'd discovered? Aren't we all just one step away from madness?' I decide to give up on work and shut the laptop lid.

'How much of that have you had?' Ed nods at the bottle and gets up again. 'Louise threatened to knife you. She was off her trolley.' He yawns. 'What are we doing for dinner?'

'Oh, hello!' I ignore him as, to my surprise, Sandrine comes into the room clutching a small pile of James's dirty washing, en route to the utility room. 'I thought you'd finished ages ago. Aren't you going to meet your friend?'

'I will leave now,' she says quickly. 'I just found this and thought I would put this in the basket. Hello, Ed.'

'Hi, Sandrine.' He looks up briefly from digging around in the freezer and gives her a little wave. She smiles, waves back, then turns to me: 'Your phone was on top of it, Jessica.' She holds it aloft. 'I thought you would want it.'

'Oh, thank you – yes, I don't want to wash that by mistake, been there done that.' I reach out for it and slide it onto the table next to me. 'Talking of phones, you'll remember to text me if you get held up and you can't be back by eleven?'

'Of course. But I will be back for sure. Good night!'

''Night, Sandrine, have fun.'

Ed re-emerges and waits tiredly until she's left the room before asking: 'I thought the curfew *was* eleven on a week day?'

'It is.'

'So just say that then.'

'My way is a bit more polite. Why, do you think I should be more like Natalia?' I pick up my wine again, take a large mouthful, and then put it back down. Ed hastens over and moves my phone out of the way as some of the liquid slops over the side of the glass. 'I was halfway through telling you how she was her usual direct self today, wasn't I? I wouldn't call Natalia diplomatic at the best of times, but today there were several points where she really should have just engaged her brain and *thought* about what she was about to say. In the space of about five minutes she covered us being cheap for getting an au pair, told me she thought I was crazy for staying at home all the time with James while Sandrine is here, even though she got "why" I do it, then she told me all women who fall for older men have daddy issues, and *then* announced becoming involved with someone who is married makes you solely responsible for destroying a family. I honestly think she has no idea how aggressive and judgemental she sounds sometimes, and' – I remember her remark about Adam not having affairs with 'the staff' – 'actually pretty snotty occasionally too. It's not just me that thinks she's borderline offensive either, the other girls have all said it… I mean, people can't help who they fall in love with.'

Ed looks at me meditatively. 'She's really upset your apple cart, hasn't she?'

'Not as much as I'd have upset hers if I'd have told her I was once Susie from Accounts, and not only did my daughter's *married* teacher get me pregnant, I lied to my husband about whose baby it was, only for the wife to find out the truth… Da Da DAAAA.' I mimic cliffhanger music and take another enormous mouthful of wine. 'She'd probably never speak to me again.'

Before Ed has a chance to ask, 'Who's Susie from accounts?', the door opens to reveal Sandrine in her coat, a scarf wrapped tightly round her neck. For a second I think she still hasn't left, and am about to ask her if there's any point in going at all, but notice that in fact her cheeks are flushed with cold, and she has a terrified expression on her face.

I straighten up immediately. 'Are you alright?'

She shakes her head. 'No. I was gone and er…' She struggles to find the words; she's visibly frightened. 'I had gone,' she corrects herself. 'I walked up the road and someone is following me.'

'What? Just now?'

'Yes – pushing a bicycle. They were standing outside the house. I think they are waiting for someone next door maybe, so I walk off, but then I turn around because I hear them, and they are – boom – *right there*,' she holds her palm right up to her face, 'breathing on me.'

Ed doesn't wait to hear any more. He steps smartly round the table and out of the room. We both hear the front door open as I hasten over to Sandrine and take her hand. She is trembling wildly and looks like she's about to cry. 'Did they hurt you, Sandrine?'

She shakes her head again. 'They tell me that God loves me, and then they are gone.'

I slam instantly back into the cold morning of seventeen years ago, like a lift lurching sideways and opening on the wrong floor. The woman on the bicycle is stood in front of me, looking earnestly at Beth playing on the grass. I drop Sandrine's hand and step back. '"God loves you"? You're sure that's what she said? And you think she was watching the house?'

She shakes her head. 'I don't know if it was a woman or man; they have a jacket with a…' she mimes pulling a hood up 'and this…' she lifts the edge of her scarf, 'on their face. They say God loves me then they leave. Who are they? What do they mean?'

But I, too, am now rushing from the room. I run up the hallway and out onto the pavement in my socks, my breath clouding in the dark around me.

Ed is walking back down the middle of the quiet road, panting slightly, and throws his arms up. 'No one here. They must have ridden off.'

'Sandrine wasn't sure if it was a man or woman,' I tell him urgently. 'They got right up close and said God loves her.'

Ed pulls a face. 'What?'

'Don't you understand? That's exactly what that woman on a bicycle said to me about Beth the morning she died. You're absolutely sure you didn't see anyone?' I push past him and take a few more steps out into the road.

'Hey!' He grabs my arm. 'Whoever they were, they're long gone. We need to go back in.' He nods at the front door where Sandrine is standing in the doorway looking petrified. 'We're freaking her out, Jess, and all of this is going to wake up James. Let's just go back in, OK?'

He slips his hand into mine, and gently starts to lead me away as I look desperately over my shoulder up the now completely empty and eerily still street.

CHAPTER FIFTEEN

'So tell me again what this person looked like?'

'I don't remember.' Sandrine is looking worriedly between me and Ed, all three of us stood in the kitchen, her leaning right up against the kitchen units as if she'd like to get further away from us, but can't.

'You're not in trouble, Sandrine, it's OK,' Ed reassures her. 'We just want to make sure we know everything.'

'Did they have glasses? Do you think it *could* have been a woman?' I interrupt.

'It was dark. I'm sorry, Jessica. I think maybe glasses, yes, but it was a big cover over their head. It was fast and I wasn't sure what was happening.'

'It's OK, Sandrine, we understand.' Ed offers her a kitchen chair and sits down opposite her. 'I don't know if you have this in France, but in this country we have people that go and visit houses to talk about God. They give out leaflets—'

Sandrine looks at him blankly.

'Sorry, um, they give people pictures of their churches and some writing about how they love God. I think this is what this person was doing, that's all.'

'But Sandrine said they were waiting outside the house,' I cut in.

'Jess, please!' Ed gives me a look. 'Everything is OK, Sandrine. I can see it was not nice for someone to come out of the dark at you like that, but I don't think they meant to scare you.'

I look at her – tiny and looking much younger than her eighteen years, trying to swallow down her fear – and get a sudden picture in my mind of Ed and I stood in front of her weeping mother, her father saying 'but why didn't you do something? She told you someone was following her!'

'I don't want you to go to your friend's house now though, Sandrine,' I say quickly and force myself to smile. 'It's late. Just stay here.'

'OK, Jessica.' She unwinds her scarf. 'I don't want to go now anyway.'

'I understand completely. Do you want to go up and watch some TV in your room, or sit in the living room? Whatever you want. I'll make you a hot chocolate?' I walk round the table, put my arm round her and just for a moment she rests against me. She's so fragile and light – I can feel her shoulder bone – it's like touching a bird.

'Thank you,' she whispers. 'That would be nice.'

She closes her eyes with relief, just for a moment, then opens them quickly and says: 'I think I will also go and speak to my mother, if that's OK?'

'Of course.' I let my arm fall away, and she stands up. 'Come and get us if you want us to talk to her and explain what happened.'

'Thank you.' She tries to smile, but leaves the room, head down.

'You'll do that then, will you?' Ed says, once we're on our own. 'My French isn't up to a rundown of what just happened. I didn't know yours was either, to be honest?'

'You know it's not.' I sit down heavily at the table and put my head in my hands. 'Do you think we ought to call the police?'

Ed looks astonished. 'And tell them what?'

'Did you not hear what I said to you earlier? That's almost exactly what that stranger said to me the morning Beth fell. A woman on a bicycle, in glasses.'

Ed looks at me steadily. 'I get why it's making you react this way, but Sandrine didn't actually say she was wearing glasses, or even that it was a "her". You suggested that. Jess, you go past women on bikes every day of your life, and it doesn't register, right?'

'Yes, of course, but that's because they don't all make a point of coming up to me or someone I know, and announcing God loves me, or them.'

'I'm coming to that. Like I said, my first assumption is that this person was probably a Jehovah's Witness. In a minute I'll go next door and ask one of the neighbours if they visited them. I expect they were coming to knock on our door – which is why they were right outside – Sandrine appeared, they followed her to talk to her, then realised she'd freaked out and rode off.'

'Ed, one of the things I was never able to explain the morning Beth died was that woman who came up to me in the street: who she was, or why she said what she did. It was something I worked really hard to let go of in counselling. You know that. I have tried to come to terms with the fact that it was an unrelated event, just a random occurrence. So imagine how it feels to have it happen *again,* tonight?'

'You honestly feel someone going up to Sandrine and saying something similar, seventeen years later, is connected? You think this person is some sort of angel of death?' he speaks seriously, no hint of sarcasm. He's really asking me.

I exhale. 'I think a stranger came up to me and said my daughter needed to be told that God loved her, hours before she died in a freak accident, and now in uncannily similar circumstances, someone has approached Sandrine and said the same thing. Yes, I'm frightened.'

'Frightened that something bad is now going to happen to Sandrine?'

'Just frightened full stop.'

'OK. Let's go next door and ask one of the neighbours if they saw or spoke to anyone. I don't think it's too late to go round. What time is it?'

'It is—' I grab my phone to check. 'Hang on—' I touch the screen quickly. 'I just called Natalia by mistake. That's weird.' I peer at the phone, and tap it again, going to the recent calls. 'Outgoing, thirty minutes? I've been on the line to her for *half an hour?* She was the last person I called much earlier, but my phone has been locked. I couldn't have dialled again by mistake.'

'You were talking about her before. Are you sure you didn't accidentally press Siri and it dialled her when you said her name? It doesn't need to be unlocked for that to happen.'

'Oh God.' I go white. 'Do you think she heard everything I said? I should call her.' I hold the phone up to my ear, but then instantly hang up again. 'Actually, what am I doing? We need to sort out what just happened.' I look at Ed in disbelief. 'I can't think straight.'

'You're right, let's focus on one thing at a time. I'll go next door. Are you able to listen for James?'

I stand up. 'Yes, but if you hang on, I'll come and—' Only, as I get to my feet, the phone starts to buzz in my hand. 'Oh God, it's Natalia calling back. I'd better pick up. You go while I speak to her.'

He leaves the room.

I take a deep breath and answer. 'Hello?'

'Hi,' Natalia replies. 'You rang, again?'

'Yes, just to say I'm sorry. I called earlier by mistake and I think I might have left you a long, rambling message of rubbish. Just—'

'Jessica, I heard it. I heard what you said about me. I picked up when you called. You were talking to Ed and I tried to shout hello, but you just carried on talking.'

I close my eyes and feel the hot shame of embarrassment wash over me.

'I've often wondered what it would be like to be a fly on the wall in someone else's house, to listen in and find out what they actually think of me. I didn't imagine for one minute it would be such an unpleasant experience.' I can hear the hurt in her voice.

'I'm so sorry, Natalia. Obviously I didn't mean for you to be party to what I said. I was a little upset earlier, and—'

'Yes, I get now why I touched a nerve. Don't worry, I'm not going to tell anyone about your past, Susie.'

I flush. 'Natalia, there are good reasons for my not having been open about what I did a long time ago, but for the record, I didn't know the man I had an affair with was married. I—'

'Jess, you don't owe me an explanation. Everyone is entitled to privacy. What was upsetting, was the way I heard you speak about *me*. I get that I wasn't supposed to hear it, but I did. And I can't pretend that I haven't. I'm going to go now. All the best.' And then she's gone.

I stare at the phone in disbelief. *All the best*? Is that it then? Friendship over?

I look up to see Ed has reappeared and is standing in the doorway, listening. 'She heard, then.'

'Yes.' I feel stupidly teary. 'Just ignore me though. I'll sort it out; it was my own fault. More importantly, you were very quick – what did he say next door?'

'Well, it was her, not him – I can never remember her name, but she'd only just got in from work, and he's still out so she didn't know if anyone had been or not. She did look through their post though, and this leaflet for a church group had been put through their door.' He passes it over to me.

I look down at it. 'Right, so it probably was one of their members attempting to speak to Sandrine?'

'I think so, yes. I'm sorry to hear that things with Natalia have kicked off though. That's bad luck.'

I glance at my phone. 'Yes, isn't it? Very bad luck.'

'It's been a shit evening full stop for you. Do you want to just go and watch something in bed for a bit? Try and switch your mind off?'

I nod. 'Yes, I think I do. I'll just check on Sandrine, and see you up there.' I grab my laptop as I leave the room and head off upstairs.

❦

I find her in her bedroom, sitting on her bed, headphones plugged into her phone. She pulls them out and smiles politely when I knock at her door.

'I just wanted to make sure you weren't still feeling worried, or frightened.'

She shakes her head. 'I only feel stupid. I talked to my parents and they think I am surprise when I turn around and a person is, pooft! – right there – you know? But not to cry about it.'

'Well, I'm glad you're feeling better. Good night.'

'Good night, Jessica.'

❦

I head into our bedroom and sit down on the bed, propping the pillows up behind me. I open the laptop – and do a Google search on 'Stranger saying God loves you'.

One of the results to come back is a forum page, where someone has asked: *'Question: Did a Christian stranger ever tell you "Jesus loves you?"'*

Someone has answered: *'YEAH! They like come up to you and are all "Jesus loves you, you're special to him, yadda yadda..." I just kind of smile and walk off. I don't need that kind of shit when I've had a long day.'*

Another answer reads: *'Yes, and it was weird. This guy came up and asked me if I wanted a bible... AWKWARD!!'*

There are actually five pages of answers. I scan through a couple – a lot of respondents mention pocket bibles being handed to people outside schools. I learnt a long while ago that's quite a common practice. I return to the results, and one of the related searches is: 'God spoke to me through a stranger'.

It leads to another forum.

'Question: A man came up to me in the street and told me not to be afraid 'cause God is with me??! Has this happened to you and what does it mean?'

Another seven pages of answers follow:

'A: It can mean whatever you want it to mean. Were you upset at the time? Perhaps he could see that and wanted to help/take advantage. If you're the kind of person who believes in clairvoyance or wants to believe it, you'll probably see it as a message. I don't personally, so I just see it as a weird thing. Just get on with your life!'

'A: Yes! God speaks through strangers all the time! He's telling me right now to tell you to give me all your money…'

'A: I think he can and these strangers are your guardian angels.'

'A: YES GOD CAN TALK TO U THROUGH PEOPLE! IT'S CRAZY SHIT AND WHEN IT HAPPENS UR ALL WHOA! BUT EMBRACE IT AND LET GOD LOVE YOU TOO STAY REAL AND LOVE!'

'A: Yes I think it's possible to receive messages – if not from God, from something, or someone – that are relayed by strangers. But you will know when it's real.'

'A: He does it for shits and giggles to freak people out. It makes him feel superior.'

'A: God loves you… and I love you. I've got a baby rabbit in my car; would you like to come and see it?'

OK, that's enough. I sit back on the pillows and stare at the screen, rubbing my eyes tiredly. It's just that the woman or man tonight was even on a pushbike too. That *is* weird, surely. That's not just me?

I glance at the window, and get up, drawing back the edge of the curtain I pulled earlier when I put James down. I peer anxiously down into the orange glow of the quiet street – lines of parked cars on either side – and jump slightly as a movement catches my eye, but it's only a wiry fox darting out and across the road into someone's garden. Everything falls still again. There's no one there.

I climb back onto the bed, and finding iPlayer, put on an old *Strictly Come Dancing*. I try to focus on the sparkly dresses and cosy smiles, pushing weird strangers in the street, close friends not talking to me now, and my husband asking about angels of death, far, far away from my mind – but it doesn't work.

Biting my lip, I return to the forums and scan through until I find the response I'm looking for:

'Yes, I think it's possible to receive messages – if not from God, from something, or someone – that are relayed by strangers. But you will know when it's real.'

And *that* is the problem. Everyone can tell me over and over again that what the woman said to me on the morning of the 22nd November wasn't related to Beth's accident. I could spend the next ten years trying to force myself to reach, or find, a logical conclusion – but ultimately, I KNOW it was real.

I take a deep breath and lean my head back on the pillow. Tonight's incident has plucked me out of the here and now, and dropped me back into the skin I was in seventeen years ago, only with the curse of hindsight, and the benefit of age and experience. Why in God's name didn't I pull Beth out of the school that very first morning Simon and Louise walked into Beth's classroom holding Cara's hand and I realised why he was there. Why didn't *he* do something? 'How did we miss our chance, Simon?' I whisper aloud, in disbelief.

Beth. My baby girl.

'I miss you so much.' My lips move with the words I have said to her so many, many times. How could I have failed her so badly?

I *know* that woman's message, or warning… whatever it was – was real.

And to think that it might just have happened again?

CHAPTER SIXTEEN

'I'm so sorry, I'll find my keys in a minute.'

I rummage around in the change bag, and then in a fit of frustration, turn the whole thing upside down on the hall floor. A cascade of spare nappies, the first aid pouch, my purse, empty raisin packets, sticky, crumb-encrusted 5p pieces, ancient receipts, numerous wax crayons, a plastic Octonaut and a small car tumbles out. I'll now also need to hoover, and I still have no keys.

'We can walk, Jessica. It's fine?' Sandrine holds onto James's hand.

'No. I'm *going* to drive you. It's a filthy morning,' I insist, the stranger from last night lurking in the back of my mind. 'You'll get soaked and toddler groups are bad enough without being wet and cold too.'

As if to prove my point, the front door suddenly swings open wildly in the wind and bounces on its hinges – sending a rush of air up the hallway, making James catch his breath and Sandrine shiver. I jump to my feet and push it tightly shut, before hurrying back over to the bag and dropping to my knees to scoop everything back up. 'Sorry, guys. I didn't close it properly when I was going to see if I'd left them in the car door, that's all. Nearly there!' I smile brightly at James. 'Mummy will just find the keys and then... off we go!'

'Off we go…' he repeats dutifully as I glance at him worriedly. His coat is so padded he can barely move his arms. He's going to start overheating wearing it indoors like this, unless I get a bloody move on. I grit my teeth, stand up and start to go through the drawers in the sideboard for the second time.

'iPad please, Mummy?' James suggests. He's quite right. Why the hell would any sane person want to go out in weather like this rather than staying in, and cosying up on the sofa? He's *two*, and he's worked it out. I hesitate, and almost capitulate – the group started at half nine and it's already ten to ten, but then he can't just sit in all morning and play with Sandrine. It's good for him to have a change of scene, and see other children. It's important to make the effort.

'Five seconds – I'll check on the side in the kitchen again.' I turn and dash through, scrabbling through the box that contains a couple of cook books, random bits of post, pens, a Calpol plunger… but no FUCKING KEYS. Where are they? Is Ed *sure* he hasn't got them with him by mistake? I'm about to reach into my back pocket for my phone to call him again, when there is a shriek and deafening crash from the hallway. *James!* I spin on the spot, bashing my hip on the edge of the kitchen table I'm trying to get from the room so fast.

Sandrine is standing pressed up against the bannisters, James clutched to her body tightly. She's completely white and staring wide-eyed at our large hall mirror that is now lying face down on the wooden floor – exactly where James was standing seconds ago – shards of splintered glass spreading outwards, making the frame appear to have landed in an iced-over puddle.

'Are you alright?' I gasp. 'What happened?'

She doesn't move; she seems to be in shock. 'We are just standing here waiting and then it starts to fall. I lift James quickly and then it is everywhere.'

James turns his head and looks at the mess. 'Bang, Mummy,' he says, pointing at it.

'It did, didn't it?' I agree, stunned, and looking at the daggers of glass in horror while trying to think straight. 'OK, here's what we'll do. There's a spare car key in Ed's study. If you give me back your front door key, Sandrine – I'll take you both now and come back to clean this lot up and find *my* keys. Just move into the kitchen for a minute to wait for me, and then we'll go. Are you sure you're OK?'

Sandrine nods, and gives a final incredulous glance back at the mirror as she carefully steps over it and carries James safely into the other room.

Once I've driven them there and come back, it's twenty past ten – giving me an hour to clean everything up and do some editing before I have to go and get them again. I slide Sandrine's key into the lock and the door opens to reveal the glass carnage. Putting the key on the sideboard, I crunch over the shards, gingerly pick up the edge of the heavy gilt frame and lift it carefully. A couple of pointed slices break free and slide down to shatter alongside the rest of it. Propping the frame against the wall I peer at the nails I hammered in years ago. Reaching out, I wobble one of them, and a tiny trail of plaster dust drifts down the white wall. It *is* very slightly loose, but still – that mirror has hung there undisturbed for the best part of four years. It was a hell of a gust of wind this morning, but enough to lift it to the point that it fell when James – and Sandrine – were right underneath it?

The clean-up takes for ever. After forty-five minutes – having stopped to answer a pointless call from the estate agents that scares me witless that something has gone wrong… only for them to tell me we are still on course for Friday, but did we agree if I was leaving the curtains because the solicitor isn't returning calls? I've swept, hoovered *and* shone a torch over the ground to catch the sparkle of any flecks of glass that I've missed but James's tiny fingers or toes will undoubtedly discover – I sit back. I've done the best I can, but he'll have to wear shoes indoors for the next few days, at least.

I get to my feet and walk slowly into the kitchen. There's no point in trying to start any work now, bar checking my emails, before I go. I sink down onto a chair and fire the computer up, resting my elbows on the table, and my chin in my hands as I wait, still deep in thought. Thank God Sandrine moved as fast as she did this morning. The weight of that frame really would have hurt her badly and James very badly indeed, maybe even… I swallow and try not to think of the woman from last night, pedalling towards our house in the dark, stopping and then waiting outside the house. An angel of death. 'That's enough,' I whisper to myself. 'That's enough, Jessica.' The two events are not connected. How could they be? HOW could they be?

I take a deep, steadying breath and click on my email, watching the spam download alongside a couple of genuine work messages, and, oh God, one from Natalia. I open it in dismay.

Dear Jessica,

I'm still feeling really upset about last night. The more I've thought about it, the more weird I think it was. Usually when something like that happens, the person's phone is in their pocket, or bag, and you can't really hear what they're saying. I could hear you very clearly. Did you actually pretend that you'd called me by mistake, when really you wanted me to hear everything you said about me? Perhaps you've wanted to tell me for a while but not been brave enough to face the confrontation, so you faked ringing me 'from your back pocket' then let rip. Or perhaps you were trying to find a way to tell me what actually happened during your first marriage, because you know I have very strong personal feelings on adultery/infidelity. I genuinely can't make sense of it. Having slept on it overnight however, while I still feel you obviously you didn't need to tell me anything about your past life, and I don't judge you for what you did then (I didn't even know you!) – I really am very hurt by what you said about me, and I'm sorry to say I don't think we can be friends any more. This isn't a decision I've taken lightly, but one of the things about being a grown-up is recognising when a friendship has, for whatever reason, run its course, and this is it, for ours. I'm going to tell the other NCT girls why I'm bowing out of the group – which presumably they won't mind about in any case, as they too think I'm 'offensive'.

All best,
Natalia

Shit. I rake my fingers through my hair. What an absolute mess. For all of Natalia's 'that's just me, take it or leave it, and I call a spade a spade' attitude, I know she feels things very deeply – sometimes to an almost paranoid level – and I can see from this intense response she's given this *a lot* of thought. Of course I didn't ring her deliberately – that's just crazy! I was privately bitching to my husband in my own house. I shouldn't have said any of it, but really, who hasn't done that? And now I'm going to have to talk to the other girls about it too. Wait… she doesn't mean she's going to tell them about me and Simon, does she? Surely not? I think she just means the remarks I made about her personally; at least, I sincerely hope so.

I glance at the computer clock. Eleven twenty – I don't have time to think about this right now anyway; I need to go. I get to my feet, shut the laptop lid and make for the door, picking up the spare car key from the side on my way out.

I arrive to find James climbing *up* a slide in the busy church hall, with Sandrine next to him, watching and smiling – but not holding his hand. He's pretty fed up to be lifted straight off it and it takes all of my strength to wrestle him into the car seat. He's also devastated to leave behind a plastic helicopter, and cries all of the way home, and is still whimpering 'James, heliclopper' when we pull up on the drive.

'You go and open up, Sandrine.' I reach into my back pocket for her key and pass it over. 'I'll carry James in.'

James flings about a bit, crossly shouting 'no', and whacking me on the head as I try to lift him out, so I take a moment to remonstrate with him by the car, telling him it's not kind to hit mummy, can he say, 'Sorry Mummy', please? before we turn and walk up to the house.

Sandrine is standing on the doorstep looking puzzled, and holding her key in one hand, and *my* set in her other hand.

'Oh my God! Where did you find them?' I say in amazement.

'They are in there.' She points to the front door lock.

'What, in the door itself? Just hanging there?'

She nods and shrugs, then hands me the keys.

'OK,' I say slowly, looking at them. 'Well, perhaps I dropped them on the drive and the postman found them, or something.' I glance around us. 'Let's go in anyway, shall we? Time to put the kettle on.'

'Sing it, please!' says James immediately.

'Polly put the kettle on, Polly put the kettle on, Polly put the kettle on, we'll all have tea,' I begin, as I slide my key into the lock, twist it and push the door open. There is no post lying on the mat, which knocks that theory into touch, but I don't say anything. 'Sukki take it off again, Sukki take it off again, Sukki take it off again, they've all gone away...' I trail off as I step in, glancing up the stairs before walking tentatively into the kitchen.

But everything feels and looks exactly as it did when I left just under half an hour ago. I can't have been stupid enough to actually leave the keys in the door, surely? I would have noticed when we left, or Sandrine would have. Although it *was* belting down with rain, and all I ever do is slam it behind me. But then I would have discovered them when I came back from dropping them off at playgroup...

'Would you like a coffee, Sandrine?' I offer, putting James down and walking over to the kettle as she takes her shoes off in the hall. 'I'll get this on and we'll make some lunch. It'd be good to get James down by half twelve, I think,' I call over my shoulder. 'What time is it now?' I say this to myself, glancing across at the kitchen clock – which is reading five past ten.

I do a double take. It's stopped. I didn't notice that earlier. I sigh and put the kettle down, before heading out into the hall to find a new battery in the sideboard drawer. I wrestle one from the packet, and look up at my dad's cuckoo clock on the wall, which he sweetly gave us after James fell in love with it on a visit to his, to see what the time *actually* is.

It is also reading five past ten.

I stare at the hands of the clock, frozen in time, and the pendulum that has also stilled. It never stops; I keep it wound myself.

'Sandrine,' I say slowly, and she looks up from fiddling with her phone, 'could you just keep an eye on James for a moment while I go upstairs? He's just playing in the other room.'

'Sure. No problem. I will make him his lunch?'

'Yes, please, a sandwich would be fine, but stay with him while he eats it, won't you, in case he chokes?'

I take the stairs two at a time, up into our bedroom. My alarm clock on my bedside table has the face turned to the wall because it lights up blue in the night – thanks to the neon paint on the hands – and irritates me. I keep meaning to get a new one. I grab it and turn it round.

Five past ten.

I gasp and, starting to shake, I hasten into James's bedroom. His Winnie the Pooh clock, bought by Ed's parents, sits on his bookshelf. Five past ten; again.

I run back into our room and grab the thermostat, but the digital display reads 11.58. It's only the actual physical clock faces with hands that have all stopped and are reading the exact time that Beth died; five minutes past ten in the morning.

My legs give way suddenly, and I collapse down onto the floor in the corner, to just sit there, staring at the clock. Without taking my eyes from it, I reach for my mobile in my back pocket and call Ed. 'It's me. I need you to come home. Yes, now. Right now.'

✻

'So your keys were missing all morning and you think someone has been in the house during that time?' Ed says in a low voice as we sit in the kitchen at the table, his work overcoat slung over the back of the chair. James is napping upstairs, directly above us. Sandrine has gone to her college course and won't be back until four. 'Can you remember when you last had the keys?'

'Um. Yesterday morning, first thing, I took James to a singalong session at the library. I'm pretty sure I had them then.'

'You must have if you drove?'

I shake my head. 'I walked, but I wouldn't have left home without them. And now I think about it, Sandrine let me in yesterday when we got back because she saw me coming up the road. I didn't use my keys.'

'Did you leave your bag open at the library?'

'Well, no, not open, but I left it hanging on the pushchair like I always do. There are about a hundred pushchairs and prams there, Ed. Everyone does it. We couldn't possibly all lift our bags off and keep them next to us while the kids sing, there wouldn't be any room for them to sit down.'

'I'm not having a go, I'm just trying to work out if someone had time to go in your bag and nick them without you noticing?'

'Yes, they would have.'

'So you didn't use your keys all yesterday?'

'No, because I didn't go out again once I got back from the library. Natalia came over in the afternoon.'

'You only realised they were gone this morning?'

I nod.

'And the clocks had all been altered when you got back from collecting Sandrine and James from playgroup?'

'Yes.'

'But nothing else – and nothing is missing? It all looks like normal?'

'I only noticed the clocks after playgroup. They could have been changed earlier while I was dropping James and Sandrine off, but I didn't realise because I had the broken glass to sort out, and a shitty email from Natalia. I was pretty distracted.'

'So someone could have been in the house – upstairs perhaps – while you were down here and you might not have noticed?'

My insides squirm at the thought of a stranger crouched in one of our bedrooms, me crashing around clearing up downstairs, none the wiser. 'Yes.'

'And tell me again what happened with the mirror?'

'It just came off the wall. James was under it, it started to fall and, thank God, Sandrine was there and snatched him out of the way.'

'So someone could have loosened it deliberately? Possibly yesterday?'

'I don't see how. One of us was here all day. Unless they let themselves in while we were asleep last night.'

Neither of us pass further comment on that hideous thought.

'I thought the mirror coming off was down to my leaving the front door open this morning,' I add. 'It was incredibly windy; I assumed that was what disturbed it… I feel ill, Ed. Do you think it's the person who was hanging around the house and approached Sandrine who's done this?'

'I don't know, but we'll get the locks changed. I'll have this sorted before you go to bed tonight, don't worry. You leave it to me.'

'But shouldn't we also call the police? Someone trespassed into our house. And Ed, five past ten in the morning is the time Beth died.'

'I know it is.'

I hesitate. 'This is going to sound crazy, but the only person I can think of that would know a detail like that and use it to hurt me is Louise Strallen.'

Ed's mouth falls open slightly. 'As in the Louise Strallen who died just before Christmas?'

'What I mean is, I know that's what Simon *told* me – that she'd died – but maybe she just left him, or he chucked her out and she's not dead at all. But then that would be a really sick thing for him to do: play a grieving widower when he wasn't, and to ask my advice about what to tell Cara. God, what am I thinking?' I put my head in my hands. 'Of course he wouldn't do that… but then breaking into our house and setting the clocks to a time that could only have a significance to someone who *knows* what happened to Beth is sick too.'

'Louise Strallen is definitely dead, Jess.' Ed says, looking at me worriedly. 'If you give me a minute I'll get the obituary details up online for you to see, but I need to phone a locksmith first. And as soon as I've done that we'll work out what we have to tell the police that's concrete, and won't make them think we're just being paranoid and weird. Not that I'm saying *you're* being paranoid and weird,' he adds quickly.

'OK. So you're going to make a few calls?'

He looks up at me sharply. 'Yes. Why do you say it like that?'

'I just mean if you're going on your phone, can you take it in the other room so you don't wake up James?' I look at him, surprised at his tone. 'We're right under him here, aren't we?'

'Oh right – I see. Yeah, sure. I'll do that then.' He gets to his feet, scraping his chair noisily on the floor anyway, and leaves the room.

I stay sitting at the table, hands clasped as I bite my lip and stare down at the pattern on the plastic tablecloth. Someone used my keys and let themselves in. They could have been in the house while I was here.

They certainly know exactly what they want to say to me, that's for sure. Five past ten. There is no mistaking that message. They want to talk to me about Beth.

They evidentially have blame to lay at my door, but what else? I think about the mirror wobbling precariously above my son before beginning to fall… retribution? Revenge? If they want to hurt me, nothing could cause me more pain than something happening to James.

They *must* be the person on the bicycle. Someone posing as a stranger, while fully aware Sandrine would be frightened enough to tell me what they'd said to her – and exactly what that message would mean so personally to me.

'Unless it's you, Beth?' I say suddenly. 'The messenger on the bike, the clocks, the mirror – you're not trying to tell me something? Or warn me? Are you angry with me, maybe?'

There is silence. I can only hear the thumping of my heart as I sit very, very still and wait.

'Or you, Mum?' I try instead. 'Tell me what you're trying to say.' But again there is, of course, absolutely nothing, and I suddenly hear and see myself – the absurdity of a woman in her forties sitting at her kitchen table, desperately talking to her dead

5-year-old daughter, and mother. A wave of intense anger crashes over me.

I said I wasn't going to make mistakes this time; that I was a different woman, and yet I've already let this person – whoever they are – get inside my head, when they've only just started their game.

CHAPTER SEVENTEEN

'You alright?' Ed rests his book down on the duvet and turns on his pillow to look at me as I lie staring up at the ceiling in one of his old T-shirts.

'Not really.'

'I can see that.' He folds down the corner of his page and rolls over to give me his full attention. 'The locks are changed, Jess. Even if someone had copied the keys, they can't get in now.'

'I know that whoever it is didn't steal anything, but I'm actually finding it *more* chilling that all they did was alter the clocks, when I can't see what else they might have touched, or done… Apart from possibly the mirror. In any case, it's still trespass, Ed, and that's a criminal offence.' I speak quietly so as not to wake James. 'We should have called the police tonight. It doesn't matter that we don't know who might have done this, that's their job, not ours. I want to contact them in the morning. Yes, of course, I can hear myself saying to them: "I think someone took my keys but nothing is missing; a mirror fell off the wall and all of the clocks have been changed". I know how that sounds, but I also know this is about protecting all of us. Especially James and Sandrine.'

'Do you still think it's Louise Strallen doing this?' Ed asks. 'Even though I showed you her obituary?'

'No,' I confess. 'I'm not worried it's her, now. I'm quite glad I wasn't the only one to consider her still being alive a possibility, though?' I glance sideways at him.

'What do you mean?'

'Well, it must have crossed your mind too, for you to have already checked so thoroughly that she definitely died that Sunday night.'

'Oh, right.' He falls silent. 'Well, yeah, I wanted to know exactly what had happened. Do you want me to sleep in with James tonight, or you can – or we'll bring his cot in here with us if you're still feeling frightened?'

'I'll go in there with him in a minute.'

Ed hesitates. 'Jess – there's something else. I heard you talking to Beth in the kitchen earlier, asking her if she's trying to get a message to you, or if—'

'Can I stop you right there?' I interrupt quickly. 'I don't want you to think that I'm in danger of becoming overwhelmed by this to the point of—'

But before I can finish my sentence, he suddenly blurts: 'I lied to you, Jess, about the person on the bike who approached Sandrine. When I asked next door, they hadn't seen anyone, but they also hadn't received a leaflet through from a church group either. I picked that up from our old recycling pile in the hall. It's been there for days. I was trying to protect you from the place I knew your mind would go to.'

I jerk my head round to look at him. 'You deliberately misled me?'

'And I need to tell you something else.' He swallows. 'I can't phone the police about what happened today because I *did* send someone to the Strallen's house to have a word with Louise. They went there the night after she attacked you and Simon came here.'

I gasp, and pull back from him on the pillow. 'That was the night she *died*.'

He nods slowly.

'Oh my God… what the hell were you thinking?' I wriggle up to a sitting position and stare down at him in shock. 'I can't believe this! I asked you outright about it, and you got really angry. You said you weren't in the Kent mafia—'

'Shhhh! I was thinking that some woman who threatened my wife with a knife had attacked her again, called her a whore – and then almost certainly found out where we lived, thanks to her husband as good as leading her by the hand, right here. I'd talked to Dan, remember, and he said legally there was nothing we could do. I was beside myself.'

'Who did you send?'

'A mate of a mate.' He looks at me, nervously. 'Not someone I actually know; I'm not that stupid. I made it clear that they were not to physically hurt anyone at the house at all. They spoke to her, warned her off – and then left.'

'And yet when Simon came home, Louise was dead in their bathroom, with a head injury. Jesus Christ.' I put my hands up to my own head in disbelief. 'So for all you know, it escalated – she was gobby and drunk with this bloke, he got angry – and then this person you've never met, but *paid*, might have killed her?'

'Yes.' He stares up at the ceiling blankly as if he can't quite believe the words he's saying. 'I've checked though, and her cause of death was written up as natural causes, not a head injury, which means they think something "malfunctioning internally within the body" caused her death – which is good, seeing as otherwise I could be looking at conspiracy to commit GBH or us being joint accomplices in a murder.' He exhales shakily. 'The bloke I paid swears blind he didn't lay a finger on her, but when he found out she'd died, he made it clear to me – via some other bloke I had to meet in a car park – that if the police came knocking at his door asking questions, he'd say I told him to kill her, so they better not come knocking at all. I gave him some more cash as a sweetener, but at the very least if it comes out I'll be looking at conspiracy to blackmail; around four years in the nick.'

'Blackmail?' I'm appalled. 'How?'

'The offence would be my trying to force someone to do something against their best interests, because blackmail isn't apparently just about obtaining money, it's to gain an interest for yourself.'

'Four years in prison?'

'Yes. Which is why I'm not overly keen to involve the police.'

'I simply can't believe this…' I'm trying to wrap my head around what he's saying, but it feels as if I'm watching us on TV. 'We're actually having this conversation? And you've obviously talked to Dan about all of this too. You seem to know an awful lot of detail that I can't think you would have been aware of in advance of pulling a stunt like this. At least, I hope not.'

'Yes, I spoke to Dan. Off the record, obviously. He hasn't and won't tell anyone, not even my sister.'

'Doesn't that compromise him horribly?'

'I asked him hypothetically. And he hypothetically told me I'd been a fucking idiot, which, of course, I know now. I thought it would be a simple solution – that Louise would stop when she realised what it felt like to be threatened, but without anyone actually getting hurt.'

'What if she'd just gone to the police herself, then and there, after your "bloke" left. Did you think about that?'

'I knew she wouldn't. She'd already threatened you with a knife years ago, and attacked you in her house. Only people with no secrets to hide go to the police.'

'I should have said I wanted to press charges after she went for me at the viewing,' I realise aloud. 'And then we wouldn't even be having this conversation now. I just didn't want to prolong any more contact with the Strallens. I wanted to walk away.'

'Yeah, well, like I said, going to the police isn't an option any more. Sorry. I can't explain to you what I was thinking. I just wanted to keep you and James safe… but we're going to have to deal with whatever has started now ourselves.'

'"We're going to have to deal with it"?' I repeat in disbelief. 'What does THAT mean? You said to me, categorically, you wouldn't do anything without talking to me first. I can't even… I don't know how to process this.' I lean my head on the wall behind me. 'You genuinely sent someone to rough-up Louise Strallen?'

'Please try and keep your voice down,' he pleads. 'No, not to "rough-up", to warn her off. She threatened you with a knife!'

'She was a drunk, someone to pity! A desperate woman!'

'Exactly! The more desperate someone is, Jess, the more dangerous they become.'

I throw back the duvet, revealing my bare legs. 'You know, I was terrified last night when I thought history was repeating itself. What happened the morning Beth died was *real* – that woman on a bike had a warning for me. For years afterwards I worried that I had some sort of gift, or insight that I wilfully ignored that morning. Then earlier, after those clocks were all set to five past ten, I realised this was about something else entirely; someone trying to play on that guilt and fear I've had all this time, by pulling something personal, nasty, and vicious… only for *you* to now tell me there's nothing I can do to protect us from whoever is doing this. How can you have made such a huge mistake? This wasn't something you did in the heat of the moment; this took effort, premeditation. I get that you were trying to protect us, but my God, Ed… what were you thinking?'

'I get it, Jess. I fucked up. Surely you of all people understand that? Look at what you did to Ben.'

I turn to ice. I am actually unable to speak for a moment.

'That was a little different,' I manage eventually. 'I was 19, recently bereaved, heartbroken and pregnant.'

He sits up alongside me. 'I'm not judging you, Jessica. I've *never* judged the choice you made. You thought at the time you were doing the right thing. That's all anyone can do. It's what I did. I can't even explain how much you and James mean to me. I'd do *anything* to keep you safe.' His voice trembles slightly. 'I was very, very scared and it seemed like a solution when I didn't know what else to do. I couldn't stop thinking about that woman Dan prosecuted who just turned up on the doorstep of her ex-partner's new wife and stabbed her. Tell me you can see where I was coming from?'

I just sit there, shivering in the cold, and he reaches out for my hand. 'I'm not saying it wasn't fucking stupid. I've been having nightmares ever since about Louise Strallen, about being locked up. I feel like I'm having a heart attack every time I so much as see a police car… I don't know how people who do this sort of thing properly live with the pressure.' He closes his eyes and rubs his head exhaustedly, as if he's trying to force the thoughts from his mind.

I hesitate, watching him visibly struggling. 'Yes, Louise was unstable. Yes, she probably found out where we lived. Would I do anything to protect James? Of *course* I would,' I admit eventually. 'And yet to hear you say you actually sent someone round to their house, like something out of a movie, and on the night she died… I genuinely don't know what to do with that. It's too surreal.'

'I should never have done it. It was wrong,' he says. 'But let's also keep everything that's happened here in perspective. Nothing has actually—'

'Ed, someone was hanging around outside the house, gave our au pair what could only be a message for me, almost certainly stole my keys from my bag – which meant they followed me and James into the town, stalking us for want of a better word – possibly loosened a mirror while we were asleep, which almost fell on James, then came back to the house and, while I was out, changed all of the clocks to the time of my 5-year-old daughter's death. Exactly what part of that do you want me to keep "in perspective"?'

'What I'm trying to say is that no one has been actually hurt, and whoever it is can't get in any more, not without *breaking* in, and they've already proved that's not their style. Get back under the covers for a moment, you're shivering.'

'No. I want to go through to James now.'

'OK, OK. But before you do, I want to say I think you're right. They've made this very personal and it's not aimed at hurting James or Sandrine. It's all designed to get *your* attention. Isn't it obvious who it is?'

'Go on?' I look at him quickly.

'Well, Simon has already been here, hasn't he? He knows where we live.'

'Simon would never do anything to hurt me,' I say immediately. 'I'm sorry, Ed, but he just wouldn't.'

'Hold your horses, I didn't say it was meant to hurt you, I said it was designed to get your attention. Everything that's happened has some reference to Beth and her dying, things that barely a handful of people would know – and you might feel compelled to go and ask him about, maybe?'

My mouth falls open slightly.

'It's not that crazy an idea, Jess. I was thinking about it earlier while you were giving James his tea. What does he have to share with you that I can't, that no one else can? Your daughter; his and your daughter. If something bizarre started happening involving Beth, isn't it natural that you'd want to go and see if anything similar had been happening to him too, or at least discuss it with him?'

'To do something like that just to get my attention, and draw me back into contact with him, would make him not only very cruel, but completely mad. And Simon is neither of those things. I know you don't like him, and I understand that completely, but he's just not that person.'

'OK, then maybe it's Ben.'

'*Ben?*' Now I really am astonished.

'Maybe he's finally somehow found out that you've been lying to him all this time, he's flipped, and this is his way of punishing you – and telling you he knows.'

'Even if that were true, and he was somehow deranged with grief and anger, he would never hurt James. Not in a million years. That falling mirror could have killed him.'

'Ben couldn't have been certain *when* it was going to fall. Maybe it was just supposed to smash full stop, and mess with your head. Seven years bad luck. Whoever did this knows that you put store by that sort of thing.'

'Right. So you think it's one of my two exes. The only two men I've been involved with my whole life, apart from you. Does this say more about you, perhaps, than you realise?'

'Hey!' he says sharply. 'I've never had a problem with you staying in touch with Ben. I've been nothing but supportive of your relationship with him.'

'I've told you before, I don't have a relationship with him. Not now.'

There is a pause, and Ed sighs. 'Alright, so who do *you* think it is then?'

I miserably draw the covers back over my shivering legs. 'I don't know. Maybe Simon's daughter? She's good reason to hate me, and whoever has done this knows how to hurt. They know that time doesn't heal grief and that you'd give anything to go back to when your loved one was still here. That's what they're doing. Taking me right back – but to the exact moment I lost Beth for ever. Although Simon and Ben know exactly how that feels too, of course.' I pause exhausted. 'When I saw all of those clocks stopped earlier, it was like someone had slammed an apple corer through me. It ripped my guts out, instantly.'

'Does his daughter even know you?'

'No,' I concede. 'I haven't seen her since she was five, and she knows nothing about what happened, or who I am.' I reach for my phone and google 'Cara Strallen'. But nothing comes up at all. 'I guess I could ask Simon about it... he'd be easy to find via whatever school he's gone to in Surrey.'

'No,' Ed says, 'because if *I'm* right, that's exactly what he's going to want you to do – get in touch with him. I say we do nothing, and wait. This person has got no way of getting into the house any more, and we're watching for them now in any case. I'll ask Mum and Dad to have James tomorrow, and Sandrine can go too. You and me will work here, and see what happens. We could park the car a street or two away, as well, so it looks like we're out.'

I shift uneasily. 'And if they do come back? What then?'

'I'll handle it.'

I exclaim aloud in frustration. 'Can you even hear yourself, Ed? You say you're terrified of getting four years for blackmail, then in the next breath you say something like that?'

'I'm not going to let anything happen to you, Jess,' he insists.

'But what if something happens to *you*?'

He snorts. 'I can hold my own against either of your ex-partners or some girl, thanks very much.'

'Natalia was here yesterday,' I realise suddenly, ignoring him. '*She* could have taken my keys, and I'm very far from her favourite person right now.'

'Natalia?' Ed frowns doubtfully.

'I really upset her, big time.'

He yawns tiredly, in spite of himself. 'Whoever it was, approached Sandrine outside the house at the same time as you were accidentally calling Natalia in the first place, so that doesn't make any sense. Like I said, no one has actually been hurt, nothing dangerous has happened. It's just upsetting for you. Genuinely upsetting,' he says quickly, 'but I don't believe any of us are in any physical danger. Get some sleep – and we'll see what tomorrow brings.'

CHAPTER EIGHTEEN

'So you feel hot and shivery?' I look down at Sandrine lying in bed, her face shiny with sweat and her hair stringy and damp against the pillow. 'You should have come and got me.'

'I didn't want to wake you when I knew James was sleeping.'

'But I wouldn't have minded.' Concerned, I reach out and place my hand against her smooth forehead. She is indeed burning up, and her eyes instinctively close at the cool of my skin. As I'm drawing it back, I realise there is a tear escaping down her cheek.

'Oh sweetheart, don't cry!' I sit down immediately on the edge of the bed. 'It's OK.' I pick up her hand and hold it like I would James's. 'You're going to be OK, I promise. I'm sure it's just a virus, but it's horrible feeling ill when you're away from home.'

'I'm sorry. I just want my family. I want to be at home.'

'Of course you do,' I say sympathetically. 'Why don't I go and get you some paracetamol and breakfast, then when you're feeling a bit better and you've had a sleep, I know it's not the same, but you could Facetime them? You definitely need to stay in bed today though.'

'Thank you,' she says, 'that would be nice. I'm very sorry to not get up with James.' She sighs and closes her eyes again.

'It's no problem. He's going to be out all day anyway. All you need to do is rest.'

I stand up and look at her lying there. Natalia is right: she's so tiny she does look like a child.

'Sandrine, if you felt like you needed to go home, and working here wasn't what you wanted to do any more, that would be fine,' I say suddenly. 'You do know that, don't you?'

She opens her eyes again and twists her head to look at me quickly. 'You wouldn't be angry?'

She does want to go then.

'Of course not. I don't want you to be unhappy, or missing your family,' I say sincerely. 'We could book you a flight for Saturday if you like? You could be at home again in just two sleeps. Think about it and let me know.' I take a deep breath and smile. 'Life is too short.'

She hesitates. 'I know that person in the dark was only trying to be kind to me, and that mirror falling was nothing, but I am still frightened and I can't stop. I am always like this. My family, they always laugh because I am the one who is—' She weakly gasps and mimes jumping. 'Always, even when I am a little girl I get bad dreams and my little sister sleeps in with me.'

'That's nice of her,' I smile.

'I miss her. My brother he pretends sometimes, still, to scare me,' Sandrine laughs but then another tear spills out, 'but not my sister.' She wipes it away hurriedly. 'I am sorry, I think it is because I feel ill only.'

'I know, please don't worry. I'll bring you some breakfast, then James is going to his grandmother.' I watch her immediately stiffen with anxiety and her eyes widen. Oh God, the poor kid is terrified at the thought of being here alone!

'Ed is taking James?' she says. 'Are you are staying here?'

'I was going to take him.' I look at her, troubled. 'But yes, Ed can do it, that's fine. You won't be the only person in the house, I promise – and tonight we *will* book your flight home, alright?'

She nods, and whispers: 'Thank you, Jessica. You are very kind to me. Helene told me that you were so nice, but I didn't know how much.'

'Ah – well it's easy to be nice to you both, you're lovely girls. Now, I'm going to go and get you breakfast. Cereal and toast OK?'

'Yes, please.' She turns away from me and faces the wall. I'm about to leave the room when she says in a small voice: 'Jessica – sometimes I wake up here and I am afraid to open my eyes all the way, or put on the light, because I know I will see someone watching me. I can feel they are there. I tell myself not to be stupid, but I know it is real. I wanted you to know.'

I freeze on the threshold of the room and turn back quickly. *Beth.*

The hairs on the back of my neck are standing up and I realise I'm not breathing… but Sandrine is right. She's a young girl, away from home, missing her family and badly frightened. If I were her, and I knew that my daughter had died, I'd probably think ghost children were watching me too.

'Don't feel afraid, Sandrine. You are safe, and I promise nothing is going to hurt you.'

She falls silent and for a moment looks at me as if there is something else she wants to say, but thinks better of it and turns away from me again. I hear a muffled sniff as I leave the room that makes me think she might be crying again.

Back downstairs, Ed is trying to persuade James to eat his last piece of toast. James is more intent on sticking a fork in the top of his Tommy Tippee mug. 'Alright?' Ed asks as I walk in. 'She *has* overslept then?'

'No. She's not well. She's got a temperature, and I've told her to stay in bed today. And she's going home at the weekend.'

'What?' Ed looks up in amazement. 'As in permanently? She's not even been here a month! Is this Headwig all over again?'

'No. She's homesick, but it's much more than that. She's completely freaked out. Show me how a grown-up boy eats his toast, James!' I kiss the top of his head and sit down at the table.

'Get down please, Mummy?'

I get back up again. 'Have you had enough? Then of course you can, darling. Can you say, "Thank you for my breakfast"?'

'You're welcome,' James says as I lift him down.

I smile at that, in spite of everything, and look at Ed to see if he heard – but if he did, he completely ignores it. 'Can we talk to her, try and change her mind? It's really bad for James, all this chopping and changing.'

'No. I'm pretty sure she's going on Saturday.' I watch James toddle over into the playroom and pick up his Thomas the Tank Engine as I sit back down again. 'I doubt she'll be well enough to travel tomorrow, and if it's the weekend you'll be off and can drive her to the airport, or have James while I do it – which would make life much easier.'

'OK.' He shrugs helplessly. 'If that's what you've agreed.'

'When she thought she was going to be here by herself while we drove James over to your mum's, she was terrified. I had to explain to her that I'd be here with her and she didn't need to panic.'

'*I'll* be here you mean. You need to take James. The two of you can't be here on your own. I'm not comfortable with that. I want to be in the house if and when whoever it is comes back.'

'Well, why don't I just ask your mum to come and get James? That's the better idea. She won't mind and that's easier all round.'

'Fine. Do that then.' Ed shrugs. 'But I'm not going anywhere today. I'm staying put, and that's that.'

I go back up at half past ten to check on Sandrine and ask her if she'd like anything to drink, but she's asleep, so I don't disturb her, just creep back down to the kitchen where Ed is staring at his screen and writing an email.

'Is she OK?' he asks as I sit back down at my laptop.

'She's flat out. I left her asleep, poor thing.'

We fall silent – I hate how quiet it is without James in the house – and I return to copy-editing chapter eight of *All That Sparkles*. The title is an ambitious claim, but it's a reasonably clean manuscript – although the author has a thing for people closing their eyes and her characters 'realising' things, which is driving me slightly nuts, as well as a penchant for ridiculously long sentences – but even that withstanding, I can't concentrate. The words are swimming in front of me, and when my mobile starts to ring, it's a very welcome distraction.

Except, when I glance at the screen, it's the estate agent.

'Hello?' I snatch up the phone.

'Hello, Mrs Casson-Davies,' a voice says warmly, and I don't bother to correct them. This is Linda from Grantly-Brocken. I've just had your purchaser on the phone—'

'And?' I ask in dismay.

'He'd like to pop over to measure up for some white goods today for when he refits the kitchen. We've got keys so we could accompany him this afternoon?'

'No, you haven't got keys actually. We had the locks changed.' I realise, feeling ill with relief that the buyer isn't pulling out. 'We'll have to drop some new ones round.'

'If you could, please,' she says smoothly. 'We *are* due to exchange on Friday, I see, and we will need to hold a set for completion to go ahead.'

'OK. Can I get back to you about this afternoon in a bit, and let you know if we'll be here to let you in?'

'That would be *super*. Thanking you, Mrs Davies... Casson!'

I roll my eyes, and hang up. 'The agents want to visit this afternoon to measure the kitchen. And we have to get them the new keys or we can't complete.'

'Leave that with me. I'll sort it,' Ed says. 'And I'll call them in a minute and fix another time for them to come round. I'm not having them in the house today.'

My phone rings again. This time it reads 'Christa NCT'. I brace myself for a more potentially difficult conversation and pick up. 'Hey, Christa. How are you?'

'I'm OK, thanks, Jess, but,' Christa clears her throat, 'I've had a weird email from Natalia…'

I take a deep breath. Here we go. 'Oh right? Saying what?'

'It was pretty strange, even by Natalia's standards. She started by going off on one about being aware she's the black sheep of the group and she knows mothering doesn't come naturally to her in the way it does for some of us. Then she went on to say that she's known our feelings on some of her methods and approaches weren't complimentary, but that she's always been grateful that we've not corrected her, or criticised her in any way. So she was devastated to be told by you that we all secretly find her "impossible, rude" and, hang on – let me double-check this – "snotty and offensive". There's then this weird bit about you, which I'm actually not going to read aloud because I know it will upset you, but it basically says you not being a first-time mum like the rest of us made her feel particularly inadequate, although you were always "really sweet" to her, so she feels especially betrayed to discover you're not the person she thought you were.'

Exhausted, I put my head in my hand. 'Right. And does she go on to say what she means by that?'

There is a horribly uncomfortable pause and then Christa says. 'Yes. She does. You fell pregnant with Beth after an affair with a married man, and told your then husband it was his baby.'

I straighten up. 'She actually wrote that in an email to all of you?'

Ed stops what he's doing and looks at me.

'Yes, she did. Jess? Are you still there?'

'I'm still here. I just don't know what to say.'

'Well I've spoken with all of the other girls about it, and while Natalia is obviously very, very upset about whatever it is that's happened between you two—'

'She heard me bitching about her to Ed,' I interrupt. 'I called her number by mistake and she overheard me say that I'm not the only one to find her difficult; we've all said at times she can be rude and offensive.'

'Ah – I see,' says Christa.

'She thought I'd phoned her "accidentally on purpose" because I wanted her to know what we all really think of her. Which is not true, obviously. I'd just had a tough day and was letting off steam. We all do it; I'm sure I've done things that have annoyed you and you've told Jack about them. You don't have to answer that,' I say quickly.

'I actually haven't,' she corrects me, 'but the point is, me and the girls just wanted to say, whatever you did back then doesn't matter to us, and Natalia shouldn't have used that to hurt you, just because she was upset. Everyone is entitled to a past and yours is – well…' she stumbles slightly. 'Let's just say we think you've suffered enough already, without all of this being dragged up again.'

I hesitate. I've suffered enough? What does that mean exactly? They're satisfied I've been more than punished for my past transgressions? Or given the fact my daughter died they're willing to overlook my being a slag, on this occasion?

But I stay silent. Like so many of the things that people say in reference to Beth that unwittingly hurt me, I don't pick her up on it; half the time, I don't know if it's them – or me.

'I'm very grateful to you for ringing,' I manage eventually. 'Obviously I'd also really appreciate it if this is something that goes no further, and stays between all of us.'

'Oh God, absolutely,' Christa says quickly. 'That was another reason for calling, to let you know we've deleted all of the emails and NONE of us will ever mention it to anyone. We can't vouch for Natalia obviously, but hopefully when she's calmed down…'

Not bowing out of the group after all then, Natalia? 'Well, thanks for calling, Christa, but I'm going to have to go now because I've got to go and get James, so—'

'We don't actually have to go for—' Ed interrupts, and I glare at him, before putting my finger to my lips. 'OK, yes I'd love a coffee soon. That'd be great. Yes do. And love to you too, Christa. Take care.'

I hang up, drop my phone and put my head in both hands.

'Natalia told them everything then?' Ed says.

'She has a thing about affairs because her brother was dumped after her sister-in-law fell for someone else. Natalia absolutely hates her. I've copped a lot of misdirected rage.' I sit up and push my laptop back across the table before exhaling heavily. 'But obviously my far bigger fear is that now seven new people know the truth about Ben.'

'Well, yeah,' Ed shrugs, 'but they don't even know his full name, so I can't see that's a problem. You're not friends with him on Facebook and there must be hundreds of Ben Davies's anyway.'

'Yes, but if Natalia looks at any of my Chichester friends, she'll probably find him in a heartbeat. I'm going to block her now so she can't see any of them.' A couple of clicks and it's done. 'I hope I'm not too late.' I stare at the screen worriedly. 'I should have done this earlier.'

'Shit! What was that?' Ed suddenly whips round and stares through the open door out into the hall.

'What's the matter?' I ask instantly, but he doesn't speak, just leans to the side, and to my horror, starts to slide one of the *knives* from the block and gets to his feet slowly.

'Ed!' My eyes widen. 'What the hell are you doing?'

'I heard something.'

'It's probably Sandrine!' I exclaim. 'Have you gone mad? Put the knife down! You'll terrify her!'

'Jessica, *shut up!*' he orders and, chastened by a tone I've never heard him use before, I do as I'm told.

We both jump as three rapid knocks sound on the front door.

'You see? Someone's out there,' Ed whispers. 'Just stay very quiet. Let's see what they try and do.'

My stomach flips unpleasantly, and I rise slowly to my feet too, convinced that at any second I'm going to hear the sound of a key slowly sliding into the lock as whoever it is tries to use the old one to get in again, but there's nothing.

What feels like minutes passes, but it's probably no more than thirty seconds before Ed sets down the knife on the kitchen table and strides out into the hall. The chain is on the door and as I exclaim 'no!' in alarm, because I realise what he's about to do, he suddenly yanks it open. The door bounces as the chain tautens, and I expect to see a face briefly in the gap, but there's no one there. Ed hesitates and then shoves the door closed, before whipping the latch off and throwing it wide. He dives out into the front garden, and I hasten to the doorway to stand on the step, helplessly, shivering, with my arms folded across my chest, as I watch him disappear round the side of the house, only to return and start a check down the other side. He comes back, throwing wide his hands.

'Nothing.' He spins on the spot and looks down the road in confusion. 'But you heard it too, right?'

'Three knocks, yes.'

We both stand there watching the empty street. Eventually, there's nothing for it but to go back in and shut the door. In the hallway, Ed turns to face me. 'Do you think that was him, just then?'

'Or her,' I say. 'I really have no idea. It could have just as easily been a delivery or something?'

'But there's nothing out there! I checked,' he exclaims. 'Something's not right. I can feel it.'

'Ed, you need to come in and sit down,' I say slowly.

He looks agitated. He can't stand still, and the red blotches he always gets when he's *really* stressed, are beginning to appear on his neck.

'I'm fine, Jess.'

'You're not,' I say. 'Picking up a kitchen knife when someone knocks at the door is not fine.'

He jumps as there's a creak at the top of the stairs, which makes us both look up. Sandrine is standing there in her dressing gown and slippers, staring at us with wide, frightened eyes.

'Oh, hi, Sandrine,' I try to sound completely normal. 'We thought we heard the door, but we made a mistake. Are you feeling a bit better? Can I get you a cup of tea?'

I watch her gaze lift past me, over my shoulder and through the door to the kitchen table, and the large knife lying between our laptops.

'No, thank you,' she whispers, then looks at Ed, petrified, and spins round on the spot before rushing back off upstairs.

'Lovely,' Ed says shortly. 'Now the au pair thinks I'm about to murder her in her bed… although, on the plus side, whoever it was that was trying to get in, didn't manage it. I feel a lot better about that.' He smiles widely suddenly. 'A *lot* better. Don't you?'

'Not really, no,' I admit, looking at him. 'I actually really would like you to come and sit down for a minute. You just picked up a knife, Ed. You do know that statistically you're more likely to have any weapon that you use to defend yourself actually turned on you in a fight – don't you? Not only that—'

But before I can finish my sentence there's another knock at the door.

Ed dives past me, practically knocking me over in his haste, and grabs the handle, flinging it open – to the obvious alarm of the delivery man stood on the step, holding a very large box, almost taller than him. 'Mrs Casson?'

I step forward. 'Yes, that's me.'

He looks relieved, but still shoots a wary glance at Ed. 'Where do you want this? It's quite heavy, just so you know.'

I hesitate. 'I'm sorry, where do I want what? I haven't ordered anything.'

He looks at the address label. 'Jessica Casson?'

'Well, yes, that's me, but—'

'Then this *is* for you,' the man says, as he props the box up against the wall. 'Happy days. I didn't even know they made them like this any more.' He flips the box round to reveal the image on the front, of two children on an old-fashioned wooden climbing frame.

I gasp out loud and stumble backwards.

He looks surprised. 'Right… Um, can you just sign here then?'

'No,' I shake my head. 'I can't. I don't want it.'

'Wait.' Ed steps forward. 'Can I see the dispatch details, please? They'll tell us who ordered this, and we HAVE to know.'

I start to shake. 'Take it away,' I repeat – and then I look at both of the men desperately. 'Take it away NOW!'

My shriek is enough to make both men leap into action. The delivery man hurriedly starts to remove the box as Ed simultaneously reaches out to grab my wrists, and hold me up, because my legs give way and I slump back against the wall. I look up to see a horribly pale Sandrine reappear, peering down through the bannisters.

'Jessica?' she calls down, although I can hear the tremor in her voice. 'You are OK? Should I get help? Ed!' she says very bravely, 'you are hurting Jessica?'

'No, of course I'm bloody not!' he says indignantly and lets me go. 'See? I was helping her up! Fuck's sake...' He holds up his hands where everyone can see him, and walks off into the kitchen.

'I'm OK, Sandrine. *Everything* is OK,' I call up, trying to reassure her, and at least stand up properly. 'There's nothing to be frightened of. I'm fine, I promise. Go back to bed. You're not well!' I give her a beaming smile, but she just looks like she's about to cry again, before helplessly turning and rushing back into her room, the door slamming shut behind her.

🐝

'No, she doesn't want anything for lunch.' I come back into the kitchen. 'Unsurprisingly. I told her I was drying up earlier, which was why the knife was on the table, and that there was a huge spider on the box the delivery bloke was trying to bring into the house, and that's why I shouted at him to take it out and was so frightened. I don't think she bought it for one second. I might actually have to look into a flight home for her tomorrow.'

'I thought you said she wasn't well enough to travel,' Ed says flatly.

'I don't think she is, but...' I trail off, exhausted. 'Maybe you're right, perhaps I should see how she is in the morning. Seriously, I can't think straight, Ed.'

'You need something to eat. I'll make us a sandwich.' Ed reaches over to the bread bin, grabs the board down, and pulls a knife out of the block again as I sit down at the table.

'In other bad news,' he continues, 'I checked online again while you were upstairs and the amount of £548 definitely *has* been charged to our card. So the woman from the toy company was right; as far as they were concerned, we ordered the climbing frame on Tuesday morning, including £25 express delivery charge to have it arrive here today before 5.30 p.m.'

'Tuesday morning when I was at the library with James, you mean?'

'Yes – while someone was busy stealing your keys they were also using your credit card. Whoa!' We both jump at a horrible grating sound of metal on metal as he starts to cut the bread. I spin round to look, but he's already lifted the loaf up and is staring down at the wooden board in confusion.

'What is it?' I ask.

He peers at it. 'There's something stuck in it.' He sets the bread knife and loaf to one side, picks the board up and angles it next to the window. Something silver and roughly an inch long does indeed glint in the light. 'It looks like a large staple,' he says, puzzled.

I wrinkle my nose. 'Why have you stapled the bread board?'

'*I* haven't done anything,' he corrects. 'Hang on a minute.' He walks over to the knife block and pulls out a smaller vegetable blade, returning and starting to dig at the wood.

I watch him in disbelief. 'Is that really necessary, Ed? If you gouge a hole in it we'll have to chuck it out.'

He turns around to face me, holding a sharp metal point, gripping it carefully between finger and thumb. It looks like a shark tooth from a kid's drawing.

I look up at him blankly. 'What is it?'

'It's the broken tip of a blade.' He clears his throat. 'Have you snapped a knife by mistake?'

'No? Have you?'

He shakes his head. 'We've pretty much only got that set, haven't we?' He points over to the block. 'And they're all there. So how did this get in the chopping board?'

I stand up, pull open the kitchen drawer and start to rifle through the jumble of vegetable spoons, fish slices, roasting forks, peelers, the pizza slicer – and some random knives that don't sit on the side. Despite the apparent disorder, I know exactly what should be there, and nothing is missing. 'That doesn't belong to us.' I nod at it, still between his finger and thumb.

There's a moment of uneasy silence. 'You're saying someone's brought a knife into the house?'

'I don't see how else it could get here.'

We look at each other worriedly.

Ed puts the sharp piece of metal down on the side, steps back over to the knife block and pulls out the eight-inch chef's blade. Returning to the board and standing over it, he suddenly jabs it down, lets go and stands back to reveal the knife stuck on end in the wood. He hesitates. 'You'd have to be going some for it to be hard enough to snap the tip of a blade clean off and leave it embedded in the board.'

'You mean, *really* stab it?'

'Jess, are you sure this isn't ours?' Ed is trying to keep his voice steady, I can tell. 'It hasn't been there for ages and we just haven't noticed?'

'I do detail for a living. Of course I'm sure.' Suddenly I'm unable to stop looking at the knife tip. 'Someone has been practising their stabbing technique? So do you still think we're not in any physical danger?'

He doesn't answer. Just stares at the lethally sharp scrap of steel.

'Ed, this has already gone much too far. A malicious campaign designed to traumatise me is one thing, hanging around outside and then breaking *into* the house quite another – now we have proof whoever it is intends to do actual harm. We HAVE to call the police.'

'We can't,' he says immediately. 'You know why we can't. And whoever is doing this knows that too.'

'This isn't a game of brinkmanship!' I look at Ed incredulously.

He is still staring at the knife. 'I really don't think they intend to do anything at all. It's all smoke and mirrors. This was just another stunt designed to disturb and upset you. And you're letting it work.'

'"Letting it work"?' I repeat, amazed.

'Or,' he says slowly, raising a finger and wagging it as if he's just made a breakthrough, '*I'm* letting it work. Maybe this isn't about you at all. He's "hurting" you to get at me. He *knows* I can't go to the police, and he knows what this will be doing to me, watching you sweat like this. The gutless fucker. He couldn't just come and punch me one, like an actual bloke?'

'You still think this is Simon doing this.'

'Yes,' he says simply, 'I do.'

'Ed – try and forget who is doing this, or why. It doesn't concern you that someone brought a knife into this house full stop? Because it scares the shit out of me,' I say urgently. 'In three hours I have to collect our son and bring him back to this house. We also have someone else's ill child upstairs, who we are responsible for. We cannot possibly sleep here tonight. It's not safe. *We're* not safe. Even if the police *had* been here, I wouldn't sleep in this house tonight.'

'I'm telling you, he's got no intention of actually hurting you at all. He'd have done it by now if he had, but if it would make you feel happier, we'll find you somewhere to stay tonight. What about at my parents'? What could we tell them?…' He pauses. 'How about that we have a gas leak here? That it's sorted, but to be on the safe side we don't want James and Sandrine staying in the house? That's plausible, isn't it?'

What on earth is he talking about? 'I honestly think you're losing a grip on what is actually happening here,' I say quietly. 'This isn't a game.'

'Of course I know it isn't a game! I should never, ever have sent someone round to their house that evening. I've let you and James down so badly, I can't even begin to think about it. I'm so ashamed. All I can tell you is what I've already said. I was I trying to protect you from that woman, that's it. I swear. If I'd have known for one second that it was going to result in Simon doing *this*—'

'It's not Simon.'

'Sorry, I don't believe you.'

'He was Beth's father!' I exclaim. 'Our daughter fell to her death from a climbing frame exactly the same as the one that arrived here this afternoon. You honestly believe he'd do that to me, just to hurt *you*? I've already said; he has his faults, but that would be an utterly sick thing to do. He loves me, Ed. I know you don't want to hear that, but it's true. He wouldn't do this to me.'

'Oh, I know he loves you, alright,' Ed says immediately. 'It's how much he loves you that's the problem.'

'What?' I'm completely confused. 'So now you're saying this is about driving a wedge between you and me? To be honest, Ed, you're starting to sound like the obsessive one here.' I stand up. 'I'm going to pack some stuff and tell Sandrine what we're doing. Will you do your bag?'

He shakes his head firmly. 'I'm staying. If he sees us all taking overnight stuff out of the house, he'll know he's got plenty of time to do God knows what in here before we come back.'

'You think he's watching us?' I'm stunned.

'I'm not going to stand by and hand him access to our house on a plate, I'll tell you that much for free. Fuck that – and fuck him. He won't try anything if I'm here, but I get why you don't want to take that risk with James and Sandrine. Don't worry about me though, I'll be fine.'

I think about him reaching for the knife when the delivery man knocked at the door and hesitate. 'Ed, I want you to come with us to your mum and dad's. This whole situation is having a serious effect on you, and I don't want you staying here tonight on your own.'

'And I'm telling you I'll be fine. I can handle this.' He smiles brightly. 'Go and pack some stuff, and I'll ring Mum to let her know about the gas leak, so she can expect you just before teatime.'

He almost makes everything sound normal, and not completely terrifying at all.

Without saying another word, I leave the room, walking past the clock that yesterday was set to 10.05, and the empty space on the wall where the mirror hung happily for four years.

Knives broken and hidden in pockets, climbing frames, people paying nasty little visits and making threats.

Leaving lovers.

Has time *actually* gone backwards? I'm really not sure what is yesterday and what is today.

I climb the stairs quietly, to go and pack my bags.

CHAPTER NINETEEN

I glance at Sandrine, her teeth chattering slightly, as she huddles on the passenger seat of the car in a huge, oversized oatmeal jumper. She's pulled the sleeves over her hands, and her matching woolly hat is rammed down over her ears too.

'You're still feeling cold?' I ask in disbelief.

She nods, shivering slightly. 'Yes, but I am OK.'

I really don't want to make the car any hotter than it already is. James will start to get too warm in his travel Grobag, and I'm so stressed out that I'm knackered – I don't want to fall asleep at the wheel. 'It's not long now until we arrive.' I glance in the rear-view mirror and can just make out my sleeping son in the back of the dark car. He's going to have had about enough to make it impossible to get him down again tonight, but I'll just have to do my best. I turn back to Sandrine, concerned. 'I'm so sorry that I had to ask you to get up and out of bed when you feel so ill, but Ed needs to fix the problem in the house and we have to stay somewhere else tonight. So that's why we are driving to stay with my father in a place called Chichester. It's really not that much further though, I promise. Only another twenty minutes. And don't worry, you'll still be able to go into college in the morning. As it's your last day, I expect you want to say goodbye to your friends. We can have you there by lunchtime.'

Sandrine looks sideways at me, and then out of the window. 'I shouldn't have told you. I am so sorry.'

'Shouldn't have told me what?'

'About being afraid in the night. Knowing that I was being watched. This is why you have taken me and James away from him?'

The car in front of me brakes suddenly, tailgating an Audi – despite the fact we're doing 80 mph in the fast lane, and I have to do the same to avoid going into the back of them. Sandrine and I lurch slightly, and James shifts in his sleep too, before we hit a more even speed again, and I quickly switch lanes to drop down to a more measured pace. My heart is still thumping as I say as normally as possible: 'Him? Who do you mean?'

'Ed,' she says in surprise and then looks down at her hands inside her jumper, arms wrapped protectively around herself. 'I saw him holding the knife today,' she mumbles. 'Sorry, I shouldn't have been looking when you didn't know I was there.'

My breath has caught in my throat. '*Ed* has been watching you sleeping?'

She looks up sharply. 'I told you that this morning when I was crying? You said I would not get hurt, and that I can go home?'

Blood starts to crash in my ears. She wasn't talking about Beth at all. 'And you can. I promise. Just like I said.'

'Ed doesn't know that I told you what he did?' she asks timidly.

'No,' I say. 'He has no idea. Sandrine, has Ed tried to touch you, or hurt you… or do anything you didn't want him to do?'

She squirms with embarrassment and tightens her arms around her middle. 'No! He just – looks at me. I didn't bring *all* of my things, Jessica,' she says anxiously. 'Was I meant to?'

Does she think I've left Ed? 'No, it's fine. You'll have plenty of time to pack properly tomorrow.'

We both fall silent. I can only hear the sound of the road beneath us, and James gently snoring.

'Thank you for believing me, Jessica. And for helping me this way,' Sandrine says timidly. 'I didn't do anything to make him think I wanted something. I promise. I would never do that. Especially to you, you are very kind to me. I want also to say I won't tell anyone this. I won't tell Helene either when I am home.'

'Thank you,' I say automatically. 'You should try and get some rest now. I'll wake you up when we get there.' I don't want to talk any more. Ed has been going into her room while she's been asleep? What the fuck?

She obediently turns her head to the side and closes her eyes.

'To very pleasant surprises.' Dad raises his whisky glass, and I lift mine in return before taking a sip. The heat at the back of my throat makes me cough as I sit back in my armchair, watching the flames flickering behind the glass of the woodburner in Dad's small sitting room.

'Are you alright?' Dad says, and waits for me to stop.

I nod. 'Sorry – and I'm sorry about James shouting for so long too. The trouble is, when he gets a bit of sleep it peps him up just enough to not want to go down again, especially when it's somewhere different and I have to mess around with putting the travel cot up.'

'It's fine. I'm just glad for you that he's finally asleep now. I offered Sandrine something to eat, by the way, but she went straight up.'

'She's not well. I'll check on her in a minute. Thanks though.'

'You're welcome. So, what's really going on then, Jess,' Dad says, sitting up a little in his armchair. 'Pretend gas leaks withstanding.'

I look at him quickly, and he raises a quizzical eyebrow.

'We're having a few issues at home,' I say eventually. 'I couldn't stay there tonight and I didn't want to go to Ed's parents. I need some space to think a little more clearly.'

Dad frowns worriedly, gripping his drink. 'Space away from Ed? That's not like you two.'

'I know,' I agree, taking a much larger mouthful of whisky that makes me cough again. 'It's not.'

'Do you want to talk about it?' Dad offers.

I consider that, swirling the amber liquid around my glass. 'Yes,' I confess, 'but I don't think I can.'

'Because?...' Dad waits.

'I don't want to put you in a difficult position. Ed did something recently that he now very much regrets and—'

'What?' Dad interrupts, shocked. 'But that man adores you. He wouldn't so much as look at another woman.'

'It's not that, Dad.' Except now I can't help but picture Ed standing over Sandrine, watching her sleeping, and it makes me feel sick to my stomach. Forcing the image from my mind, I continue: 'He's done something that could have devastating consequences, if he's caught. I'm also having a few problems with someone else at the moment, but because of Ed, I can't sort everything out in the way that I would like to.'

'*You're* involved with someone new, then?'

'No. I'd say they're more of a blast from the past.'

'Ben?' Dad says incredulously. 'Is that why you've come here? You're going to go and see him?'

'Jesus, no.' I'm appalled. 'Look Dad, I can't really tell you more than that, but it's all been really disturbing, and has had a very significant effect on Ed. He's...' I shift uncomfortably. 'He's behaving in a way that I don't really recognise right now. Sandrine is actually frightened of him.'

'Is that why she's going home the day after tomorrow?'

'Partly. That reminds me, I need to book her flight – shit, except I need her passport number to do that and I bet it's back at ours.' I rest my head tiredly back on the chair.

'Jess, does this blast from the past want to pick up where they left off?' Dad asks carefully.

'No. They're very angry with me. Very angry indeed. To the point that I've felt afraid in my own home.'

Dad frowns, and sits forward, about to say something, but is interrupted by the sudden loud jangle of the old-fashioned bell pull in the hall. Someone is at the front door.

Dad looks at the clock on the wall quickly. 'Ten past nine on a Thursday night?' he says. 'Does anyone know you're here?' He begins to move stiffly to the edge of his chair.

'No one except Ed.'

Dad says nothing, just hauls himself up to a stand, and leaves the cocoon-like warmth of the room. I shiver as much cooler air whispers in around the door from the hall, and pick up the baby monitor to listen for James. He hasn't been disturbed; he can't have heard the bell. I ought to check that Sandrine is OK up in the top bedroom in a minute though. Low voices carry through to me, and I'm craning to listen anxiously, when the door pushes open wider still, and Laurel appears in the doorway, wrapped snugly in her coat and hat, clutching car keys and her phone.

I gasp with delight. 'What are you doing here?'

'That should be my question to you, surely?' she says. 'You were going to sneak down to Chichester under the cover of darkness and not tell me?'

'Tea, Laurel?' Dad offers, standing behind her. 'That is – I assume you're driving?'

'Yes, sadly, so tea would be perfect, thank you,' she says, and as he disappears off to the kitchen, Laurel comes into the room properly, unwinding her scarf and putting her things down on the coffee table so she can undo her coat. I get to my feet and we hug tightly. The skin of her face is cold and, as she pulls back, she sniffs and laughs. 'Sorry! It's freezing outside. Let me blow my nose.' She fishes up her sleeve for a tissue and makes her way over to a chair, kicking off her boots, sitting down and folding her legs underneath her.

'You're looking lovely.' I smile.

'Oh thank you!' She glances down at herself. 'I feel really mumsy today. I just can't shift this last half a stone and it's doing my head in. I'm just going to have to stop eating completely, or something. You're looking *very* skinny malinky, though. Are you on the extreme stress diet, by any chance?'

I give her a tired smile. 'What gives you that idea?'

'Well,' she rearranges the velvet cushion behind her. 'I had a text from your husband telling me you were coming down unexpectedly, and that he thought you could use a friend.' She smiles, but I can see the worry she's trying to hide. 'So, what's he done then?'

The silence that follows is only punctuated by the hiss and fizz of the fire – another log catching – and the static crackling on James's baby monitor. 'Um, it's not really him that's the problem as such, although he did something *about* the problem that's so mind-blowing, I don't even know where to begin.'

Laurel looks confused. 'Mind-blowingly *bad?*'

I look straight at her. 'The kind of thing that you read about in the papers, and wonder how someone could have been stupid enough to take a risk like that.'

Her expression changes completely. 'Something illegal? Something *dangerous?*'

I don't know I'm about to tell her everything. It's not a conscious decision – but I suddenly simply reach my limit and disconnect from what has become my twisted reality. So much so that, as I begin to discuss it aloud, it doesn't even feel real. 'You know I told you about that afternoon I wound up doing a viewing at Simon Strallen's house, and his wife went for me?'

Laurel frowns. 'That was before Christmas, wasn't it?'

I nod. 'Well, last night, Ed told me, because of what she did, he sent someone round to "have a word" with her... the night she died.'

Laurel blinks, and her lips slowly part in shock as she simply stares at me, open-mouthed.

'He says the bloke concerned didn't touch her, but the police found Louise dead on the bathroom floor, apparently having had a seizure, but also with a head injury.' I clasp my glass tightly. 'Her death was written up as natural causes, so they think she hit her head after she had the seizure. Ed seems to have got away with it, which is lucky really given that his brother-in-law – a barrister – has told him if it does ever come out he's looking at four years, minimum.'

'Jesus Christ.'

'The reason Ed told me this,' I drain the last of the whisky and set it down on the table, 'is because this week I've been on the receiving end of a hate campaign. I wanted to go to the police, but Ed asked me not to involve them because he can't risk them finding out what *he* did.'

Laurel raises her eyebrows in shock. 'And the two are connected how exactly?'

'Ed thinks Simon is behind everything that's happened to me this week. Someone stole my keys from my bag on Tuesday while I was out at a singalong session at the library with James, then they let themselves into the house and changed all of our clocks to the time of Beth's death.'

Laurel gasps in horror.

'They also used my credit card to buy a climbing frame which they had delivered to the house, and approached Sandrine on the street in the dark to tell her God loves her. Ed is convinced it's all for show, but I'm pretty sure whoever is doing this would very much like to drag me down a dark part of memory lane and hurt me. Today there was a knock at the front door, but when Ed opened it, no one was there. The day before, the hall mirror fell off the wall and nearly crushed James, and then this afternoon, Ed found the point of a knife embedded in our bread board in the kitchen, where someone had stabbed it with such force it simply snapped. Ed conveniently didn't think that showed any real intent however—'

'Because you can't call the police for fear of them finding out *his* little secret?'

'Exactly. Oh – and Sandrine told me in the car on the way here that Ed has been coming into her bedroom at night to watch her sleep.'

Laurel stares at me, speechless – and then we both jump horribly as the door opens and Dad reappears clutching a mug of tea. He looks between us, puts it down on the table and quietly leaves again without a word.

Laurel hesitates, then takes a deep breath. 'Well… let's take the last bit first. Ed is the only bloke in the house responsible for the safety of his wife, child, and a teenager – right? I think I'd be checking everyone in their beds at night too. Have you explained to Sandrine what's going on and that someone is targeting you?'

'No,' I admit. 'I didn't want to frighten her.'

'So then she's not going to understand why Ed is appearing in her bedroom, is she?' Laurel says reasonably. 'Of course she's going to think it's weird without any context.'

'But to hear her talk in the car today, you'd have thought I was liberating her from the clutches of a predator. And the thing is, it's not as if she's a voluptuous, looks-older-than-she-is bombshell. You haven't seen her, but she looks like a little kid. Even one of my friends remarked on it at the beginning of the week, about how at least I wouldn't have to worry about Ed shagging the hot au pair.'

'Well that backs up what I've just said, doesn't it? He feels responsible for her safety, as any parent would when a child is staying under their roof. I have to ask though, what makes Ed so certain that Simon is behind all of this?'

'His main theory is that Simon's engineering a situation I'll feel compelled to discuss with him – thus drawing him back into my life – because he's obsessed with me.'

'Re-bonding over the death of your daughter seventeen years ago?' Laurel wrinkles her nose. 'I can't see that, somehow.'

'Me neither.'

'Hang on – didn't you say someone approached Sandrine in the street? She must have given you a description?'

I shake my head. 'It was dark, they were wearing a hoodie and had a scarf up over their face. She wasn't even sure if they were male or female. I also fell out badly with one of the NCT girls on Tuesday: she heard me bitching about her to Ed – I accidentally rang her – but unfortunately also overheard me discussing my cheating on Ben. She's gone a bit nuts about the whole thing, firing off intense emails to our group of friends left, right and centre. It's possible she could have already found, and contacted, Ben before I had a chance to block her on Facebook, which lends some weight to Ed's other theory that this is Ben's doing.'

'What?' Laurel says sharply. 'Ben? That's actually offensive. Ben would NEVER do anything like that, even if he had found out you'd been having an affair with Beth's teacher. If Ed is coming out with crap like that, I'm not surprised you've left him.'

I pause. 'I haven't left him, Lau. I just refused to stay in the house after finding the broken knife, and he equally refused to leave.'

'Well, given he's behaving so oddly perhaps he ought to be careful we don't start thinking this is in fact all *his* doing,' she snaps. 'I can't believe he suggested Ben would torment you in such a cruel way for finding out you had a fling nearly twenty years ago. I think that says a lot more about him than he realises.' She picks up her tea.

I sigh. She's known Ben so long, I know why she's defensive, but equally, this isn't fair to Ed. 'It's not as simple as that. He has good reason to think that it might be Ben.'

'Like what?' Laurel says immediately. 'You couldn't find a nicer, kinder man than Ben! He's one of the good guys, the kind that set the bar impossibly high for other men.'

I have no right to feel this way, but her words start to prickle me. I do know that; he was *my* husband. 'That's true, Lau. But even the nicest person has their limits.' The whisky is loosening my tongue.

'I'm sorry, Jess, but it's been a long time since you saw Ben. I see him often now socially and he's happy. Really happy. He doesn't think about you any more… well, not like that. If he did find out you'd had an affair, I'm sure he'd be hurt, but it would hardly be the end of his world. He's moved on.'

'He wasn't Beth's father.'

My blurted words have the desired effect – Laurel instantly pales and for a brief second I am the triumphant victor – but it is the cheapest of thrills and I want to claw the words back the moment they have left my mouth.

'Simon?' she breathes, and I nod.

'Oh, Jess…' She puts her hands to her mouth. 'You told Ben… you let him *believe*…' she trails off and stares at me.

I have to look away, as the pendulum swings back and I begin to see myself through her eyes.

'All this time you've let him think he was mourning a daughter that was never actually his?'

'She *was* his daughter, in every way except one. She *is* his daughter,' I say fiercely. 'She loved him, and he loved her.'

'That's true, but you've also told him a lie that he's been living with all this time.' She puts down her tea.

'I did it to protect Ben. It would have devastated him to find out after she'd gone that there was a chance he wasn't her father – but anyway, I don't know for certain, and to have no possibility of conclusively knowing one way or the other… I couldn't do that to him.'

'So instead you thought you'd wait seventeen years and let a stranger tell him?'

'I'm actually terrified at the thought of that,' I admit. 'I've spent years preventing that happening by keeping it secret – I didn't even tell you – but in the last couple of days, the number of other people who know the truth has gone from two to nine. It was just Simon and Ed, and now thanks to my friend, Natalia, my whole NCT group knows.'

'And Ed thinks one of them might have contacted Ben, who – insane with fresh grief – has decided to make it clear he now knows *everything* by exacting some kind of revenge for what you've put him through?'

'Pretty much.'

'You wanted to protect him…' she repeats slowly. 'You didn't think he had a *right* to know the truth?'

'Of course I did! But Laurel, nothing is that black and white.' I sit forward with energy. 'You cannot understand what it's like to lose a child unless it happens to you. It's every pain you have ever felt turned up so loud you can't think, move, speak – and nothing drowns out the agony, not even for a second. It's what annihilation actually means. Even breathing hurts.' My voice begins to crack. 'You wanted me to confess to Ben when he was like that? You weren't there; you didn't hear the sound he made in the hospital when I had to tell him. You think I should have taken away the one truth that he had left, that he was her dad? Because he *was* her dad!' I am now crying. 'More so than Simon ever was. Ben was the one who was there for Beth when Simon stayed with Louise, and you know what? If Beth was only going to get five years on this planet, I'm glad – I'm GLAD I gave her the love of a father like Ben, and I know he would feel the same. So don't lecture me on rights.'

Laurel looks down at her feet while I wipe my eyes with shaking hands and clear my throat.

'Is that why you're here then,' she says after a moment more. 'To find out if he knows the truth, and if not – tell him before someone else does?'

I shake my head. 'I came here because I knew we'd be safe. I was only thinking of James, and my duty of care to Sandrine. I didn't consider Ben.'

She snorts lightly and gets to her feet, bending to pick up her coat, keys, and phone. 'You need to tell him, Jess.'

'You're going?' I say in astonishment.

'I have to get back to the kids. School tomorrow and all that.'

'Please don't go like this,' I beg. 'You of all people – I thought you'd understand.'

'You just told me I *won't* ever understand!'

'Oh come on, you know what I meant.'

'I actually don't. Of course I'm sorry that you've had such a horrendous week, and that you can't call the police, and you don't feel safe. I don't know what to say about Ed's mistake – if you can even call it that.'

I feel cold to my bones with sudden fear. 'You won't tell anyone, will you? PLEASE, Laurel, he could go to prison. We'd lose everything.'

'I won't tell anyone about that. I promise. But I really have to go now. And for what it's worth, I'd stake my house on it not being Ben that's done this to you.' She leans over and kisses me briefly. 'Take care.'

Take care? I watch incredulously as she lets herself out of the room and walks down the hall, opens the front door and then quietly shuts it behind her.

Dad reappears as I'm staring at the flames of the fire wondering how that all just happened, and sits down on his chair.

He looks at my fresh tearstains and passes me a tissue from his pocket.

'I'm so sorry, Jess. I can't believe I was so stupid,' he says as I'm wiping my eyes. 'When you said this trouble was all down to a blast from the past, I assumed you meant a man, and then I went and just let Laurel in without so much as a second thought. It never occurred to me you might have been talking about *her*.'

'Oh, she's not who I've been having problems with.' I rub my eyes tiredly. 'She's not happy with me, but she'd never do anything to deliberately hurt me. Don't worry, Dad, you didn't do anything wrong.'

That night, I have a horrible nightmare about Beth. Like all of the worst ones, it's very simple. She is sitting on the floor facing away from me, in pyjamas, and I'm brushing her long, blonde hair while singing to her. I'm desperate to see her face, but for some reason, she can't – or won't – turn around. I just keep brushing, growing more and more distressed that I can't see her, and becoming increasingly anxious that it actually is her.

I wake with a jolt in the still silence of my parent's house and listen to James breathing in his travel cot at the end of my bed. The sound should calm me, but all I feel is guilt. He doesn't deserve this shit – being dragged out for two hours in the car just so he can go to sleep safely, or a mother who's living in the past when she's so bloody lucky to have him in her present, because I am lucky. I *am*. I turn on my back and look up at the ceiling and think briefly about my mum. James deserves better than this from me. Tomorrow I will sort this, even if Ed can't, or won't. I think about my husband back at our house, alone. He should have come with us. I should have made him.

I close my eyes, desperate to try and get some sleep, but I'm unable to stop thinking about my dream. It doesn't take Freud to work out why I'm dreaming about identity, but all I can really see in my mind is the back of that little golden head that is never going to turn around again.

CHAPTER TWENTY

'Are we going back to the house before college?' Sandrine asks as she does up her seatbelt, and I lean forward so I can blow a kiss to my father, standing in the front sitting room window waving to us.

'Bye, bye, Grandpa!' James shouts, and I wish Dad could hear his enthusiastic farewell.

'We won't have time, no,' I tell Sandrine as I start the car, wave one last time and pull away. 'But are you sure you're actually feeling well enough to go in anyway?' I glance across at her. 'You could just come to Ed's Mum's house with me?'

Sandrine shakes her head. 'I am much better, thank you. I would like to go to say goodbye to everyone, like we said.'

'Oh God.' I remember suddenly. 'Your passport! We need to go back and get it so I can book your flight.'

She hesitates. 'Jessica, my mother has booked it already for me, for tomorrow morning. I had a copy of my passport details on my phone and I just texted them to her. I hope that is OK?'

'Of course!' I say immediately. 'That's great.'

Sandrine looks uncomfortable. 'I just didn't want to leave it and for everything to be full. And I know you are busy.'

'I would have happily done it,' I say quickly. 'But now I don't have to. I'll still take you to the airport tomorrow though.'

'Thank you.' Sandrine smiles gratefully. 'That would be very kind.'

'No problem. We're going to miss you!'

She hesitates again and then, God love her, she says politely: 'I'll miss you too.'

'We are actually just going to stop off very briefly somewhere before we head back.' I put the indicator on. 'It won't take long though, I promise.'

I pull into the petrol station on the main road, which also has a mini Waitrose. Ducking in quickly, I re-emerge with two bouquets which I place carefully on top of our overnight bags in the boot.

We've done another three minutes driving, before I indicate left again and we turn onto the private road that leads to some very nice houses indeed, and the small church where Mum and Beth are buried.

'Would you just keep James busy for a couple of minutes?' I ask, as I undo my belt. 'I'll leave the keys in the car in case you need them for some reason, but I'm literally just popping in and out.'

Sandrine looks at the churchyard, and I see her make the connection with the flowers. She nods. 'Of course. We will be fine, Jessica. Take your time.'

'Thank you.' I close the door and grab the roses from the boot. Mindful of my promise to get her back to Kent for lunchtime, I hasten quickly through the gate and under the wooden arch, but slow down over the uneven cobbles of the path, which must be lethal for an ageing congregation to negotiate on Sundays. I glance back quickly to see that Sandrine is already sitting in the driver's seat with James on her lap, letting him pretend to drive. He is pleased as punch; bouncing up and down and suddenly beeps the horn, which makes me smile for a moment at his obvious delight, before it also occurs to me that if he grabs for the handbrake switch they're going to start rolling backwards down the road. I almost double back, but the look on James's face stops me. I honestly can't remember the last time I saw him so happy.

Sandrine glances up, sees me watching them and lifts James's arm to wave to me. I wave back and turn slowly, rounding the corner of the church. Why can't I do it myself – let him just have fun like that? I'm *always* the one putting the brakes on.

I crunch onto the offshoot gravel path which leads me to the two side by side headstones, one slightly older and larger than the other. There are no flowers on Mum's grave, and on Beth's sit the withered remains of an earlier bunch. Ben perhaps? I step forward onto the damp, soft grass and take the dead blooms out of the metal stand, to put my fresh ones in. I lift my gaze finally and look at the engraved letters. Beth Davies. Every time. *Every time* there is the sense of disbelief that it can be real. I turn to Mum's and prop her flowers carefully too. Then, straightening up, I step back and look at them both, steeling myself to leave.

'Jessica?'

I jump at the sound of a voice behind me, and turn to find a plump, older woman in an expensive-looking caramel-coloured coat, holding an enormous bunch of lilies and staring at me in disbelief. My former mother-in-law. In seventeen years, she has barely changed. I'm always amazed at how some people genuinely manage to cheat the ageing effect, but right now it's incredibly unnerving, making me feel as if I walked out on her son only yesterday. She steps forward and draws me into a warm, perfumed hug. 'I can't believe it! How are you? Do you know, I almost didn't come this morning because the usual florist I go to doesn't open until half past nine, but I thought, no, I'll do it anyway – and here you are! I've always hoped one day I'd bump into you here, and now I have. It was meant! How lovely!'

My mouth falls open at her words. Good grief, could I be as generous to any woman who walked out on James just before Christmas? She is amazing. 'It's lovely to see you too,' I say truthfully.

'You've been to visit your dad, I expect?' she says, as if we last spoke only recently. 'He's well, is he?'

I nod.

'What lovely flowers for your mum,' she says kindly, acknowledging them leaning on the headstone. 'I've always liked yellow roses.' She looks down at the lilies she's holding. 'These are too funereal for my liking really, but they were the nicest they had.' She looks up and smiles again bravely. 'So, how's your little boy doing?'

'He's very well, thank you. He's two now and into everything.'

She rolls her eyes. 'That's boys for you, they don't just sit there and colour, or build towers, like girls, do they?'

'No, they really don't.'

We both fall silent.

'I should probably go.' I gesture uselessly behind me. 'James is in the car now with our au pair.'

'Of course, you get on. And safe journey back. You're very sensible to be leaving at this time on a Friday. You're still in Kent?'

'Yes.'

'Oh good, not too long in the car, then. Bye, bye, Jessica. Take care, darling. It really has been lovely to see you.' She gives me another hug, a little longer this time, and a kiss on the cheek. I can feel her silently willing me strength and love. It makes me want to collapse into her arms and sob.

I manage to smile, and dig my hands in my pockets as I turn to walk away. I know she sees the tears in my eyes but is kind enough not to come after me. I don't ever think of her – only Ben – in relation to what I've done and yet, here she is, seventeen years later, still visiting the grave of her 'granddaughter'. Somehow her still being the human equivalent of a cup of tea – she was always so supportive to me – only makes my lie a hundred times worse. While it's clear she doesn't know the truth for one second – and that means Ben doesn't either, because he tells his mother *every-*

thing, always has done – it's so small a comfort it vanishes before I've even properly felt it.

Is she right – was our meeting here meant? Is this supposed to be my opportunity to turn back and tell her the truth now, just as Laurel said I should? I hesitate and stop on the path – but then carry on walking, even speeding up determinedly.

Yes, probably, it is meant. Laurel is almost certainly right – the way this week has gone so far, whoever is doing this to me does plan to tell Ben. But they might not – and I'm prepared to cling to that sliver of possibility, because actually Laurel is wrong – it doesn't matter who tells the Davies family the truth; they will be devastated either way, and I'd rather they have as long as possible in blissful ignorance… before their hearts are broken all over again.

❦

Once I've dropped Sandrine off at college with a promise to collect her at 4.30 p.m, and firm orders for her not to go back to our house before then, I drive to Ed's parents'.

Bob answers the door. 'Hello, sweetheart!' He kisses me, but also looks slightly dismayed to see James back again. 'We've got the boy this afternoon then, have we? I had half an eye on the driving range. Still, I'm sure Sheila knows all about it. Come in, come in!'

Sheila has already appeared behind him, and scoops James into her arms, covering him with kisses and snuffles – which make him giggle with delight – while cooing 'hello my little Jim-Jam! Nanna's got some lovely lunch for you! Yes, I have! Come on in, Jess, love. Big day today, then! Have you heard from the solicitor yet?' She calls over her shoulder, already half way down the hall with James, towards the kitchen. By the time I arrive in the doorway, she's already putting him in his high chair and there's a little plastic plate on the table, ready and waiting, containing pitta strips, hummus, carrot sticks, cheese, and cucumber.

'OOOh! Yummy!' James exclaims, as if he hasn't eaten for a week, and tucks in happily. Sheila ruffles his hair fondly and smiles at me. 'So you were saying? Any news?'

'No, not yet.' Although on cue, my phone rings and it's the solicitor. 'Hang on. This could be it now.'

'Good morning, Mrs Casson,' a crisp female voice says when I answer. 'Rebecca Lomas from Burnett & Co. We're ready to exchange and I'm just ringing to make sure you still want to proceed?'

'Yes, definitely,' I say.

'Great, I'll call you back when we have.'

I hang up. 'Cross your fingers – it should be about to go through any second now.'

Sheila pulls an anxious face. 'Don't think about it. A watched pot... tell me instead how your dad is? Feeling better?'

That catches me off guard, I have absolutely no idea what Ed has said to them about last night. I must look like a rabbit in the headlights, but I answer slowly: 'Yes, much better thanks.' I wait to see if she mentions anything about the gas leak – which is presumably why we are here now, but she doesn't, so I have no idea what it's safe to say next.

'Well now, Jess, are *you* staying for lunch?' she asks politely, 'or have you just got to go straight off?'

Where am I supposed to be going? I flounder around slightly. 'Um, actually I'll just get on, if that's OK, Sheila. I'll be back to get him around four? That's what you agreed with Ed?'

'Whenever you're ready. I can give him tea too if you like? He slept in the car, I expect, so he doesn't need a nap?'

'Yes. Sorry.'

'Oh, no bother at all. We'll just go and feed the ducks after lunch then, Jamesy. Get that Grandad to come with us too, shall we?' She looks up at me and winks. 'All taken care of. Off you go, love and good luck for the house. Look forward to hearing your good news later!'

I park round the corner, to try and gather my thoughts, as my phone rings. It's the solicitor again. 'Congratulations,' she says. 'We just exchanged with completion set for three weeks today.'

'Oh, thank you so much!'

'Not at all, I'll put the confirmation letter in the post to all parties tonight. Have a good weekend.'

I feel weak as I hang up. Thank God for that. I want nothing more than to be out of that house now. I call Ed, but he doesn't answer. I text him instead, and get one back saying he's in a meeting, can't talk but that's great, and he dropped a new set of keys with the estate agent before work this morning.

Feeling suddenly very flat and totally exhausted, I wonder what to do next. I can't go home; I don't want to go and see any of the NCT girls; I don't want to see anyone actually. I ought to go and do some work, but perhaps I'll try and catch up on *All That Sparkles* tonight instead. I close my eyes for a moment, and Ben's mother pops back into my head, smiling and holding her flowers. I can't bear that someone might be poised to devastate her too, and I'm suddenly sick of feeling so completely powerless to prevent all of this from happening, bar telling her myself. I hesitate, and then reaching suddenly for my phone, I google 'Simon Strallen headmaster', which brings up a news article from the school in Surrey that Simon is now at, 'delighted' to be announcing his appointment. I look at the school's website – it's only an hour away. I could be there and back, *and* have time to talk to Simon for twenty minutes, by four o'clock. Ed would be furious, but I think I need to see Simon. I want to know if anything has been happening to him too – if he has any answers for me at all.

His PA – because it's that kind of school – informs me regretfully that Mr Strallen is meeting with the Chair of Governors, and can't be disturbed. I ask her to tell him Jessica Davies is here to see him, and it won't take long.

It doesn't. I look up from my seat at the sound of brisk footsteps on stone floors, echoing around the Abbey school corridor, to see him walking towards me, today in expensive pinstripe. He looks absolutely in his element.

'Mrs Davies.' He smiles widely, as if I'm a prospective parent, and offers me his hand. I take it, but as we shake, his fingers slide briefly to the inside of my wrist, and he gently presses, as if taking my pulse. It completely unnerves me and I step back as we drop hands. He leans in through the door of his PA's office and says: 'I'll just be five minutes, Penny.'

Did I just imagine him touching me like that?

'No, I won't have tea, thank you. Mrs Davies, can I offer you a drink?'

I shake my head mutely and, unfazed, he calls back over his shoulder: 'We'll pass thank you, Penny. I'll be in my office if you need anything. Now, Mrs Davies.' He turns his attention back to me, opening the door to a vast, plush room containing an imposing panelled desk in front of a large leaded window, and several armchairs round a roaring wood burner. 'Do come in.'

Simon can't quite mask the hint of pride in his voice as he watches me absorb it all. Those are replica Old Masters, surely? 'I'm in a meeting with the Dean at the moment over in *his* office in the Abbey, so I'm afraid we'll have to be brief, but I'm certain we can achieve what we need to.' He stands to one side as I walk in, closes the door behind me, turns and then allows his professional bonhomie to fall away. He just stands there looking astonished. 'You came.'

I hold up a hand. 'The first thing I need to know is, you didn't do it, did you, Simon?' It's almost a throwaway comment – a disclaimer – because I don't believe that he did, but actually he looks startled, almost shocked, and tries to re-compose himself. It stops me dead in my tracks.

He clears his throat. 'Did I do what? I'm not sure I know what you're talking about?'

'Oh no…' I whisper. It's as if someone has just trickled icy cold water down my spine. I shiver and take a step back. 'You *do* know what I'm talking about. I've defended you when all along…' My hands fly up to my mouth. 'I insisted you'd never do that to me… the clocks and the mirror were bad enough, but the *climbing frame*?'

'I'm sorry?' He looks completely blank. 'What am I missing here?'

'An exact replica of the climbing frame that Beth fell from was delivered to my house.' I glance at the door. He is stood right between it and me.

Simon pales. 'My God, Jess. That's horrendous.' Then his mouth falls open slightly. 'Wait – you think *I* did that?' He frowns worriedly. 'That's not like you, jumping to such wild conclusions. You're obviously very shaken up. Come and sit down and tell me exactly what's been going on.' He speaks without anger and gestures to one of the chairs by the fire, before glancing at his watch and swearing under his breath. 'Lord – I've got to get back to my meeting… but someone's been targeting you?'

He looks genuinely concerned, and is also so calm that I'm momentarily wrong-footed, although I don't move.

'They broke into the house,' I watch him carefully, 'and set all of the clocks to the time of Beth's death. We found the tip of a knife in the house that someone has stabbed so hard it's actually broken off. There was other stuff too – mirrors have fallen down within inches of my son's head. We heard three knocks at the door and no one was there.'

Just for a second, a strange expression flashes across his face.

'What?' I say quickly. 'You looked like something occurred to you, just then.'

'No, no' he says uncomfortably. 'It was just…' He hesitates. 'Three knocks at the door and breaking mirrors were regarded as signs of impending death in the Middle Ages. Shattered reflections and fracturing souls, that sort of thing. Look, just ignore me. Once a history scholar…'

I stare at him, horrified. 'Omens, you mean?'

He avoids answering. 'Jess, have you been to the police?'

I realise I'm on very thin ice now myself. 'Not yet, no.'

There's a light rap on the door and the PA sticks her head round. 'I have the Dean's office on the line, Mr Strallen. They're asking if you need to reconvene?'

Simon exhales tightly. 'Tell them I'll be there in literally five minutes. Thanks, Penny.'

She disappears again, and I take a step towards the door myself. 'I'm sorry. This was a mistake. I shouldn't have come.'

'No, no – you were right to. I can absolutely see why you did now; you're desperate to try and make sense of this – I expect you wanted to come and see if anything has happened to me too – but I promise, I know nothing about any of it at all. Nothing out of the ordinary has happened to me and I'm so sorry that this is happening to you.' He hesitates. 'You don't think it's Ben? Some sort of post-traumatic reaction?'

'That's just what Ed said.' I feel suddenly weary.

'Who's Ed?' He says.

Oh FUCK – I remember a second too late that he thinks Ed *is* Ben. Christ – this is absurd. I can't cope with all of these lies any more. 'It doesn't matter. I'm really sorry for coming. I just thought it would help to talk to you, that's all.'

I push past him, but he grabs my wrist again, pulls me back, ducks suddenly and kisses me. His slightly wet, open lips crush against mine, and repulsed, I wriggle free. 'What are you *doing*?' I gasp, stumbling back away from him. 'I'm married!'

'But, I thought—' he begins.

'That actually I'd come here for you?' I finish, wiping my mouth with my hand. 'I wanted your help, Simon!'

'But I miss you, Jessica,' he replies eagerly.

'Did you not hear what I just told you? About what's been happening to me this week?' I look at him in disbelief. Have I learnt nothing in nearly twenty years? 'My husband said this was about you engineering an intimacy, using something only we shared, and I didn't listen.' My eyes fill with tears. 'You had no right to force yourself on me like that. How dare you?'

He laughs incredulously and steps towards me again. 'But my darling, *you* came *here*!'

'Don't call me that!' My voice is trembling wildly. 'And stay away from me and my family. I want no more contact with you. You are to leave me alone!' Stifling a sob, I reach out, fling open the door and sprint down the dark, echoing corridor as if he's only two steps behind me, and reaching out his fingertips, ready to pull me back, wrap his arms tightly around me and never let me go.

Sandrine smiles happily as she climbs into the front of the car in which James and I are waiting. 'Hello, James!' She twists in the passenger seat, reaches into the back and takes his hand.

'Nice to see you!' he says dutifully, and she laughs.

'I will miss you, little man!'

I glance in the rear-view mirror at my smiling boy. He's going to miss her so much. We're going to need to revisit the whole au pair thing and go for a more permanent, stable solution that, as Ed said, isn't so disruptive to our son. 'Have you had a good afternoon?' I force a smile for Sandrine as we pull away from the college.

She nods. 'Yes, thank you. It was sad to say goodbye, but I am happy to be going home. My sister is going to meet me from the airport with my mother and then we are going out to eat, just the girls!'

'That sounds lovely,' I say truthfully.

'I am very excited!' she says, and I can see the flush of colour in her cheeks as well as hear it in her voice. 'Are we going back to the house now? I would like to pack my things, if it's possible?'

'Of course, we just have to pick up Ed from the station first.'

Her face falls instantly. 'Oh, OK.'

'Sandrine, you really don't need to be afraid of Ed.' I glance sideways at her. 'Some things happened at the house this week that he was trying to keep us safe from, that's all.'

She doesn't say anything, just looks down at her hands and starts picking at the quick of one of her nails. We lapse into silence for the next ten minutes, during which she no doubt thinks about how after tomorrow – if she can just hang on for one night – she never has to see any of us again, and I consider how the hell I'm going to tell Ed that I went to see Simon this afternoon, and he kissed me. I shudder involuntarily at the memory as we arrive at the station just in time to see Ed walking down the concourse in his work suit, holding a bunch of flowers.

'Hello!' He leans over to kiss me once he's climbed into the passenger seat, Sandrine having moved into the back with James. 'And hello, Sandrine, and hello, you.' He twists round and tickles James's tummy, who laughs delightedly and says: 'Daddy on the train!'

'I was, yes, James, but I'm home now. So, who fancies fish and chips for tea?'

'Me!' James says immediately – having heard the magic word, chips. I open my mouth to say I was going to do a slightly healthier option at home, but think better of it. It can't hurt, just this once, and we certainly do have bigger fish to fry.

Back at the house, Ed stands on the step holding the full carrier bag of wrapped warm chip papers, as I open the front door warily and push it wide, before reaching my hand around the corner to turn on the hall light. All without actually going inside myself. 'There you go. Are you alright to go in now, if I go back and get Sandrine and James?' I nod back at the car where they're waiting for me.

'Yes, of course. So everything was fine then, at your dad's?' he lowers his voice.

'Yup. And you?' I nod at the house. 'All quiet here?'

'Yeah, although I'll be honest, I didn't get much sleep.'

'I'm not surprised. Thanks for coming back early tonight.'

'Don't be daft. There's no way I would have left you to go in like this on your own... We're so nearly there, Jess. Two weeks and we're out of this place.'

'Let's talk some more in a minute... Can you have a quick check upstairs as well, please? Right, in you come, you two!' I call, walking back towards them. 'Let's have tea!'

In the kitchen, I put James in his high chair and give him a drink while he tries to reach round me and grab a too-hot chip. Sandrine pops upstairs to go to the loo and wash her hands. I'm sitting down and Ed is re-emerging from the cupboard, clasping the ketchup, when there is a sudden scream from upstairs. Ed and I glance at each other in horror, before my husband drops the bottle and explodes out of the room. I hear him taking the stairs two at a time up to Sandrine's room and then another scream. *I thought he had checked everywhere...*

My hands shaking violently, I undo James's straps and pull him out of the high chair. He's gone very quiet, and leans against me as I rush to the bottom of the stairs, and place one hand on the front door.

'Ed!' I yell desperately, looking up the stairs as James buries his face in my shoulder. 'Are you OK?'

There is a muffled thump, then the sound of a door flinging open and bumping off the wall. Sandrine appears, eyes wide with fear. 'It's a bird!' she jabbers. 'I walk into the room, and it's in there on my desk, just sitting there! Then it starts to flap, and smash around crazily.' She shudders. 'Ed is catching it now.'

James whimpers and reaches for my hair, twisting it round his finger.

'It's OK, darling,' I reassure him. 'Nothing's wrong. A bird?' I repeat, beckoning her down towards me. 'In your bedroom?'

'Yes,' says Ed, appearing at the top of the stairs. 'A dirty great magpie, cool as you like, just sitting on the desk.'

'Where is it now?' I put my spare arm around Sandrine, who is shaking.

'I put it back out of the window. It's just a bird, guys. It doesn't mean anything. It's my fault – I didn't check in Sandrine's room when I should have. Let's just go and eat our food.'

But before he can say anything else, there is a knock at the front door, right next to me, making me leap with fear.

'If that's the magpie again…' Ed jokes shakily.

'Should I open it?' I look up at him worriedly.

'Of course,' he says. 'I'm right here, Jess. In fact, I'll do it. You three go back into the kitchen.'

We do as we're told and I'm just slotting a very confused James *back* into his chair, when Ed appears in the doorway flanked by two uniformed police officers.

He stares at me, utterly terrified, and just for a second, I wonder how on earth he thought he was equipped to send someone round to intimidate Louise Strallen. He has four years minimum written all over his face.

I step forward quickly. 'Can we help you?'

'I'm sorry to disturb,' the older of the two officers nods at the table, and our rapidly cooling food, 'but we received a call from one of your neighbours about an hour ago, concerned about someone loitering around outside your property, possibly about to break in. They noticed a man standing outside, apparently watching the house, at around half past four. He approached and knocked at the door, peered in at the window and went around the back. They called us, and we sent a squad car down, but he'd gone. They didn't find anything. You haven't discovered anything missing? No signs of any attempted break-in? Nothing out of the ordinary?'

A *man* loitering?

I glance at Ed who implores me silently not to say anything incriminating. I inwardly steel myself and reply carefully. 'Nothing odd has happened today at all, apart from us coming back to find a magpie in our au pair's bedroom. Which I guess means we accidentally left the window open.'

'Perhaps that's what the man was interested in?'

'I don't know' I shrug. 'It's good to know there's no sign of anyone now though.'

'OK,' the police officer says. 'Well, if you do have any concerns later, just call us again. And maybe make sure your windows are closed and locked before you leave the house.'

'We will do.' Leading the way, I open the front door for them. 'And thank you again for your help.'

Once they've gone, with my hand still on the latch, I think about how there is no way Ed would have left a window open.

There was a man outside our house.

It's hard not to imagine that the magpie was put in Sandrine's room deliberately.

One for sorrow…

Isn't that how the nursery rhyme starts? Seeing one magpie is meant to be bad luck – which instantly makes me remember Simon talking earlier about omens.

I walk slowly back into the kitchen. Ed is already on the phone. I go to open my mouth, but he holds a finger up to his lips as he waits for whoever he's called to pick up.

I glance across at Sandrine who is helping James with his fish and chips, cucumber sticks and diced avocado she's done for him, and soften. 'Thank you, Sandrine,' I say and she gives me a small, tight smile. She's done so amazingly well to hang on in there like this.

'Hey, Mum, it's me,' Ed cuts in. 'I've got a massive favour to ask you. I'm so, so sorry – but can we come and stay tonight? Yes, all of us. I know – but we've had a gas leak… I know, tell me about it! They think it's fixed, and I might be able to stay put here, but I don't want to run the risk of something happening again with James in the house, until we're sure it's OK. I'll pop back over once I've dropped off the girls and James, just to double-check… OK, thanks. No, we've already eaten. We'll get our stuff together and be there in a bit. No, they've been already, and it's fixed; it's just like I said, I don't want to take any chances. Ok. See you shortly.' He hangs up.

'So this time it's the gas leak?'

'Please don't,' he says. 'I just want you safe, that's all.'

'Sandrine, could you go and start packing *all* of your things when you've finished your food?' I turn to her. 'We'll leave tomorrow from Ed's parents' house, so it needs to be everything. Is that OK?'

'Of course.' She stands up immediately.

'There's no rush, you can finish eating,' I assure her.

She shakes her head. 'It's OK, I'm not hungry anyway.'

I know what she means; I've got no stomach for this either.

As soon as she leaves the room, I turn to Ed. 'The police didn't know anything, it was just a routine enquiry.'

'Shhh!' he says immediately. 'You say that, but a bloke was hanging around outside. What if they'd picked him up and he'd spoken to them? After all, I think we can safely assume it was Simon.'

I open my mouth to tell him about Simon kissing me – but there is *another* knock at the door. 'For God's sake!' I explode, as poor old James says simultaneously 'What's that noise?' and Ed jumps too. We are all so horribly unnerved.

'Do you think it's the police back again?' Ed looks like he's about to be sick.

'It's just someone at the door, darling.' I stroke James's hair. 'It's nothing to worry about. I'll go and get it, and you finish your tea, and then we'll go to Granny's house for a bath and some stories, shall we?' I get back up, look at Ed over James's head and put my finger to my lips. 'Just calm down. Take a deep breath, OK?'

Taking my own advice, I approach the front door, pause for a moment and then swing the door wide open with a confident smile. 'Can I – oh my GOD!'

My smile falls away completely, however, because stood right in front of me, clutching a piece of paper tightly in his fist, is Ben.

CHAPTER TWENTY-ONE

I have imagined this moment a hundred times, in various incarnations. Now that it's real, and *this* is the one that's actually going to happen, a strange acceptance coolly floods my body, like an injection of saline. I know better than to fight it. My mind is clear and calm. I only want to make this experience survivable for Ben.

'Hello,' he manages, in barely a whisper. 'Just tell me it's not true?'

I've not seen my ex-husband – the first boy I slept with – for so long that we ought to be strangers now. He's had a whole other life since me, just as I have had him, and yet I have no hesitation in stepping forward and taking his hands in mine, just as I did all those years ago in the hospital room, seconds before he made that cry I will never forget – the sound of a heart breaking.

He jumps at my touch, and he's right – I have no right to assume this level of intimacy, it's just an instinctive action. He is still desperately clutching his piece of paper – and briefly glancing down at it, I see it's a screenshot that he's even gone to the trouble of colour printing out. The familiar blue branding of Facebook is unmistakable, and it appears to be a message conversation. 'Who was it who contacted you?' I ask.

He shakes his head. 'I don't know. It's an empty profile. Someone who opened a fake account just to send it to me.' He moves the hand holding the paper lightly, as I still have hold of him – then meets my gaze full on. 'Is it true? Beth was never mine?'

'I slept with someone else around the time I fell pregnant with Beth, yes.'

'That teacher, the one who took her to the hospital the day she died?'

'Yes.'

'Oh my God.' He breathes in deeply, and looks up at the dark, moonless sky. 'So she's his daughter – and you knew that, all along?'

'No,' I say truthfully. 'I don't know for certain which of you is her biological father.'

Ben pulls free and steps back – away from me. 'But given all the time we spent trying for a second baby, and it didn't happen, it's pretty likely it's him and not me, isn't it?'

I shake my head. 'Not at all. Second time round infertility is a very common problem. I honestly don't know who Beth's biological father was, and I never will, but I can tell you exactly who her dad was – you.'

He's clutching the paper more tightly now. 'Don't, Jess. Don't do that bit. Try and imagine how it felt to be just lying in bed reading last night, only for my phone to buzz with a message from a complete stranger telling me that I should know the truth, and I've been lied to for twenty-two years. I've known you the best part of my life. I know we were kids, but I loved you, and you loved me. I *know* that was true. So how could you do this? When the three of us were together were some of the happiest times of my life. And now, all I can see when I think about them, is you wondering how I could be so STUPID...' He looks at me with tears forming in his eyes. 'Every anniversary I've sent you a rose, knowing that you would be out there somewhere and wanting you to know you weren't alone – that I was missing our daughter with my whole heart too; my *whole heart*, Jess.' He is openly crying now, and I am too. 'Only it wasn't real. None of it was real.'

'Yes, it was!' I step towards him again and desperately grab his arm. 'Of course it was! Everything we experienced; those were beautiful, real days. We loved her and she loved us. I wouldn't have denied her – or us – any of that by telling you something I didn't even know for certain was true. And I gave everything to try and protect you from this after she died.'

'"Protect me"?' he says in disbelief.

'Yes!' I exclaim. 'From how you're feeling now! It was *my* burden to live with – my guilt, not yours. You were, and are, her dad, Ben. And you were amazing. I loved you so much for how good a father you were. You have no idea.'

'Is that why you left when she died then?' He can't help himself from asking. 'I'd fulfilled the role you needed – one *he* presumably turned down?'

'Of course not,' I whisper. 'He never even knew I was pregnant. His wife found out about the,' I swallow, struggling for the right word, 'fling and came to our house after the funeral. She threatened that unless I moved away, she would tell you that you weren't Beth's father. I couldn't bear for that to happen, Ben. I left the next day.'

'It wasn't just an excuse to go?'

I shake my head. 'Beth dying broke me. You know that. I didn't know where to put myself. I thought I was doing the right thing. Like you said, we were so young, Ben, but I did love you – and I was desperate for you not to be hurt any more than you already had been. I was trying to shield you.'

'I *still* love you.' He wipes his eyes with his free hand. 'I always will. Not like I did back then, in that doomed, obsessive way; I mean in that I've shared so much with you… but to now find that it was him that you were really sharing it with?' He closes his eyes as if he's in physical pain.

'But I didn't share anything with him at all,' I insist. 'He didn't know Beth existed until she started at that school. It was only ever you.'

'Except when she had her accident – he was with her then. Not me, and I hate him for that.'

'You know she died instantly, Ben. But yes, I wish that you or I had been there with her. She's your daughter in every way that matters. She loved you so much.'

He stares down at the ground and I know he's rerunning scenes, seeing her face, hearing her voice, her laugh… trying to remember. I hold my breath, suddenly conscious of now not wanting to say the wrong thing.

'You saw my mother today,' he says suddenly. 'She phoned me to say she'd seen you at the grave, and that she was worried about you; you looked too thin, and as if you had the weight of the world on your shoulders. Do you know what it would do to her, to find this out?'

'I'm so sorry.' There is nothing else I can say.

'You're "sorry",' he repeats slowly. He exhales deeply, his breath clouding around him, then he shakes off my hand.

'Please, can you forgive me?'

He loosens the fingers of his other hand, and the paper falls to the ground. He turns quickly and begins to walk away.

'Ben?' I call desperately after him, wrapping my arms around my body at the chill of the early evening darkness creeping through my clothes, but he doesn't turn, even though I know he hears me. He keeps walking – his straight, upright back, clad in a waxed Barbour, briefly illuminated under the street light – before he disappears round the corner and is gone.

CHAPTER TWENTY-TWO

'You didn't need to ask for his forgiveness,' Ed says quietly, as we drive to his parents'.

'Shhhh.' I look out of my window, drying my eyes and rubbing my cheeks clear of tearstains, certainly not wanting to discuss this in front of Sandrine, who is in the back with James, holding his hand and singing lively songs in French to keep him awake.

'You made a mistake. You are not a bad person.'

'Please, Ed.' I don't add that, of course, Ed would say that right now.

'And just because there was last night's date on that printout conversation doesn't mean it all happened as he said it did,' Ed continues, ignoring me. 'He could have doctored it. The whole thing could be faked.'

I close my eyes briefly. 'He's just as much a victim in this as we are. Can we *please* leave it now?'

'I suppose at least we know who it was that the neighbours saw hanging around the house earlier. He was obviously waiting for you to come back.' Ed glances sideways at me. 'You look knackered. At least you might get some sleep at Mum and Dad's tonight. Listen, when we get there, I'm going to get you all settled, and then I actually do need to pop back out.'

I lift my head quickly and look at him. 'To where?'

He hesitates. 'I'm going to go and see Daniel.'

'In his professional barrister capacity?' It's all I feel comfortable saying in front of Sandrine.

'Yes,' he says equally evasively. 'I won't be long. An hour at most.'

Which is about how long it takes me to get James to sleep, even though Sheila has very kindly made up the cot they keep at theirs, so at least he doesn't have to cram into the travel cot again. Sandrine seems much more relaxed, and happily goes off to the second spare room, saying she wants to get plenty of rest ahead of her day of travelling tomorrow. I watch *Coronation Street* with my in-laws – which I haven't seen for years – while drinking a strong and very milky cup of tea that Ed's father has made me, and think first about Ben driving back to Chichester in pieces, and then – my jaw clenching – Simon trying to kiss me. Just as the credits start rolling, Ed suddenly bursts into the room, his eyes sparkling and his step positively jaunty, as he clutches a bottle of champagne.

'Evening all!' he smiles widely, holding it aloft. 'Can I get anyone a drink?'

'Ooh, lovely!' says Sheila. 'Yes please!'

'Jess? Will you give me a hand?'

He leaves the room, and picking up the baby monitor, I heave myself up out of the sofa and follow him through.

He's waiting for me and before I'm even through the doorway, he grabs me round the waist, picks me up and whirls me around delightedly.

'Ed!' I'm slightly alarmed. 'What on earth are you doing?' He puts me down unsteadily, and I wobble to stay on my feet. Has he been drinking already? Before I can ask, he holds a finger up to his lips and whispers: 'No. I'm not drunk. Ask me where I've just been.'

'To your sister's. You said that was where you were going.' I can't help my irritated tone. I'm sick of games.

He shakes his head. 'I didn't go to Katie's to see Daniel. I made that up. I actually went to see that bloke.'

'What bloke?' I draw back. 'The one you paid? I thought you told me you didn't know him?'

'I don't. I had to ask my mate to tell me where I'd find him. I wanted to be upfront that the police had come to see us today, but make sure he knew he had nothing to worry about; we didn't say anything to them about what I'd paid him to do. Anyway, I went to this pub, and he was there. He was massive – not fat as such, but really solid. I was shitting myself – I felt like I was in a Guy Ritchie movie or something – but when I told him why I'd come, he just started laughing. Proper belly laughing. He told me to sit down and then proceeded to tell me he never went to the Strallens' at all that night. He just took my money and *told* me he had. He said he was going to give me a piece of advice; I should never try and do anything criminal ever again, because I'm shite at it, and I'll definitely get caught. Then he told me to piss off and that he never wanted to see me again.' Ed looks at me, delighted. 'Don't you see? It means Louise Strallen's death really was an accident – I had nothing to do with it at all! AND it means if anything else malicious happens to you – or us – we *can* now call the police! How great is that? This has been a fucking brilliant day.'

'Edward Casson!' his mum says sharply, coming into the room carrying the empty cups in time to catch his last sentence. 'Potty mouth! I take it your gas leak *is* mended then?'

'Certainly is!' Ed grins. 'Everything is fixed. We'll definitely be out of your hair tomorrow.'

His mother looks almost disappointed. 'It's never a problem. I love having you all here. Why don't we have a quick round of Scrabble in a minute with that bubbly?' she adds hopefully.

'I'll just go for the drink, Mum, if you don't mind?' Ed opens a cupboard and lifts some glasses down. 'We've had a long week and

I could really use an early night. Plus Jess needs to get Sandrine to the airport in the morning, so she ought not to be long either.'

'I'll go a quick round with you if you like, Sheila?' I offer, seeing her disappointment. 'And Ed, you can come and play too. Open the booze and come through to the other room.'

It's a bizarre end to a surreal week; sitting in my mother-in-law's sitting room drinking champagne and playing board games, still aware that I need to tell my husband about my ex kissing me today.

'Don't you two want to pop out to the pub?' his father asks after we've exhausted Scrabble and Sheila suggests moving onto Pictionary with a glass of Baileys. 'You might as well. We can call you if James stirs.' He eyes the turned off television wistfully.

Ed looks at me and shrugs. 'Want to?'

'I'll pass, thanks. Like you said, I've got to take Sandrine tomorrow. I'll go up now I think. Do you mind if I go through the bathroom first?'

'Go for it.' Ed sits back on the sofa happily. 'Put the telly on, Dad.'

Sheila starts to put the sherry glasses back in the drinks cabinet rather sadly and I feel bad, but not so much that I offer to stay up any longer.

As I walk past Sandrine's room, I can see under the door that her light is already off. I creep into our room to pick up my toiletries bag and freeze as James stirs in his sleep… but manage to tiptoe back out and to the bathroom. Once I'm finally alone, I lock the door, reach into my back pocket and pull out the piece of paper Ben dropped at my feet before he walked away, and sit down on the closed loo.

'26 Jan 22.33

Hi. You need to be told the truth, Ben.

Who is this?

Jessica has been lying to you. Ask her who Beth's real father is.

WHO IS THIS?
Ask her about your daughter's married teacher.
Do you mean Simon Strallen?
Hello?
Please answer me. Who are you?
WHO ARE YOU?
27 Jan 9.05
Please tell me who you are.
Are you Simon?
ANSWER ME!!!!'

I exhale. The sender could be Simon, it could be Natalia…
it could even be Laurel. I scrunch the paper into a ball, unable
to look at the evidence of Ben's suffering for a second more.
Getting up – I throw it into the loo, weigh it down with tissue,
and flush. But the damn thing won't go. I flush it noisily again,
and then a third time before it vanishes, at which point I hear a
small, frightened voice shout: 'Where are you, Mummy? I can't
find Mummy *anywhere.*'

I force the image of Beth frantically looking for me from my
head and hurry into the bedroom to James. Everything that has
happened this week has slowly unhinged my thinking to the point
that now I'm no longer picturing Beth as smiling and happy –
which is how I want to remember her, and is a place I have worked
so hard to get to. All of the old feelings of guilt, powerlessness and
fear have been unlocked by whoever it was that stole my house
keys. My nightmares have all returned. Which is, no doubt, exactly
what they wanted.

I begin to sing James back to sleep, sitting on the carpet and
holding his hand through the bars. I love him so much. Thank
God, he is safe in his cot, and Sandrine is safe in her room. I have
managed to protect them, and if anything else happens now – I can
call the police. That at least is a huge relief. I must hold onto that. I

think about the two officers earlier, asking if we'd noticed anything out of the ordinary… I'm so glad they didn't arrive in time to find Ben peering in at the windows looking for me, and have to add to his distress by picking him up. But, thinking about it, I realise that actually none of it is Ben's style. He certainly wouldn't go round the back of the house – he's far too polite for that. He would have knocked, and if he'd had no answer – he'd have simply come back later. It wasn't him that our neighbours saw. A man loitering…

It must have been Simon. I'd bet my life on it.

✣

'You're certain you don't just want me to do the drive to the airport while you stay here?' Ed asks, hands in his pockets, all three of us shivering beside the packed car on the pavement outside his parents' house. Sandrine looks at me, alarmed, silently imploring me not to take him up on his offer.

'No, it's fine. I'd like to do it,' I assure him, and smile at Sandrine as she looks relieved and turns to Ed.

'Thank you for everything,' she says to him. 'You have a lovely little boy and I will miss him.'

'He'll miss you too,' Ed says sincerely. 'Thank you for all of your help, Sandrine.' He offers her his hand, and she delicately shakes it for the briefest of moments before darting into the car and shutting the door.

Ed looks at me in disbelief, and gestures in frustration. 'I give up. Tell me later what I'm supposed to have done, OK?' He leans in and kisses me briefly, before whispering: 'Do you think she's secretly got the hots for me?'

'No, I really don't. I'll be back as soon as I can, OK?'

'No rush,' he yawns. 'James and I are just going to chill here. I'll probably put him down for a nap this morning, because Mum's offered to do lunch too, so come back when you're ready. You've got your phone?'

I nod – and wave to the sitting room window, where James is being held by Sheila, his bottom lip starting to tremble. 'Oh dear – you better go in,' I say hastily, as James begins to lean forward behind the glass, his arms outstretched for me, and begins to cry.

I jump into the car so as not to prolong the goodbyes any further, and pull away sharply. 'I think James just worked out that you're leaving,' I say to Sandrine, only to glance across and realise she's sniffing and teary. 'Oh no! Are you OK?'

'Yes,' she gulps. 'I'm just going to miss him very much.'

She *is* talking about James?

God – of course she means James. Ed's old enough to be her father. What on earth would a girl like her see in him? That again reminds me of Simon and I shift uncomfortably. When I get back, I'm going to tell Ed everything about yesterday. I should have told him last night.

'Jessica…' Sandrine's voice jolts me back to the car, and I look over at her, to see her rummaging frantically through her bag. 'I'm so sorry – but I've left my passport at the house.'

'OK, no problem. We'll go back; we've got just enough time, don't worry. I'll ring Ed and ask him to start looking for it. Do you know where you left it?'

'No, I mean it's at *your* house.'

'Oh…' I fall silent.

'I'm so sorry. I hid it under my mattress to keep it safe—'

I can't say I blame her for that.

'But we left so quickly yesterday, I forgot I'd taken it out of my file.' She looks at me desperately. 'I could run in quickly? I know exactly where it is.'

I hesitate. Shouldn't I go back to Ed's parents' and get him so he can go into the house for us? But by the time I've gone back, driven to the house, and dropped him back again, we'll be starting to cut it fine if anything else happens. I don't want her to miss her flight. It *is* broad daylight, and she's only going to be seconds…

'OK,' I agree doubtfully. 'But we'll have to be very quick. Literally just in and out.'

As we pull up outside the house, I survey it carefully – it looks totally normal, just as we left it last night. I unlock the front door, but Sandrine pushes past me before I have a chance to tell her to wait and let me have a look first – her feet thump on the stairs as she dashes up. 'Sandrine!' I call up nervously.

'It's OK! I've got it!' she shouts delightedly from her room. 'Can I please go to the toilet, as well?'

'Alright,' I call back reluctantly. 'Quick as you can though… I don't want to be late.' Or have to be in here any longer than we need to be… I hear the bathroom door close, and decide I'll just open the front door right out and keep it like that while we wait. The house badly needs ventilating in any case. It smells stale, a stuffy airless heat having built up thanks to all of the locked windows and central heating. I turn round to throw it wide, only to swear violently and leap out of my skin. Natalia is stood motionless on the doorstep, right in front of me, like something out of *The Shining*, only clutching a huge bunch of flowers.

'Jesus, Natalia!' I breathe. 'You scared the shit out of me! Where did you spring from?'

'Can I come in?' she smiles. 'There are a few things I need to say to you.'

'Um, now's not the best time, actually.'

Her smile becomes a little more forced. 'Please don't be like that. It took a lot of courage for me to come here today.'

'I'm not trying to be difficult, I'm just in a rush, that's all.'

'It'll take literally five seconds.'

I glance up the stairs again. 'Sandrine!' I call, 'we don't want to miss your flight.' Having made my point that I wasn't lying, I turn to Natalia: 'I honestly don't have more than a moment right now.'

'That's all I need, don't worry.' Without waiting any further, she steps past me into the hall. 'Firstly, can I give you these then, and tell you how sorry I am – for everything.' She holds out the flowers, but I don't take them. 'I overreacted in saying our friendship was over. I know you didn't mean for me to hear what I did, and I'm sorry I span out. Everyone bitches about everyone else – it doesn't mean anything! We're all grown-ups really, aren't we? We all do and say things we don't mean.' She tries a relaxed shrug, but she's so tense, it's more of an odd jerk, or twitch.

'Yes, we do,' I say slowly.

She takes a deep breath. 'Like I've done something I wish I hadn't. I went through your friends list on Facebook. I found Laurel, who was listed as from Chichester, then I searched her friends list, and a "Ben" came up. I messaged him—'

I gasp. She did it before I blocked her. She actually did it.

She holds up a defensive hand. 'But I'd really like to just move on now, and put this behind us. I'm genuinely very sorry, and I know I shouldn't have, but I was very, very upset. You hurt me very deeply, Jess.'

My heart is thumping faster, the adrenaline kicking in as our confrontation gathers steam. 'You think doing something like that is something you can just apologise for, and everything will be OK?'

She grits her teeth. 'No. It wasn't a rational response to what I'd heard you say about me. I recognise that now and hope you'll understand that I'm having a few challenges at the moment, but that I genuinely am sorry for my over-reaction. Perhaps we can go out for coffee soon, or something?'

Coffee? She really is crazy. I think about Ben walking away from here in pieces. Silently furious, but refusing to give her the satisfaction of shouting or anything she could repeat to the rest of the NCT girls, I reply icily: 'How about I give it some thought? I'll be in touch.'

She hesitates, but before she has a chance to say anything else, I pointedly stand to one side and hold the door for her. Realising she has been dismissed, she flushes, drops the flowers and darts out of the door, before jumping in her car and speeding off so fast her tyres squeal at the end of the road. I bend down and snatch up the bouquet that has already dropped a bright orange staining pollen on the floor, which I know, for a fact, is toxic to pets and children. Swearing under my breath, I march straight over to the black bin, hurl them in, turn around and slam back into the house. How could she? *How could she?*

'Sandrine!' I yell. 'We're really going to be late unless we go *now*.'

Ben was devastated. Natalia seriously thinks my bitching about her, and her deliberately hunting Ben down, are in *any* way comparable? She's mad! She's—

My phone goes off in my bag suddenly, interrupting my thoughts and making me jump again. I reach in and pull it out. It's the estate agent. I almost don't answer, but am too confused not to. They must know we exchanged yesterday? There can't be a problem now. Not unless it's going to be a very expensive one for our buyers.

'Hello? Mrs Casson? I mean Davies,' the agent corrects himself quickly when I pick up. 'Congratulations and sorry to disturb you again, but it's—'

'I'm so sorry, but I don't really have time to talk. Is everything OK? Nothing's wrong?'

'Your purchasers were wondering if they might be able to pop in and measure up for the white goods and the kitchen now that exchange has taken place. They were thinking later this morning, if that's OK?'

Oh God, I forgot about that. 'I'm afraid we won't be here. I've no objection to you bringing them round though.'

'Well that's not going to be possible, is it?'

I frown at the phone. 'Well, if you're fully booked up already with other viewings, they'll just have to wait then, won't they? I'm really sorry, but I must—'

'No, I mean we don't have a key any more. Your husband collected them this morning.'

I turn to ice. 'But I've just left him having breakfast with my son at his parents. You did ID him and sign them out?'

There's an uncomfortable silence. 'Well, he said he needed some clothing urgently for your son but was locked out. It's cold and we thought—'

'First you give out my address without my permission, now this?' Sandrine and I have to leave. We have to go *now*.

'We'd never release address details Mrs Casson-Davies.'

'Mr Strallen contacted you, and you told him where we live. How else did he know how to find me? Are you calling him a liar? Look, I have to go.'

'No, no! I'm just—'

But then I hear what I've just said aloud. Simon *is* a liar. He always has been.

He already knew where I lived.

And someone collected the keys this morning.

My heart stops, and the phone almost slides from my fingers as I hang up.

The house is completely silent.

'Sandrine?'

There's no reply.

My heart thumps. 'Sandrine? Can you answer me, please?' I look up the stairs, but all I can see is the empty hall. I go up a step, but I'm too frightened to go any further. We should never have come here. Not even for a moment. Ed *told* me not to come here alone.

'Sandrine!' I call frantically. 'Answer me right now!'

Nothing. Oh Jesus. He must be in the house right now. Upstairs, with her. Does he *want* me to go up and look for her? Is that what he's hoping I'll do?

A paralysing fear overtakes me and my fingers start to shake as, stepping backwards, I glance frantically down at my phone and start to dial 99—

I feel myself back into what I think is the door – but it isn't. There is someone stood right behind me. I realise too late, and scream – dropping the phone – seconds before a searing pain explodes in the back of my head and the hallway begins to slide sideways. I know I am falling, and there is absolutely nothing I can do to stop it from happening.

CHAPTER TWENTY-THREE

My eyelids flutter but, as I lift them, the shapes in front of me are blurred. Struggling to focus, I draw my head back in an attempt to see more clearly, but instead it lolls heavily on my neck because there's nothing behind me. I appear to be sitting bolt upright. There is now, however, an intense throbbing at the base of my skull, a pain so hot, all I instinctively want to do is touch it, to try and work out what's happened – but I can't move my hands. In fact, I can't move my arms either. There's a familiar smell in the room too, that I can't quite place. I open my mouth to try and speak, but it's horribly dry; I cough instead and lick my lips – only to taste copper. Blood. On my mouth? Have I had a nosebleed? I blink again, and realise that someone is standing very close, and peering into my face. I can feel their warm breath on my skin before they draw back. I scrunch my eyes shut and then, with effort, force them wide open, determined to focus.

Their features drift and settle, but with such an intense sense of relief that I feel sick, I recognise the face searchingly looking into mine. 'Sandrine!' I exclaim croakily. 'You're OK!' I swallow with effort. 'I think someone attacked me. We have to get out of the house now. Can you help me up? I can't seem to move.' I blink again and the rest of my surroundings start to settle into order. I *am* sitting on a chair – in the kitchen, facing the table, upon which sits my open laptop. Sandrine is just standing, staring at me. I think she's in shock. Have I been so badly hurt I just can't feel or see it?

'We have to get out of the house,' I repeat. 'We need to get help.'

She starts to back away from me.

'It's OK. Don't be scared,' I begin, but to my surprise, she just leans on the kitchen units, crosses her arms and says flatly: 'Thank you, but I'm not. Don't worry.'

Gone is the shy soft lilt of our French teenager. Her voice is well-spoken, British. Almost a drawl. Her face is now equally expressionless. 'Hello, Jessica. My name is Cara Strallen.'

The air draws into my body so slowly I actually hear it... it reminds me of the slow rasp Mum was making when I found her in the bedroom.

Cara? This is impossible.

'What have you done?' I can barely get the words out.

'All of it. It's all been me.' There is no pride in her voice. She's merely stating facts.

I try and stand – but I am unable to move.

'You're taped up. Hands and feet.' She reaches her own hands behind her and pushes up onto the kitchen unit so she's now sat on the work surface. 'Ed thinks we're on the way to the airport. No one is expecting you. Well, almost no one.' She leans her head from side to side, and shrugs her shoulders, like she's limbering up for some sort of intense physical exercise. 'So. I expect you have questions. Go for it.'

'You've been in my house for weeks!' The depth of her duplicity is beginning to sink in. 'I trusted you,' I whisper in disbelief. 'I tried to protect you.'

Oh James. Oh my God, James. I am so sorry. What have I done? I should never have come here. I had no idea. I have been so stupid. So, so stupid. I close my eyes again and see my son's smiling face; feel him leaning his soft cheek against mine, while twisting his hair in his small fingers. I have to get back to him. I cannot lose him too. 'But I had an email from Sandrine, Helene's friend!' I blurt. 'She knew I was still looking for someone to replace Helene.'

'No, that was me using a fake email address.'

'I spoke to someone on the phone who said they were Sandrine, and we made the arrangements. When I rang it was an overseas dial tone. That was you too?'

'Yes – I was in France when you called me, but I'll confess – I don't actually know Helene.' She holds her hands up in mock surrender.

'I don't understand. How did you know to use her name then?'

Cara brings her arms down, inspects her fingernails carefully, and bites the hangnail on her thumb, before spitting it out. 'I saw the email you sent to Helene asking her if she had any friends who were looking for work – and if so, would she pass your details on? I also saw the emails you sent to several agencies looking for an au pair at short notice. I knew you were desperate and you'd be only too eager to hear back from one of Helene's "friends".' She shrugs and looks back at me blankly.

'But how have you been reading my emails?' I'm still confused.

She jumps down from the side, reaches into the kitchen cupboard and gets a glass. Filling it with water and taking a gulp before wiping her mouth with the back of her hand, she asks: 'Do you know what ratting is, Jess?'

How is she so calm? It's as if she's having a perfectly normal conversation. I shake my head.

'It's when someone sends a mundane email pretending to be a trusted source, maybe a bank or a charity,' she continues, slamming the empty glass down on the side and jumping back up. 'The recipient opens it because it looks legitimate – it seems harmless, and then they forget about it. Except the mail contains a Remote Access Trojan – or a RAT. It downloads the moment the email is opened and, from that moment on, the sender has access to their victim's entire online world. It's like peeking at someone's laptop whenever you feel like it – only from the comfort of your own living room.' She points at me suddenly. 'If your life depended on it, do you think you could tell me which email it was that *you* unwittingly opened?'

I shake my head.

She shrugs again. 'No such thing as privacy any more, Jessica.'

'When you say everything was you,' my voice is starting to shake, 'we're talking about the mirror, the clocks, the climbing frame…'

'The stolen keys, the magpie.' She moves her head from side to side as she lists each item in turn, 'calling Natalia – although I only really did that because she was so rude to me. The person on the bike who came up to me on the street I made up, but technically, that was me too.'

'How did you know about *that*?' I say quickly. 'Someone must have told you.'

'It was in my mother's diary. I say diary… notebook full of devastated outpourings is more accurate. I found it among her things after she died. It runs for a month or two, starting from the day she found out about the affair. You showed up in my father's office at work with some cock-and-bull story about needing him to investigate a stranger on a bike coming up to you outside the school gates, etc. etc.' She rubs her face tiredly, then yawns. 'I've got to say, I'm with my mother on that one, Jessica. It was a shockingly rubbish excuse to get him alone. The rest of her fulsome account of my father's betrayal is a heart-warming read though: "He can't look at me or Cara. We are the wrong lover and daughter". That was nice to see, as was "Is this what madness feels like?".'

I lower my gaze.

'So, in answer to your question, yes, pretty much everything was me.' Cara's face clouds momentarily. 'Although I don't know what that weird knocking at the door the other day was all about. And I didn't tell Ben, either. Honestly, I have no idea why you're even friends with Natalia. She's such a grade A bitch.'

'I thought it was your father. Does he know you're here?'

'I don't know, actually,' she says, more quietly.

'It wasn't him that told you about Beth?'

'No – like I said, it was all in the diary… but Mum had already called to enlighten me anyway the day before she died.'

'Oh my God, Cara, I'm so sorry.'

'Are you? What for?' She starts to swing her legs, idly kicking the cupboards.

'You must be feeling very angry and very hurt right now.'

She watches me. 'Go on.'

Her complete lack of emotion is unnerving. I falter slightly and try to think. 'I don't know if you are aware of this, but my mother died when I was a similar age to you. It was a huge shock. She killed herself actually, after a long battle with depression.'

'How did she die?'

I am taken aback by her outright question. 'I'm not going to tell you. That can remain private, at least.'

She gives a brief flicker of a smile. 'Did you know, most people think women don't go for the messy suicide options, when in fact someone who really *wants* to kill themselves will use whatever is to hand and is most effective?'

'I did know that, yes.'

'A gun is what you really want. You're looking at an 85 per cent success rate there.'

I don't say anything for a moment. 'My point is, Cara, I don't think I registered my loss for some time. I was in shock. Possibly as you are now.'

'My mother really didn't like you very much.' She's not moving at all now, just watching me.

'No. She didn't. I don't blame her, and I don't blame you for being angry with me, for what I did to her. What happened hurt her very deeply.'

'Yes, it did,' Cara agrees. 'But that's also because she let it.' She continues to regard me unflinchingly. 'It actually made a lot of sense, what I read, and everything she told me about you and Beth. My mother has always been completely unable to let go of the past. Most of my life has been spent with her looking backwards to some golden age in Chichester that, as far as I could work out, never really existed. Either that or she was just drunk.'

'She wasn't always like that.'

Cara ignores me and continues: 'Don't get me wrong, when I got the phone call that Mum had died, of course I felt sad. But it was also a relief. I can't sit here and tell you I hadn't secretly wished she'd just get on and die sooner than this – at various points – rather than slowly drink herself to death. So, I'm sorry to disappoint; I don't think you and I really can share a "sad mum" history that we then bond over, where I'll realise that you're nice after all, we'll hug, I'll be just like your dead daughter, only I'm not, you'll be the Mum I never had, blah blah blah…'

'I would never try and do that. Your mother loved you very much.'

'Based on what evidence?'

'The lengths she went to, to keep your family together.'

'My mother wasted her life,' she says. 'It was frustrating to have to sit by and watch it happen, but also very frustrating to have to be around someone like that. They tell you the same stuff over and over and over again because they've fried every synapse in their head. They have no room in their life for anyone. They are inherently selfish. Sometimes that goes on for years. You're going to think I'm lying, but I'm not even angry with her any more, and I'm not interested in avenging her. That's not what this is about.'

She jumps down again, and this time takes a step towards me. I think suddenly of the children's game 'What's the Time, Mr Wolf?' Someone creeping inevitably ever closer.

'Then you're angry with me?' I say slowly, 'because I'm the reason this all happened? That's what you think? I am so very sorry, Cara. I didn't know your father was married when I met him.'

Cara rolls her eyes. 'In some ways you're no better than my mother, you know. James is *really* cute – and yet all you see is Beth and what happened to her. You're obsessed by it.'

I clench my teeth defensively – and my head throbs blindingly again. Don't react – it's what she wants. Think about James. Think about getting home to him. 'You're right. James needs me. Could you let me go? We don't need to tell anyone about this.'

She sighs and takes another step. 'Oh, come on, Jessica. You know that's not going to happen.'

'Tell me then, what do you want from me?' I'm starting to panic.

She puts her hands on her hips. 'I just said. This isn't about you.'

'What do you mean? You've spent all week trying to hurt me!'

'No, I've been sending messages.' She walks determinedly right up to me and I shrink back into the chair, but she moves instead to the table and my laptop.

She twists the screen to face me, looks critically and then tweaks the angle again.

'What are you doing?' I feel suddenly very frightened indeed. 'Why do I need to be sitting in front of my computer like this?'

She ignores that too. 'Do you remember when we drove past my house, just after Christmas? I was in the back with James. You slowed right down. Were you looking for him, or just being nosy?'

'Him? Your father, you mean?' I ask, confused.

'You don't actually still love him, do you?'

'No. I don't,' I say truthfully. 'I did a long time ago. But not any more.'

'Jolly good,' she says absently, and then taps on my computer. I gasp as she's through my password in seconds and my screen saver of Beth comes up. 'You see,' she nods at it, 'that ought to be James. It wouldn't mean you love Beth any the less. It just means you acknowledge you actually have a son still living.'

'Don't talk about Beth like that, please.' I blink again; my head is killing me. 'Jesus – what did you hit me with?'

'It's completely irrelevant.' She turns back to the screen. 'It's the fucking great hole in the back of your head you should be worried about. That's exactly what I mean, Jessica. You waste so much time focusing on the wrong details.' She shakes her head again and mutters 'Idiot' under her breath. I don't know who she's referring to: her or me. She taps a couple of keys on the screen. 'Right. I think we're ready.' She straightens up.

My guts tighten. 'Ready for what? What are you going to do to me?'

'So – what would you normally be doing on a Saturday at this time, Jessica?'

'Um…' Confused, I try to think. 'James would be going down for his morning nap or out with Ed. You'd be out. I'd be working probably.'

'On your laptop.'

'Yes, of course.'

She leans forward and speaks directly to the laptop screen. 'So you're on the laptop most Saturday mornings at this time.'

'Yes. Why are you speaking into it like that?'

She ignores me. 'Hello,' she says to the screen, 'I know you're there. Come join us. Jessica's here too.' She moves out of the way and gestures expansively to me. 'I could make the obvious comment about her being a bit tied up, but I'd rather just tell you I'm going to give you up to fifteen minutes, OK? Then it's going to get a bit more complicated.' She shuts the lid suddenly.

'Who were you talking to?' I say slowly.

She looks surprised. 'My dad, of course. Oh, sorry – did you not know he watches you through your computer?'

This time I don't even blink. I just stare at her in shock.

'It wasn't me that sent you the infected email. It was him. He has access to everything of yours. Your emails, your files, your pictures, your searches, your notes… and your camera.' She opens the lid again and points up to the small round circle in the middle of my laptop screen. 'That's how he watches you. How – as far as I can make out – he's been watching you for the last four years. He's pretty dedicated.'

Bile starts to swirl in my stomach and rise up my throat. 'You're lying.'

Cara shrugs. 'I don't care if you think I'm lying or not. But I am interested to see what my father does next. Will he come straight away because he's worried for your safety, and thus have to admit his dirty little secret, or is he going to protect himself and do nothing? In other words – who is the most important person in Dad's life? You – or him.'

'You're insane.' I can't help myself.

'No, I'm not.' She is unafraid to meet my eye. 'I'm just desperately sad.'

I'm reminded suddenly of the tearstained little girl sat on the carpet holding hands with Beth that morning – as Ed's warning echoes in my mind; *the more desperate someone is, the more dangerous they are.*

'Please just let me go back to James, Cara.'

'No,' she says. 'Be quiet now. Although – I do need to tell you something else before he arrives. When I spoke to my mother the day before she died, she said that seventeen years ago I was asked to do something.'

She pulls out a chair and sits down opposite me, folding her legs up and under her so that she's sitting in the lotus position. She still looks no older than fifteen.

'"Hurt her." That's apparently what I was told. I think Mum meant *she* told me to hurt Beth rather than it was my dad who said it, but as you can imagine, Mum was pretty incoherent and I'm not entirely sure who said what, but I was definitely told: "At playtime, hurt Beth. It's part of a secret game".'

I feel myself start to shake despite the fact that I am tightly bound. 'You're lying. It was an accident.'

'I have no reason to lie.'

'Of course you do! You hate me!'

She hesitates. 'I thought I did, but I don't, actually. I was told to hurt my friend – and I did it because I was a good girl. And she fell.'

I stare at her, unable to speak. A single tear courses down my cheek. Beth holds up her arms to me, asking for her hug goodbye. 'You're lying.' I'm now pleading with her.

'It wasn't an accident, Jessica. When Mum told me… I think I even remembered doing it. I could see it all happening, reaching out…' She closes her eyes and frowns intently as if she's trawling through her thoughts, replaying it back to herself, but just as suddenly, her eyes snap open and she looks straight at me. 'I'm sorry. I'm sorry that I didn't know what I was doing.'

I scream. The pain at what she's just said is just too much to keep in. That woman on the bike with her message… *someone* knew what was going to happen. They tried to warn me. *Was it Mum?*

Cara looks down at the floor. 'He's not coming from Surrey, in case you're wondering,' she says quietly. 'He just works there. He bought a house just around the corner from here.'

'You're not serious?'

'Of course I am.' She looks at her watch, before standing up, walking over to the side and picking up a large kitchen knife I don't recognise.

My pulse begins to flutter with panic, but we are interrupted by hammering on the front door. Cara stiffens, and takes a deep breath. In a couple of quick steps, she is right next to me and slips the blade under my chin. The sharp edge rests on my skin as she shouts: 'Come in Dad. It's open.'

CHAPTER TWENTY-FOUR

Simon bursts into the room, gasping for breath. He was clearly unprepared for running several streets today, dressed in a checked shirt, jeans and brogues, but the high colour in his cheeks literally drains from his skin as he takes in the scene of his daughter stood holding a knife under my chin.

'Shut the front door,' Cara says calmly, 'then come in and stand in the doorway. No closer than that though – and I mean it.'

He turns and does as he's told. When he reappears, he just stands there for a moment, puts his hands on his head in shock and whispers: 'I'm so sorry.'

Cara sighs heavily. 'Well, that makes it all much better. Thanks, Dad. I'm not even sure which one of us you're talking to.'

'Is Jessica badly hurt, Cara?' he asks quietly. 'She's got a little boy who needs her.'

Cara says nothing.

'I don't want to call the police, but I will if you don't answer me.'

'No, you won't,' Cara says. 'They'll uncover everything and then you'll lose your job, your reputation – the lot, which we both know would really bother you; "Headmaster at £30k-a-year school found guilty of ratting, to be sentenced next week. Simon Strallen had been cyberstalking Jessica Casson for several years, using the camera on her laptop, monitoring her emails, and keeping tabs on her Internet searches. Aware that Mrs Casson was selling her property, Strallen followed her activity on the property portal Rightmove, before also deciding to 'sell' his house so that his victim, also known as the lover-that-he-had-a-secret-child-with"—'

Simon looks at the floor and closes his eyes.

'"Might want to go and view it, with no knowledge of whose house it was". Ratters call their victims slaves, you know, Jess, in their online forums.' Cara addresses me as if we're having a cosy chat. 'Most of them have several "slaves" they're watching. Dad just has you. It must be a lot easier to do it *that* way than the good old-fashioned stalking he used to indulge in though, which involved accepting a new job and moving his wife and daughter to the town his ex-lover had also moved to. Like we said earlier, there's no such thing as privacy any more. Isn't that right, Dad?'

Simon takes a deep breath. 'I don't want to call the police because you're my daughter, Cara. I want to help you.'

'Is what she says true, Simon?' I can barely get the words out.

Simon looks down at the floor again.

Oh God, it is. 'You've watched me?' I can't keep the horror from my voice. 'All this time? *Years* of watching me, and I never knew?'

'I was watching *over* you – there's a difference. I kept my promise; I didn't interfere with your life. I stood by when you married Ed. I let you live it exactly as you wanted to.'

Cara exclaims. 'You "let" her live it? Wow Dad. Just… wow.'

'I never intruded on anything intimate,' Simon says quickly. 'I'm not a voyeur, or a pervert.'

Cara bends down and the knife slips diagonally across my throat, making me catch my breath as she whispers in my ear: 'Now might also be the time to ask him about the pushing incident.'

This time Simon turns completely ashen and his mouth falls open. 'What pushing incident?'

Oh Jesus Christ – that's true too? It can't be! He can't have done that. 'Cara tells me that either you or Louise told her to hurt Beth the day she died. Cara did as she was told and pushed Beth.' I swallow, and the blade gently presses on my skin with the pressure of the movement of my throat.

'*What*?' Simon whips his head round and looks at his daughter in astonishment. 'That's an outright lie. I would never do that, and I don't believe your mother would have either. Just stop this at once! This is an unforgivably cruel thing to do to Jessica. You were *five*, Cara! You couldn't possibly have remembered that, even if it did happen, which it didn't.'

'Mum discussed it all with me the day before she died,' Cara insists, unfazed by her father suddenly adopting such an authoritarian tone. 'She told me it wasn't an accident.'

'Don't listen, Jess,' Simon says. 'This simply isn't true.' He turns back to Cara again. 'Mum said I told you to *hurt* Beth? Why on earth would I have done that? Darling, Mum was very, very ill. You know that. Please don't tell me you believe her? You didn't do anything wrong. You didn't hurt anyone. Least of all Beth. It was an accident. You were just a little girl.'

There is a pause. I can't see Cara's face but I feel the slight tremble of her hand before I hear her say: 'The problem is, Dad, you're a habitual liar. Even if Jessica and I were to believe what you just said, now, we're always going to have that element of doubt. Anyway, I think I can remember doing it.'

'You can't. Cara. It didn't happen. Stop this. Please.' Simon takes a step forward.

She pushes the flat of the blade against my throat so hard I cough. 'Don't! Don't come any nearer!'

'Is that what this has all been in aid of?' He is aghast. 'You think I made you *kill* someone?'

'You completely disgust me!' she cries suddenly. 'I am angry, really angry. I can't keep listening to my friends' shitty little problems that aren't really problems. I don't fit in any more. I can't concentrate. I can't sleep. My head feels fucked.'

'You're grieving, Cara,' I say. 'That's exactly what it felt like after I lost my mum.'

'Shut up!' Cara says. 'I told you already, we're not doing the bond over our dead mothers bit. Was it you here yesterday, Dad? You were the man the neighbours saw looking in at the window, weren't you?'

Simon nods. 'I found your Larsen trap hidden in the shed at home. When your daughter suddenly develops an interest in trapping magpies, you can't help but be a little concerned. Then Jess came to see me about the nasty little tricks someone had been playing on her: broken mirrors, messages from beyond the grave – omens, frankly. It wasn't hard to put two and two together. I came here yesterday to see if I was right, to see if you were here, and if I could persuade you to stop, but the neighbours called the police.'

'Bloody hell.' Cara laughs incredulously. '*That* was what you noticed? The trap? Something offline and in real life... How ironic. I'm pleased to hear you went to the school though, Jessica. I hoped you might. Did you think she was about to fall back into your arms, Dad? That you were about to get everything you'd ever wanted?'

I see Simon's jaw clench.

'She doesn't love you,' Cara says. 'She told me.'

'But I heard you,' he turns to me. 'I heard you say that you miss me. You were in bed, on your laptop, and you said out loud that you didn't understand how we'd not taken our chance, and that you missed me so much.'

My eyes widen. 'Simon, did you deliberately come to teach at the school Beth was going to attend?'

'No. That was actually the first time I'd seen you since we split up. It really was coincidence – or fate – I swear.' He takes a deep breath. 'Yes, I decided to accept a job in Kent after you had moved to this area from London, and yes, I did put our house on the market before Christmas with the same agents you were selling with, and I was aware you were looking to buy something exactly like our property, but no, I don't apologise for coincidence creating opportunities for us.'

'And there you have it.' Cara looks at her father incredulously. 'Playing God and creating opportunities… is that what I was doing when you told me to push Beth?'

'I didn't tell you to do *anything*! I would never—'

'When Mum phoned me the night before she died,' Cara talks loudly over him, 'she told me she had made some terrible mistakes. She told me about Jessica, what you told me to do and what then happened to Beth. She tried desperately to keep us together as a family, and it hadn't worked. She admitted she had finally accepted your marriage was over. She was going to quit drinking for good this time, she was going to leave you – and she was going to be a better Mum to me. I told her to detox safely and take her meds, and she swore she would.' Cara takes a deep breath and continues: 'Then when she died, I came home, and *you* told me she'd been trying to detox so we could all be a family again. Pretty much the exact opposite of what Mum said. Not only that, but when one of your parents dies, you kind of expect the one left might lift their head up out of their computer for more than five minutes, come out of the study and sit with you in the sitting room for a bit. I get why you used to live in your room while Mum was alive – but I really could have used some company when I got back from France. Do you know, I took James to the park the other day and there was a father on the seesaw with his little girl. She was sat on one end, looking confused, just holding on, and he was sat on the other, bouncing up and down while staring at his phone. That's bad enough – but you take that shit to a whole different level, Dad.

'I actually couldn't believe what I found on your laptop when I went through it while you were at the solicitors. Not only was the woman I'd seen driving away from the house the morning I got back clearly *not* the estate agent, like you said – it was Jessica in a hundred different files, screen grabs, and emails. I can only suppose you didn't feel the need to hide it all away as Mum wasn't there any more; perhaps you didn't think I cared. Well, I'm sorry to tell you this, Dad, but you've *always* been a fucking disappointment as a parent and do you finally see what you've done, now? What your actions have caused?' Her hand starts to tremble again. I can't tell if it's with fear, or excitement. Then she steps to the left of me so we are side by side. 'Jessica doesn't get Beth, Beth doesn't get a life, I don't get a Mum… you don't get Jessica…'

She suddenly lifts her hand aloft, the knife high above my head.

My mouth falls open in horror, and I hear Simon shout: 'STOP!'

Cara pauses, as if she can't quite believe what she's about to do, and then says in a tiny voice: 'and you lose another daughter too.'

She closes her eyes and swoops the knife in a graceful, determined arc towards her stomach.

'CARA!' Simon shouts in fear, and strikes out across the room. He grabs her arm, forcing her hand to twist outwards and the metal to flash as the blade changes direction. He stumbles though, and knocks her completely off her feet. They crumple to the floor and I hear Cara exclaim 'No!' in disbelief, and then sit up, confused, her hands empty and open, as if she's praying.

Her eyes widen with horror and she looks at Simon – we both do – lying on the floor, slumped in the foetal position. All I can see is the arch of his back, the back of his head, and his knees drawn up to his chest. Cara starts to shake her head and whisper: 'No, no, no… I've stabbed him,' she says in disbelief. Her whole body starts to shake, and she slams backwards violently, banging into the kitchen cupboards, instinctively trying to get away from the sight in front of her.

'Cara,' I shout. 'CARA, listen to me! I need you to listen. Use my phone, call an ambulance right now.'

She simply stares at Simon in horror and shock as if she can't hear me.

'CARA! We need help. We need to help your dad. Can you hear me? I want to help you, Cara!'

She looks up at me, then reaches out and picks up the bloodied knife, wobbles to her feet, comes over and slices through the tape on my wrists, round my ankles and middle, then lets it clatter to the floor next to Simon, as she herself half collapses, half slumps back down, devastated.

'Where's my phone?' I demand, and she points to the basket on the side that I keep the odds and sods in. Rifling through it, I grab it and dial with shaking fingers.

'Hello? Ambulance please. A 52-year-old man has been stabbed. I can't see… I don't know. No higher than that, I think, but lower than his heart. Simon? Can you hear me? I don't think so, no. No, there's no danger now. It wasn't like that,' I glance at Cara, 'it was a suicide attempt. The knife has been removed, yes. Yes, it's—'

I give the operator our address and place the phone on the floor for a moment. 'They're on their way. Can you hear me, Simon? I need to lift your shirt so I can see what's happened and help you.'

He moans as I untuck it and, horrified, I can't help but audibly say 'Jesus Christ' – as I see a deep, single wound, blood oozing from it.

'No, no,' he mumbles. 'Leave it, I'm OK. You shouldn't do this – not after your mum.'

'Shhh,' I say and return to the phone. 'I'm not sure if his stomach looks swollen or not. Possibly. Simon, don't try to sit up – and don't look either.'

'I feel sick,' he says. He looks clammy and pale.

'I'm not surprised.' I make a huge effort to keep my voice steady and calm. I get up to grab a handful of tea towels from the drawer, but Simon reaches out and knocks the phone from my hand. It clatters across the floor.

'What are you doing?' I say in astonishment, thinking he's in shock. 'They're helping me to help you. I need—'

'Jess. Shhh. I'm OK, Cara,' he says. 'It's all OK. You didn't do this; it was my mistake. I'm fine. Don't cry, darling.'

I glance up at her; she has silent tears streaking down her face.

'Go and open the front door,' he says; he's starting to breathe rapidly. 'Watch for the ambulance, for Jess, and wave to them as soon as they turn into the road, OK? Go now.'

She does as she's told, immediately.

He turns his head to me. 'Jess, she needs to go home. This is going to ruin her life forever if she's here when the police arrive. She'll be arrested to keep her safe from herself – they've done that with Louise before. They'll do her for the GBH to you,' he swallows painfully, 'no one will believe she was trying to kill herself, and if I die it will all go to court. She'll get manslaughter or worse. Please.' He closes his eyes and grimaces.

'You're not going to die,' I insist, trying to mask my fear. 'You're doing just fine.'

'Please send her home now, before it's too late. Tell them it was me – all the things she did – that I was the one who was waiting here for you. I attacked you, and then tried to kill myself in front of you. They'll find everything at the house Cara told you about. It'll convince them. I'll take it all for her. She's just a kid. She's a good girl.'

Frightened tears are forming in my eyes. 'I can't, Simon.' I shake my head. 'I'm sorry. I can't lie for you again. I've got a little boy to think of, and the truth always comes out.'

'No, it doesn't. You'd be surprised by what you can get away with. *Please*, Jess,' he whispers. 'She didn't mean to do it and you know that. She didn't push Beth either, I promise you. That's Louise lying, not Cara. Tell her to go home now, before it's too late.' He tries to reach a hand out. 'I'm begging you! Send her home. Help me look after her, please!' He's becoming increasingly distressed and starts trying to sit up, but it's clear he's in too much pain.

'Simon, there's a knife right there covered with her fingerprints!'

'Of course it is, because I took it from our house. She lives there with me.'

I shake my head. 'It's not enough. Her prints will be all over *this* house too.'

'Because she came the day before yesterday to warn you what she'd found at home, to tell you I was watching you. You didn't believe her. Louise has annihilated her. She's grieving and lost. She needs help, not prison. You can do this, Jess. Please. She's Beth's sister. Help her. Just tell them I did this to myself.'

'Please,' I whisper, 'try not to talk. It's too late now anyway, I think they're here. I can hear voices.'

'Fine, so just tell them the truth then.'

He reaches out, curls his fingers round the knife, and before I realise what he's about to do, plunges it deeply into his gut, and then quickly does it again, before the knife clatters onto the floor.

I cannot move. I literally can't move a muscle. I am too shocked to breathe.

'Jessica?'

Someone is calling me.

'Jess?'

I manage to look up to see Ed standing in the doorway holding a set of keys in his hand with the estate agent's gaudy tag hanging from them. 'I needed to get the spare Grobag and you've taken my keys by mistake. Sandrine's sitting crying on the doorstep, she's—' He looks down and sees Simon. 'Whoa.' I watch his eyes travel to the knife. 'Oh Christ. *Shit!* What's happened? Is this him?'

'I think he's just killed himself,' I say in disbelief and I start to shake violently as I look down at Simon, who is now lying still and quiet on the kitchen floor. 'Is he dead?'

Ed rushes over to me, then gasps. 'You're hurt.' He reaches out to touch me. 'What's he done to you? Get up; get away from him.' He puts his hands under my arms and tries to pull me to my feet.

'That girl isn't Sandrine. She's his daughter, Cara. She's been pretending to be our au pair.'

He doesn't seem to hear me. 'Get up, Jess. I don't want you next to him like this. Come on.'

'She was going to kill herself and he stopped her, now she's lost him too. He's right – she needs help, not arresting.'

'She definitely needs help. Something psychiatric that's way beyond us. You're not thinking straight yourself, Jess. Good girl, that's it – stand up – no, look at *me*. LOOK at me, not him.' He starts to lead me towards the door. 'I want you away from here. Just keep looking at me, OK? Everything is going to be alright. OK… now, I can hear sirens. They're here.'

'I can't lie.' I grasp my husband's arm desperately. 'I can't do it.'

Ed looks at me in bewilderment. 'Lie? About what?'

I don't answer, but look back over my shoulder at Simon. He hasn't moved.

'Jess – you must tell the truth, alright? Promise me?' Ed says urgently. 'The truth, Jess, and then everything will be alright…'

EPILOGUE

Eleven Months Later

CHAPTER TWENTY-FIVE

Sunday, 19 November 2017

'She's in here. You're sure you're OK? Ready to do this?'

I nod apprehensively; the counsellor knocks on the door, and walks in.

Cara is sat on a sofa by a large bay window that overlooks the gardens. Even despite the appalling weather, the room is very light, and I can see that she actually looks really well. Although she's wearing an oversized jumper and leggings, I can tell she's still very thin, but there is natural colour in her cheeks. The only surprise is that her hair – tied back in a ponytail – is now Louise's reddy-brown. I guess she dyed it when she was with us.

I walk in and sit on the sofa opposite her, placing my coat across the arm. The counsellor sits in an armchair between us, and smiles. 'So, I'm going to stand in today.' She turns to Cara. 'Are you OK?'

Cara nods, and takes a deep breath. 'Thanks for coming, Jessica.'

'You're very welcome. How are you today?' I'm careful to add the 'today'. I remember that being helpful when people did it for me after Beth died.

'I'm… nervous.' She smiles shyly, but then it's gone, instantly, and she just looks very uncomfortable. 'You know what, I'm really sorry – I don't think I can do this after all.' She turns to the counsellor.

'That's fine, Cara. Would you like to stop?'

She nods. 'Yes. Maybe we could try next Sunday instead?'

'We'll be able to arrange something, I'm sure.' The counsellor stands up, and I follow her lead, despite having driven an hour and a half to get here, and it'll be the same back again. I also said no to a weekend in Chichester staying with Laurel – which James would have loved, being around her boys – but then I knew this might happen. 'It's not a problem, Cara. Just be in touch when you're ready.'

I pick up my coat and have just reached the door when she says desperately: 'Wait!'

Both the counsellor and I turn back.

'Sorry.' She tries a smile. 'I'm just really… anxious… today. It's partly knowing that I'm leaving here in a couple of weeks. I'm ready – don't get me wrong. I'm so ready this time, but it's still hard. The trouble with private treatment is it's mostly too nice. You get used to having everything organised for you, so you don't have to think… which is of course why they sling you out again before you get too comfortable and never cope in the real world again.' She laughs nervously. 'I'm just trying… to wrap my head round it all.' She stops her tumble of words and makes a visible attempt to gather herself. 'Please don't go. You've come a long way. I want to do this.'

The counsellor holds out a hand in invitation for me to sit down again, and I do as I'm told.

'OK, Cara?' she says, when we're back where we started.

'Yes.' Cara looks up to the ceiling, then straight at me. 'So, as you know, I've been here at Pathway on a voluntary basis for the last six weeks and, as I said, I've got two more left. As part of my ongoing treatment, I wanted to see you to talk to you about a few things, if that's OK?'

She's obviously been practising what she wants to say. 'Of course.' I wait in the silence that follows, wondering if I should elaborate more, be more encouraging. 'It's very peaceful in here. That's probably why they call it a quiet room, I expect,' I finish lamely.

Cara smiles properly for the first time. 'I expect so. How's James?'

'He's very well, thank you. We finally move into a new house next week. We ended up renting a lot longer than we thought we would, but he's really excited about having a new big-boy bedroom.'

'That's nice,' she says, almost wistfully, and I inwardly kick myself. She hardly needs me telling her about our new family home when her new start is going to be so different to that.

She clears her throat, and apparently reading my mind, says: 'When I leave here I'm going to my grandparents in Chichester, to live there for a while. We've got some good aftercare in place for me, so it won't be like when I was discharged from the ward after my six-month involuntary section.' She instinctively pulls her jumper sleeves further down over her wrists.

I avert my eyes. 'I'm sure it won't be.'

'This place has been really helpful for me, although sometimes I can just hear Dad saying: "*How* much did you say it costs?"'

I choose my words very carefully. 'I think he would have been pleased to see how well your recovery is going this time and would have considered that money well invested.'

She frowns, and instantly worried that I've said the wrong thing again, I hold my breath in the silence that follows, but rather she looks out of the window and, in another rush, says: 'I'm so sorry, Jessica. I wanted to say, face to face, that I should never have hit you. I've never done anything like that before and I never will again. I also never intended the mirror to fall that close to James. It was just meant to smash. I would *never* have hurt him.

The broken knife wasn't actually meant as a threat either – I was just… practising.' She looks down. 'I also shouldn't have called your friend, Natalia; that wasn't even part of it. Like I said to you that day, I only did it because she was so rude about me. I didn't know she was going to be nasty enough to tell Ben. I hope you don't see her any more?'

'No, I don't.'

'Well, that's good at least.' She pauses to gather herself. 'There's something more I want to say about Beth but I don't want to upset you, especially when I know it's her anniversary on Wednesday?'

I take a deep breath. 'It's OK, I assumed we would be talking about her today at some point, so go for it.'

'I've been exploring a lot in counselling whether Mum or Dad really did tell me to hurt Beth because, as you know, I was sure I could remember actually doing it? I've come to the conclusion that I don't think it was real. I'm almost certain that Mum made the whole thing up to hurt Dad. I don't believe she would have been able to do that, and Dad wouldn't have either. He was a lot of things, but he wasn't a murderer. That said, he also *wasn't* a hero – as someone helpfully told me in group the other day – for killing himself so I would only be charged with what I did to you. It's important to me that I tell you, in my opinion, there was nothing selfless about what he did. He knew he was going to be exposed and ruined when they found everything in his study. He took the easy way out rather than face his punishment. I wish knowing that would also make me stop caring about him. I wish I'd not wasted so much of my life waiting for him to care about *me*.'

I exhale slowly. We seem to have stumbled into surprisingly deep and dangerous water very quickly. I glance at the counsellor for guidance, who nods encouragingly. Again, picking my words very carefully, I respond: 'While I agree with you that your father was a very selfish and delusional man, there's also no doubt in my mind that he wanted to keep you safe. That's ultimately all you want as a parent, Cara. It's an instinctive thing. He wanted to protect you.'

My voice trembles slightly as I speak, and I know she hears it. She considers that for a moment, but her expression betrays no reaction either way. Instead, appearing to gain strength, she looks at me directly and says: 'I'm also truly sorry for suggesting to you that Ed checking on me at night while I was in your house was any way inappropriate. I imagined that's what a girl of 18 would do in that situation if she didn't understand or hadn't been told what was actually going on, but I played my part too authentically, and it wasn't fair. I'm also really sorry that at first you thought I meant Beth was watching me at night. I heard genuine hope in your voice and I am ashamed that I manipulated you like that. I want you to know, I never got that feeling in the house. Although I still can't explain those weird three knocks on the front door that time when you and Ed were there.' She shudders. 'Which still freaks me out a bit, to be honest. I don't like things I can't explain…'

I think about the woman on the bike all those years ago. 'Me neither.'

'Mostly though, I'm sorry I was so angry with Beth.' Cara darts an anxious glance at me. 'From the moment I found out about her, it very quickly became unhealthy and obsessive. I was not well.' She trails off for a moment. 'I don't even remember her… my sister.' Her voice is small, but I can still hear the echo of loss. 'I'm just really sorry. For everything.'

'I forgive you, Cara,' I say simply.

She raises her eyebrows in surprise, as if it can't be that easy. 'Um, thanks.'

There's a moment of silence before she looks at the counsellor. 'I think I'd like to go now, if that's OK?'

'Of course.' The counsellor smooths the creases from the front of her trousers and stands up. Uncertain if I'm meant to follow suit, I get to my feet too, and Cara walks quickly past us to the door.

'Will you stay in touch with me?' She turns back suddenly. 'Maybe you could come and see me at my grandparents if you're coming down to see your dad, or something?' She nervously balls up the pulled over jumper tightly in her hands.

'I'd like that,' I say sincerely, and watch as she slowly releases them. 'Perhaps someone could call me with the address details just before you leave here, if you still want me to have them, then we'll sort something out. But no pressure if you change your mind.'

'Thank you.' She looks relieved. 'Thank you for your kindness to me, and your support, Jessica.'

I look at her pale, smooth skin – unable to resist searching for a trace of any similarity to Beth. 'I want to thank you too, Cara, for everything you said to me about James and letting me enjoy loving him without feeling so afraid all of the time – or guilty. It's made a real difference, to both of us.'

She hesitates, then suddenly darts forward and gives me an impulsive hug. I can't help tensing in surprise, and she backs off immediately – her arms must be round me for less than a second. It's like being embraced by a sprite. Her touch is so light I'm not even entirely sure it happened. I don't even have the chance to say goodbye before she disappears round the door, and is gone.

Back in the privacy of my car, I burst into tears. It's not unexpected; I knew today was going to be challenging. They aren't tears of sadness as such, more a release of tension. Once I've stopped crying, I start the car and begin to pull away from the converted Georgian manor house and manicured gardens. I think about Cara going to live with her grandparents; picturing the kindly – if exhausted – couple I remember seeing at Simon's funeral. What a thing to bury your daughter, then her husband after his well-publicised suicide, and still be there for your troubled granddaughter. Cara's right, *they* are the heroes, not Simon.

I sweep out of the long drive onto the main road, and think about him – the man I met that first evening, bouncing down the steps into the basement bar. How transfixed I was by his confidence and easy charm, how that first kiss promised me the world... I can only assume he was telling me the truth; that it really was coincidence when we all wound up at the same classroom on that first day of the girls' school term. It would have been an odd lie to maintain in the face of everything else that Cara ultimately exposed, but who really knows? Who knows... He didn't tell Cara to hurt Beth though, I'm certain of that, at least.

Louise, however? I'm not so sure. A spiteful little push in the playground, an impulse born from the shock of Simon's betrayal? Maybe. Still, I know she wouldn't have dreamt that Cara would do it while on a climbing frame. If it even happened at all. It was an accident. I take a deep breath, *an accident*...

And then, of course, I think of my baby, my girl... her gentle eyes shining up at me, full of unconditional love. I would have wanted someone to go and see *her* if she'd been alone in that room today, so bravely trying to overcome everything to start again, in spite of the hand she's been dealt, through absolutely no fault of her own at all.

Back at the house, once I've settled James to sleep – closing my eyes blissfully as he sighs and contentedly twists his fingers in my hair – I come downstairs to find Ed reading the Sunday papers at the kitchen table with a glass of wine waiting for me.

'I thought maybe the fire, a silly movie and some chocolate might be in order,' he says, reaching out his arms.

I go and sit on his lap. 'Ow, get off,' he yelps instantly. 'I love you, but you really have got bones of steel. It's mental, you're like a female Wolverine.'

I roll my eyes and stand up – he gets to his feet and rubs his leg melodramatically before wrapping his arms round me. 'That's better… I'm sorry, you're just *really* heavy for someone so slight.'

'Alright, don't go on about it.'

He kisses the top of my head gently. 'Are you OK?'

I sigh. 'I think so, yes.'

'Do you want to—' he begins, then we both glance at my mobile on the table which has lit up and is whirring – 'talk to *Laurel* about today?' he finishes deadpan, and releases me.

'Sorry.' I look at him. 'I ought to pick up. She'll be worried otherwise.'

'Sure.' He lifts his wine. 'I'll be in the other room when you're ready.'

'Hey, Laurel.' I say as he walks out of the room. 'How are you?'

'I'm OK. I'm only going to be quick; I know you'll be knackered. I just wanted to check in with you and see how it went?'

'I'm fine, thank you. I know you were concerned, but it really wasn't that bad. She was OK. I really think she's going to be alright this time.'

'Hmmm,' Laurel says doubtfully. 'It's not really Cara I'm worried about. Do *you* want to talk about it?'

'Not really, if that's OK.'

'That's fine. You must be shattered, and you've got a big week. Finally moving – yay! New home, new start, my darling.'

'Thank you.' I hesitate. 'I was thinking though, you know we don't actually move until Friday, don't you? We're here until then. In case anyone wanted to know…' I trail off. 'You will give Ben my *new* address too, if he asks for it, won't you?' I add suddenly. 'I mean, I know he's got this one already, and he won't ask in any case, but…'

'Of course I will. If he asks for it.'

'And he's got my mobile number and email too, if he ever wanted to talk?'

'Yes. I gave them to him too.'

There's a pause, and I take a deep breath. 'Anyway…'

'He *is* OK, Jess,' she interrupts. 'He was out at a thing we went to a couple of weeks ago and he was fine. Honestly.'

'He didn't mention me?'

'No, sweetheart. We don't go there, Jess. Not now.'

'Right,' I say. 'I understand. Look, I'm going to shove off. Like you said – big week. Thanks for checking on me though, and I'll call you in the morning. Love you.'

'I love you too, Jess. Sleep well.'

When Wednesday morning arrives, I sneak an extra ten minutes to lie in bed, and listen to the sounds of Ed getting James up, before going through the shower and appearing in the kitchen to find them both having breakfast.

'I'll do the pre-school run this morning,' Ed says. 'What have you got planned today?'

'Nothing,' I say, forcing a smile. 'Just work. And more packing.'

'You don't want to go down to Chichester to see your dad?' Ed asks doubtfully. 'I could pick James up too, if you could be back by half three?'

I hesitate. 'I've asked Laurel to take Beth's flowers to the church this morning, just because we've got so much to get sorted for Friday.'

'You don't want to – I don't know – share today with someone who knew Beth?'

In truth, yes, I do. It's her eighteenth anniversary and I feel lonely alongside that knowledge. It feels wrong and weird that it's just me now; as if I've cost Beth all over again, as well as Ben. And I can't even bear to think about how Ben must be feeling today. I wish I could call him. But I know I can't.

Once Ed and James have gone, I decide, instead, to pop to a coffee shop I particularly like. Partly I just want to get out of the house, but it's also because when we were all expecting I used to meet the NCT girls here. In fact, when I arrive there is a group of seven girls, heavily pregnant and sitting in the window seat we used to go for, eating cake, drinking tea and laughing together. It's slightly bittersweet now – given what Natalia did – to watch them for a moment while my hot chocolate with extra marshmallows (Beth would have approved hugely) is made.

Walking back home afterwards, I think about how scared I was when I first found out I was pregnant with Beth – and even James – but how I know I would choose to have them both all over again in a heartbeat, if I had my time again.

'You were such a joy and a privilege, my darling,' I say out loud, as I cross the road back towards the house to start some more packing. 'And I will *always* love you.' I remember suddenly what Ben said at the funeral and add: 'I love you billions and billions, and that's a very big number.'

I swallow a lump down in my throat as I open the gate, and then stop in my tracks, covering my mouth with my hand. I must have missed a delivery while I was out.

For there, on the doorstep, half boxed up, with the top wrapped in clear cellophane, sits a single white rose.

The End

A LETTER FROM LUCY

Thank you so much for choosing to read *The Daughter*. If you enjoyed it, and want to keep up-to-date with all of my latest releases, you can sign up at the following link. Your email address will never be shared and you can unsubscribe at any time.

www.bookouture.com/lucy-dawson

Should you have the time, I would be very grateful if you would write a review of *The Daughter*. Feedback is really useful and also makes a huge difference in helping new readers discover one of my books for the first time.

If you'd like to contact me personally, you can reach me via my Website, Facebook page, Twitter, Instagram or Goodreads. I love hearing from readers, and always reply.

Again, thank you so much for deciding to spend some time reading *The Daughter*. I enjoyed writing it immensely and look forward to sharing my next book with you very soon.

With all best wishes,
Lucy x

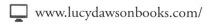 www.lucydawsonbooks.com/

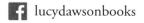 lucydawsonbooks

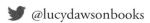 @lucydawsonbooks

ACKNOWLEDGEMENTS

My thanks to Neil White, Steve Cavanagh, Andrew Cox, Ellie Dodson, Paul Dodson and Janette Currie. Any errors made are, of course, all my own. I am very grateful to Wanda Whitely for being the first, and as ever, insightful reader of *The Daughter*. I have been hugely supported by all at United Agents. My thanks to Sarah Ballard, Margaret Halton, Eli Keren and Alex Stephens for the enormous work they do on my behalf. Thanks to all at Bookouture for making this book such a pleasure to publish, in particular Kathryn Taussig, Jenny Geras, Kim Nash and Noelle Holten for their input, energy and expertise. Thank you to all of the bloggers and readers who so kindly spread the word, and my family and friends for their support and kindness. Last but by no means least, thank you to the writers who know who they are, and without whom I would laugh a lot less, when I really should be working.

Made in the USA
Middletown, DE
05 May 2018